A Story Every Day of SPRING

Edited by John Howes and Fran Neatherway

Copyright © 2024 The Rugby Cafe Writers.
Copyright remains with the individual writers of each story. All rights reserved.

This book or any portion thereof may not be reproduced or used in any manner whatsoever without the express written permission of the publisher except for the use of brief quotations in a book review.
Printed in the United Kingdom.

This is a work of fiction. Unless otherwise indicated, all the names, characters, businesses, places, events and incidents in this book are either the product of the author's imagination or used in a fictitious manner. Any resemblance to actual persons, living or dead, or actual events is purely coincidental.

First Printing, 2024

ISBN: 9798883050359
Imprint: Independently published

For more information about The Cafe Writers of Rugby, visit their website, www.rugbycafewriters.com

The text of this book is set in Georgia, 10.5pt. This is a typeface designed in 1993 specifically for reading on computer screens and named after a bizarre newspaper headline, *Alien heads found in Georgia*. It has since become increasingly popular and was adopted by *The New York Times* in 2007.

Introduction

The Wonder Of Spring

As I write this introduction, it is a fairly gloomy Monday afternoon in January. At times like this, I long for the start of Spring - the early warmth of sunshine and nature starting to raise itself from the rest of Winter. So Spring can be a time of optimism and moving towards better times.

Here at the Cafe Writers of Rugby, we have been busy throughout the darker months working hard on getting our stories ready for the Spring anthology. This is our fourth seasonal collection, having already published books for Summer, Autumn and Winter. We are delighted to have completed this project which now offers a short story for every single day of the year.

We continue to welcome new members to the group and are very pleased to be publishing their work for the first time. We exist to support existing writers and encourage new writers, whatever genre they like to work in - maybe memoir, poetry, romance, fantasy, crime or whatever. So if you are interested, please come along to one of our meetings or contact us via our website. You will be most welcome.

This book gives you a story for every day of March, April and May, with themes including April fools, Easter, and VE Day.

I leave the final word to Patrick Garrett who has recently joined the Cafe Writers. Here is his explanation of Spring:

'Spring. Now isn't that a strange word? Sometimes a noun, other times a verb or even an adjective with multiple meanings. Say 'Spring' and, depending on who you are, the first thing that comes to mind is a compression spring that returns to its full size after being depressed. Secondly, perhaps that water that issues from the earth that had fallen from the sky and been absorbed into the darkness, sometimes re-emerging back to the light cleansed after only days or possibly hundreds of years. Or for those of a meteorological bent, that time of year when nature emerges from the dark days of winter. Or for many a good Spring clean ready for warmer days.

There is of course one constant and that is an emergence ready for the cycle to start all over again.'

If you enjoy the collection, please consider buying another in the series and, if you enjoy writing, please visit our website and get in touch with us. We would love to hear from you.

John Howes
www.rugbycafewriters.com

Contents

March

March 1 **About Mary** Ruth Hughes	11
March 2 **The Game Show** EE Blythe	13
March 3 **A Second Chance** Madalyn Morgan	15
March 4 **A Valuable Opinion** John Howes	21
March 5 **A Youth Club Story** Kate A Harris	23
March 6 **Police Report** Chris Wright	26
March 7 **Growing Pains** Fran Neatherway	28
March 8 **Two People** Ruth Hughes	31
March 9 **Working At Home-Two-Timing** Jim Hicks	33
March 10 **The Rightful Heiress** Chloe Huntington	36
March 11 **My Life Of Crime** Wendy Goulstone	41
March 12 **A Metropolitan Day Out** Chris Wright	42
March 13 **Learning To Swim** Kate A Harris	45
March 14 **Pip** Patrick Garrett	49
March 15 **The Journey Home** Rosemary Marks	55
March 16 **A Bit Of A Shock** EE Blythe	60
March 17 **Flower Power** Patrick Garrett	62
March 18 **Springtime** Simon Parker	63
March 19 **Morning Chorus** Wendy Goulstone	65
March 20 **Goodbye Miss Maudsley** Chris Wright	68
March 21 **First Day Of Spring** Ruth Hughes	70
March 22 **Hot Cross Buns** Christine Hancock	71
March 23 **A Change of Location** Steve Redshaw	72
March 24 **Real Life** Theresa Le Flem	74
March 25 **Two Spring Days** John Howes	78
March 26 **The Dancer On The Green** Wendy Goulstone	80
March 27 **Falling Down** EE Blythe	82
March 28 **The Diaries of Sylvia Starr** Madalyn Morgan	84
March 29 **The Woodland Wedding** Chloe Huntington	89
March 30 **No Good Deed** Fran Neatherway	91
March 31 **Gryphon** EE Blythe	97

April

April 1 **The Glorious First of April** Wendy Goulstone	101
April 2 **The Bells of St Mary's** Martin Curley	103
April 3 **Say It With Flowers** Fran Neatherway	109
April 4 **April In Harwich** Martin Curley	112
April 5 **Menage A Trois** Wendy Goulstone	119
April 6 **The Nest** David G Bailey	121
April 7 **Judge Not** Rosemary Marks	124
April 8 **A Change Of Air** EE Blythe	127
April 9 **Firey Fenzoy** Kate A Harris	129
April 10 **A Number** EE Blythe	131
April 11 **Fighting The Black Dog** John Howes	133
April 12 **Missing My Wife** Lindsay Woodward	136
April 13 **The Tree Branch** Christopher Trezise	141
April 14 **Oops** Kate A Harris	144
April 15 **Creative Thinking** Fran Neatherway	146
April 16 **Cucumber Fields Forever** Wendy Goulstone	148
April 17 **The Power of the Pen** Rosemary Marks	150
April 18 **More, More, More** EE Blythe	154
April 19 **Talent Spotting** Chris Rowe	156
April 20 **Yorkshire Holidays** Ruth Hughes	158
April 21 **White Rabbits, White Rabbits** Wendy Goulstone	160
April 22 **Incident In Berlin** John Howes	162
April 23 **That's What Friends Are For** Rosemary Marks	164
April 24 **Seven Deadly Sins** Fran Neatherway	169
April 25 **Dear Luke** Martin Curley	172
April 26 **Springtime** Kate A Harris	175
April 27 **A Ghost Of Golden Daffodils** EE Blythe	177
April 28 **Excitement In Norwich** Pam Barton	179
April 29 **Sounds like Spring** Rosemary Marks	181
April 30 **Driving North** Wendy Goulstone	183

May

May 1 **May Queen** EE Blythe	187
May 2 **Heart of Gold** Theresa Le Flem	189
May 3 **The Bucket List** Rosemary Marks	195
May 4 **The Enemy** Fran Neatherway	202
May 5 **Roses And Poppies** Chris Rowe	204
May 6 **Drama In The Hen House** Ruth Hughes	207
May 7 **Grey** EE Blythe	208
May 8 **VE Day** Lindsay Woodward	210
May 9 **Vera Lynn** Jim Hicks	212
May 10 **Italian Job Allowance** Chris Wright	214
May 11 **Food** Kate A Harris	215
May 12 **Midsomer Move** Chris Wright	217
May 13 **Horror In The Car Park** John Howes	218
May 1 **Pyrenean Spring** Simon Parker	220
May 15 **To My Dear Departed Son** Patrick Garrett	225
May 16 **The Lobby Of The Ritz Carlton Hotel** Martin Curley	227
May 17 **Unexpected love** Christopher Trezise	233
May 18 **Blue Dye** EE Blythe	235
May 19 **Wizards** Jim Hicks	236
May 20 **Goodbye, Humphrey** John Howes	238
May 21 **A Village Evening** Ruth Hughes	239
May 22 **Friday The Thirteenth** David G Bailey	241
May 23 **The Ghost of Grandma** Patrick Garrett	244
May 24 **Dear Cousin Blanche** Simon Parker	246
May 25 **Sorry You Are Not Well** Ruth Hughes	247
May 26 **Write What You Know** Fran Neatherway	248
May 27 **Two Days In May** John Howes	250
May 28 **Cheese Rolling** Wendy Goulstone	252
May 29 **Mr Jeff At The Park** Chris Wright	254
May 30 **One May Morning** EE Blythe	257
May 31 **Plat du Jour** Fran Neatherway	259
About the authors	267

A Story for Every Day of Spring

A Story for Every Day of Spring

March 1

About Mary

Mary really didn't like getting old; it meant aches and pains and having to slow down, but the one good thing about it was her long life of experiences which meant that she knew an awful lot. Yes, she had to do everything a lot more slowly now, but that gave her time to observe more.

She knew the signs that heralded the beginning of Spring. Firstly, and from quite early, the birds seemed to guess and start singing from early dawn, and also at night, even in the dark. She would hear their beautiful songs as they let the world know they were there. She also knew because of keeping hens when the night drew out and it slowly got light earlier in the mornings. This affected the times she had to shut them up at night and release them in the mornings.

The early flowers started to push their way into the light: snowdrops, aconites, celandines too. Then she would notice the hedges begin to shoot little green buds, hawthorn and blackthorn first and wild cherries getting white blossom on them.

To Mary, the air smelt different too. She could smell the spring coming and it made her joyful.

It made her remember things from her childhood. They had lived by a pond and, when the ice had cleared, she and her brother would go and look for tadpoles. They would catch some using their hands as sieves to catch ten or twelve each. They carried them home sticking to their palms half dead, then scraped them onto a saucer of water to revive them and put them into a big jam jar with some weed.

Mary had nature lessons watching them develop, growing their legs and seeing their tails disappear when they became little frogs to be put outside to continue their lives. She would gather glorious golden marsh marigolds for her mother, never noticing how quickly they faded.

Mary remembered the yellow hazel catkins she called lambs' tails and furry pussy willows that felt as soft as a kitten's paw. So many memories Mary remembered of childhood springtimes. Every year connected again with her past memories, adding new recollections to them. She was happy.

Ruth Hughes

March 2

The Game Show

I should never have agreed to do it in the first place, but you know how it is, trying to save face, trying not to show any weakness. All the other lads were going to do it. We all filled in our forms, one Sunday afternoon in the pub. 'We' being the Dodged The Bullet Gang: six schoolboys, now adults, and in our various responsible jobs, post university. And the bullet we dodged? Marriage.

We'd all been engaged at some point, and then broken it off. Except me. I said I'd got engaged in my last year of college, and had finished it at the end of my course because we had very different goals. Not true. The other lads teased me enough as it was, and I didn't want any more stupid nicknames. Thus I pretended. And said I didn't want to talk about it.

So, we'd all completed forms for the pilot show of a new quiz on television. And in time, we'd all received acknowledgements, and a date to present ourselves at the studio. The closer that date got, the more nervous I became, and I really wanted to pull out.

It wasn't 'til I got to the studio that it dawned on me that the others weren't there; weren't coming. Their names were not on any of the lists that the runners had, and one, seeing my puzzlement and near panic, shot off with a 'hang on a sec', and reappeared with a printed sheet listing all the applicants' names. Even the rejected ones. None of the Bullet Gang names were there, except mine. They'd done it again; made a fool of me. Once more I asked myself why I bothered with them. Because I'd have no social life, if I didn't.

I met the other contestants at the buffet lunch, and then we spent a day and a half running through the format of the game, learning the on-screen choreography so that we didn't crash into each other when we had to change places, and how to spot when the camera was on us, so that we looked suitably excited. It was Hell!

Our 'genial' host was downright cruel, especially to me and a young lass with a terrible stutter under stress. He thought he was so funny. But he wasn't.

The audience were seated, and we were all being sorted into the right order to be called onto the set. Too late to back out, but I was so angry; angry with my friends, angry with myself for being so gullible and for being too weak to leave. I could feel it rising inside me. My head roared, and I started to overheat.

The host called my name. I clenched my fists, gritted my teeth, and walked right up to his stupid, grinning face...

EE Blythe

March 3

A Second Chance

Jenny tinkered with the spoon in the saucer of her coffee cup. She had booked a table for two at her local restaurant and had arrived twenty minutes early. The waiter, whom Jenny knew, showed her to a seat in the bay window and brought her a cappuccino while she waited for her lunch guest to arrive. Jenny sipped her coffee and tried to relax. It wasn't easy. Every time she thought about the letter she'd received the week before, the same question came into her mind. Why, after two years in Canada, had Steve Hurst come back to England?

Jenny met Steve at university in London. They were both looking for accommodation and had both arrived to see the same room in the same house at the same time. Steve, a Londoner whose parents had just moved to Canada, was able to live in the family home until it was sold. Jenny had come up from Devon, so Steve graciously gave up his interest in the room on condition Jenny invited him to the housewarming party – which she did. They fell in love that night and were blissfully happy until the day they received their final exam results three years later. What should have been one of the happiest days of their lives turned out to be the worst!

Jenny found her degree course easy and got a first, but Steve struggled. He was under pressure because anything less than a 2:1 meant he couldn't take up the post he had been provisionally offered with a company called Harper Lincoln Industries. He got a 2:2, which was not good enough. That day Steve was inconsolable. He told Jenny he needed to be on his own to think and to get his head together. Jenny, as always, gave Steve the space he needed, thinking he would come back after a walk, but he didn't.

By eight o'clock that night, Jenny had telephoned all their friends. No one had seen Steve. After scribbling a note, saying she had gone to

The Jolly Pot-Man pub as arranged and would see him there, Jenny left the flat.

The pub was wall-to-wall with university students celebrating or drowning their sorrows, but there was no sign of Steve. At midnight, Jenny went home. She telephoned their friends again before falling into bed.

At six o'clock in the morning, Jenny woke to the shrill sound of the telephone ringing. Yawning, she reached out, swept the receiver from its cradle and put it to her ear. 'Steve?'

'I would like to speak to Miss Bailey?'

'I'm Jennifer Bailey. Who am I speaking to?'

'PC Thompson, Sterling Road Police Station.'

'What's happened? Is it Steve? Has he been in an accident?'

'Mr Hurst has been helping us with our enquiries.'

'Is he all right?'

Ignoring Jenny, the police constable continued, 'If you will bring Mr Hurst some clothes, we will release him.'

Jenny blinked back her tears. If she had listened to Steve that night in the police station, things would have been so different. But she had been angry and hurt when the police told her that Steve had been found naked in the bed of a hooker, and had left. Back at their flat, Jenny packed some clothes, took a cab to the station and caught the first train home to Devon.

Some weeks later, Jenny received an apology of sorts from the police. They told her that Steve had been drinking heavily and had been mugged by local youths who, guessing he was a student, thought it would be fun to strip him, tie him up and leave him in an alley – in the rain. A young woman known to the police had arrived home in the early hours of the morning and found Steve huddled in her doorway, shivering. Feeling sorry for him, the woman untied him and, with the help of a neighbour, managed to get him into her flat, where they left him on the bed. The young woman threw a blanket over Steve, and the neighbour went home and called the police.

Having learned the truth about that night, Jenny went to London to see Steve, to tell him she was sorry for not listening to him. She was too late. He had left for Canada the day before.

In her heart, Jenny knew she would see Steve again and had rehearsed many times what she would say to him. Now the day had arrived, she was lost for words. Once, Steve had been her best friend as well as her lover. They had shared everything. Now, Jenny knew it was time to share the most important thing in her life with him. It wasn't going to be easy – for either of them.

Remembering how she and Steve had loved each other woke the butterflies in the pit of Jenny's stomach. She cleared her throat, sat up straight, and shook her head as if to shake the love that she once had for Steve from her memory. In doing so, she shook out her hair. Steve had always loved her long red hair. Was it for him that she had left her hair loose today? She smiled, dismissed the idea and ordered another coffee.

Jenny glanced at her watch: Steve was late. He was often late when they lived together. It mattered to her then; it didn't now. Jenny sat back in the comfortable chair and looked away from the window. The last thing she wanted was for Steve to arrive and see her looking for him. 'If he arrives,' she said aloud.

+ +

Steve had arrived at the restaurant early. He waited in his car until it was time to meet Jenny for lunch. Seeing her in the window, Steve knew there would never be anyone for him but Jen. He had dated in Canada, but there was no one he could have loved, not as he had loved, still loved, Jen. He wanted to rush into the restaurant, take her in his arms and tell her how much he loved her. But something was holding him back.

Steve watched Jenny drink her second cup of coffee and decided that if he didn't go in now, she might think he had let her down and leave. Steve smiled to himself. He was often late in the old days, but his timekeeping had improved, and it would have to remain so when he started his new job. He ached to be with Jen, to speak to her, tell her about his new job and celebrate with her, but most of all, he wanted to tell her how much he loved her.

+ +

'Would you like a menu, Madam?' a voice behind Jenny asked.

'No, thank you, I'm waiting for a friend…' As she turned and looked up, her eyes fixed on the man she had always loved.

'I hope I'm not late,' Steve said, smiling nervously.

'Not at all,' Jenny replied. 'I think I'm a little early.'

'I wasn't sure you'd come.'

'Why wouldn't I?' Jenny asked.

'Oh, I don't know, but I'm glad you did.'

'Actually,' Jenny said, 'I wasn't sure you'd come.'

They both laughed as the waiter showed them to a table.

They discussed the menu, and Jenny decided on seafood salad to start.

'Make that two salads,' Steve said, not taking his eyes off Jenny, 'and a bottle of Chardonnay. Chardonnay all right for you, Jen?'

Jenny froze, unable to answer. No one had called her Jen since Steve left. She was Jennifer to her mother and Jenny to her work colleagues. It was only Steve who—

'Madam?' the waiter said, waiting for Jenny to confirm the choice of wine.

'Yes, lovely,' she said, smiling up at the waiter to give herself time to recover. 'Chardonnay is my favourite.'

'A toast,' Steve said when the waiter had poured the wine. 'To the most beautiful woman I know.'

'You haven't changed,' Jenny said, laughing. 'You still don't know fact from fiction.'

Steve and Jenny chatted naturally, reminiscing about their friends at university. Steve told Jenny about his two years in Canada and how he had worked during the day and studied at night to gain the qualifications he needed to do the job he had always dreamed of.

Jenny told Steve how lucky she had been to get a job with a subsidiary of Harper Lincoln Industries when she moved back to Devon, how she worked from home, going up to the London office once a week.

'And that is where I shall be for the foreseeable future,' Steve said, 'Harper Lincoln's head office in London. I start in six weeks.'

Putting her hand to her mouth, Jenny gasped with surprise. 'Congratulations, Steve, I'm really happy for you,' she said, genuinely pleased for him. 'I wondered why you had come back to England.'

'I came back because you're here, Jen,' Steve said. 'I had to see you to tell you how much I love you and ask you to forgive me. I understand why you didn't reply to my letters, but—'

'Letters? Except for the letter last week, I haven't had any letters from you.'

'But I wrote to you every week for the first three months I was in Canada, telling you how sorry I was. When I didn't hear back from you, I buried myself in my work.' Reaching across the table, Steve took Jenny's hands in his, 'I couldn't live with the thought of never seeing you again, Jen, so to make sure you read my last letter, I sent it to your mother's address, assuming you had moved.'

'I did move. I cleared the flat and handed back the keys the day after you went to Canada. I came home to Devon, but I left a forwarding address, in case—'

+   +

Jenny's mother hugged her before handing her a dozen unopened letters, postmarked from Canada. 'I'm so sorry, Jennifer, I had no right to keep Steve's letters from you.' Turning to Steve, Helen said, 'If you come with me, I'll show you why I felt I needed to protect my daughter.'

Steve followed Helen upstairs to a small, pretty, pink and cream bedroom, where a golden-haired child of around eighteen months slept soundly in her cot.

'This is Charlotte,' Jenny said, following her mother and Steve into her daughter's bedroom. 'She's having her afternoon nap, but you can meet her when she wakes.'

'Charlotte...' Steve whispered, wiping tears from his cheeks. 'She is beautiful, Jen. She looks just like you.'

'Now, do you understand why I didn't want Jennifer hurt again, Steve?' Jenny's mother said.

'I do.' Looking from Charlotte to Helen, Steve said, 'I give you my word, I will never hurt Jen again. I will spend my life loving her, loving them both.'

During the following weeks, Jenny and Steve fell in love again, and Charlotte got to know her daddy.

The morning Steve had to leave for London to start his new job came all too soon. Jenny promised she would go up to London mid-week. 'If Mum will look after Charlotte,' she said, smiling.

'You know I will, Jennifer.' Jenny's mother lifted Charlotte from Steve's arms. 'Come on, darling, let's go in and make some tea. You'll see Daddy again at the weekend, won't you?' Helen said, leaving the newlyweds alone to say goodbye.

Madalyn Morgan

March 4

A Valuable Opinion

Recently, I attended a private hospital for an opinion from a consultant. He kindly gave me his opinion and directed me towards the reception to pay for the opinion. However, I was feeling naughty, and a bit skint, so I nipped into the gents' restroom and leapt out of the window, with the opinion in my pocket. I legged it down the road, dodged a couple of security guards, and jumped into my motor before smashing through the gates of the private car park.

Before I reached home, and once it had got dark, I stopped in a local park and buried the opinion next to a large oak tree. Nobody noticed.

Later that evening, I was relaxing at home when there was a knock on the door.

"Excuse me, sir," said a tall male police officer, looking rather threatening. "Are you the Mr Haynes who visited Grantworth Private 'Ospital this afternoon?"

"Yes, that would be me," I replied, somewhat hesitantly.

"Are you in possession of an opinion which you 'aven't paid for?" said plod.

"Well, the consultant gave me his opinion, and I didn't like it. So I decided to leave without it," I replied.

The police officer looked puzzled.

"Anyway," I continued. "I thought all opinions were free in this country. I mean, my opinion is just as valid as your opinion, isn't it?"

"Well, in a way, sir," said PC 49, increasingly perplexed.

He paused for a moment.

"Well, I'm going to let you off with a warning, sir. In future, keep your opinions to yourself," added Plod.

"I will, officer. I will. And thank you for your opinion."

"That's no trouble, sir. Any time," said Sherlock, turning away, delighted in his moral victory.

The door closed. I realised that the opinion would never be safe under that tree, so, as soon as Starsky had reversed his cop car out of the street, I made my way back to the park with a shovel.

I dug where I thought I'd left the opinion but, when I uncovered it, the opinion was that Brexit had been a great idea. This certainly wasn't my opinion, though I could understand why someone might want it buried. I dug again: "Liz Truss will make a great Prime Minister." No, not mine, though I know this one came from the *Daily Mail* because I'd seen it hanging around the park late one night.

I dug and dug but I couldn't find the consultant's opinion. Someone had clearly stolen it.

Weeks later, I bumped into a man in the supermarket with only one leg. I asked him what had happened to the other one?

"Oh," he said. "I had it removed. It was my consultant's opinion."

He said he'd been surprised because he'd only gone to the hospital with a sprained ankle.

John Howes

March 5

A Youth Club Story

Every Friday I walked to the local youth club in the nearby village hall. It was a short walk from the end of our dark, unlit drive. I ran as the trees rattled and their leaves rustled with unexplainable eerie sounds, especially on the return home when it seemed to be an even darker pitch black. At the end of the evening, I sighed with relief as I slammed the old, green wooden front door tightly shut. Although we didn't lock the doors back then, I was home at last and warmed my backside against the Rayburn in our farmyard kitchen.

Our youth club was held in an old First National school building that opened in 1836. It later became a village hall when the council purchased the building in 1954. We were cold, and kept our coats on during the winter without heating. The large room had plain white walls and by the late 1950s it was warmer with curtains. In those days it seemed colder in the winters and warmer in the summers. The only heating added later was electric strip heaters suspended on chains from high in the rafters of the hall. Naturally heat rises and kept the heat in the high roof space warm, not the large hall beneath.

We were young and coped with the cold. We were busy enjoying ourselves, dancing and singing to The Beatles, including *Please, Please Me*; *I Wanna Hold Your Hand*; *Can't Buy Me Love*; *A Hard Day's Night* and *I Feel Fine*. There were risky words to a young country girl: *Love Me Do*; *Hold Me Tight*; *I Want To Be Your Man*; *I Should've Known Better*! It was wonderful to sing and dance to the Beatles, music I loved. There were more boys than girls but nobody I really fancied. Even if I had, I wouldn't have told anybody.

There was one occasion when somebody switched off the lights and one of the boys kissed me. Shock, horror! I think the girls were chatting in the kitchen, but, by the time the lights were put back on, there weren't any boys around and it was never mentioned. Just a mysterious first kiss, a quick peck on the cheek.

The village hall youth club provided a small table for us to play snooker, pool or maybe table tennis. Visiting the village website recently, it could be the same one that's there today.

That must have been when I began an interest in snooker as my husband used to play and my son still plays but not competitively these days. In 1982 it was exciting to watch the first official maximum break of 147 to be televised. It was scored in professional snooker, by a favourite player, Steve Davis. We would watch the famous snooker players in the 1980s, including Ray Reardon, Cliff Thorburn and the Welsh Terry Griffiths, late into the middle of the night.

One of the highlights of my youth club experiences was the Country Dancing Weekend when I was 14. Mother made me a special dress for the occasion. To save money, as I was the middle sibling of three sisters, Mother made most of our dresses and we could choose the material and pattern. I felt the bee's knees. My dress was a sleeveless blue and green tartan, Black Watch material pinafore dress with a drop waist skirt and pleats that swished when I twirled. Underneath I wore a long blue sleeved blouse, and navy stockings held up with a suspender belt, as it was 1963 before I wore tights.

It was a thrilling weekend in an old stone building in Grendon, Northamptonshire. We danced in a huge dark room with few ceiling lights. The dances included *The Dashing White Sergeant* and *Gay Gordons* when we galloped around the large hall and did the 'do-si-do' to the left and to the right, in a circle of boys next to girls when ordered to do so.

I felt great, my full skirt swirling this way and that to the fast music. Suddenly there was an order from the Master of Ceremonies to grab your lady and whisk her across the floor. Before I knew what was happening, this older man, tall with unkempt longish dark hair (he must have been in his 30s which seemed very old) grabbed me and flung me over his shoulder and carried me to the other side of the room. Wow, I was stunned.

By the time I regained my breath, he was gone. I don't remember speaking to him. I was shy and totally out of my comfort zone.

That night the girls slept in a large dormitory room in the hall, with beds lined up on each side of the room.

A youth club weekend to remember in Grendon, over sixty years ago!

Kate A Harris

March 6

Police Report

Date: 22 December 2023
Location: East Meadows Shopping Centre, Franks and Smith department store.
Reporting officer: PC Clifford Ward for Inspector Bea Stone, West Midlands FHQ.
Type of report: Theft with staff collaboration.
Time: 10.20am. The shop was very busy with the Christmas rush.
Report: Security Guard Allen reported to me that he noticed the old lady was struggling through the detectors with at least four bags of shopping.

He gave a description of eighty years old approximately, grey hair, lined face, grey tweed coat, three-quarter length possible grey skirt. beige shoes and nondescript glasses that he couldn't identify.

When the alarm sounded, he saw the suspect struggling through the detector showing no sign of progressing. He inquired if anything was wrong. Rather than go through the bags he looked at her and promptly allowed her through saying she must have made a mistake in the technology.

He didn't think that an inoffensive OAP could be on a shoplifting expedition.

Security guard Baldwin approached at marching speed to inform Alan that all bags were full with stolen goods taken predominantly from the home jewellery sections plus perfume section. Both guards gave chase.

The suspect in grey's faltering gait became a fast march and her posture more erect, while continually increasing speed.

The guards almost lost sight of the now rapidly jogging suspect; unsurprisingly, her glasses and grey wig were soon ejected along with false nose and old person make-up.

Guard Baldwin felt he was chasing a Paula Radcliffe simultaneously able to run at pace and carry four bags of kitchenware.

Only when a handle burst on one of the carriers did the suspect stumble over their stolen goods and was soon apprehended by the out of breath guards.

The suspect later was identified as Di Foster, well-known confidence trickster and thief. recently having lost weight in one of his majesty's detention centres

As Guard Baldwin said to me "We should help the aged who don't help themselves."

PC Ward reporting.

Chris Wright

March 7

Growing Pains

It was late afternoon when Daisy reached the glade at the centre of the forest. She'd been walking all day and her bag was heavy. Everything she owned was in that bag or stuffed in the pockets of her dazzling bright garments. Not for her the drab black of the crone - she chose the vivid colours of youth. She didn't want people to be afraid of her; she wanted them to admire her. Besides, she looked dreadful in black.

Her feet ached and she sat down on a moss-covered log to consider her situation. The trees cast long shadows over the grass, but the clearing wasn't a gloomy place. It was light and welcoming and Daisy felt safe. A tangle of blackberry bushes promised to bear plenty of fruit in the autumn and mushrooms dotted the ground beneath an ancient oak. A small stream ambled past her and fish darted through the clear water. Flashes of sunlight glancing off their scaled bodies turned them into tiny rainbows.

Her eyes filled with tears as she re-lived her last morning in the village. Her father had been so angry with her, calling her harsh names that still burned, saying she was no longer his daughter. He'd turned her out of her home as her mother pleaded with him and her sisters wept. Her neighbours' jeering laughter and their pleasure in her disgrace stung her deeply; she'd thought they were her friends. But, as she relaxed and enjoyed the warmth of the sun on her back, her sadness and her shame slowly melted away until she was at peace, harmony restored.

She removed a tiny black velvet drawstring bag from her bodice and fumbled with the complicated knot. For a moment she thought she'd never be able to untie it, but then the knot fell apart of its own accord and the bag was spread open before her. It contained a single large seed, an odd-looking thing, all straight edges not oval, black and white not green or brown. The instructions were written in a small, crabbed hand on a slip of parchment. Although some of the words were difficult to make out, their meaning was clear and she knew what to do.

Finding the right spot didn't take her long. She dug a small hole twenty paces from the stream, opposite the path leading back to her village. Now she had to wait for the moon to rise. There was enough time to eat and she was grateful to her mother for the bread and cheese. She ate and drank water from the stream while twilight fell and the forest grew quiet.

The full moon rose and illuminated the clearing with its pearly light. Daisy picked up the seed and blew softly on it.

'The air of my body.'

She took a silver knife from her pocket and cut her finger, allowing three drops of blood to fall on the seed.

'The fire of my blood.'

She placed the seed in the hole and covered it with soil brought from her garden.

'The earth of my home.'

Finally she watered the seed with tears shed for her lost home.

'The water of my eyes.'

She curtsied to the moon to complete the ritual. She watched and waited, afraid nothing would happen.

Then, in the soft moonlight, she saw a small swelling appear in the ground. It grew and twisted and turned, stretching and groaning, all angles and lines, until after one loud groan, the earth heaved and a small cottage shook itself free, showering clods of soil and clumps of grass over the glade.

She opened the door and stepped inside. The moon shone through the window and showed her a small room with a fireplace. A sleeping loft was tucked beneath the eaves of the thatched roof, next to the chimney to keep her warm in winter. It was perfect for her. She would be happy there.

Daisy had been afraid that her father had been right, that the pedlar had swindled her, but now she felt vindicated. The pedlar had not lied. It was a houseplant.

Fran Neatherway

March 8

Two People

Algernon Wallis Smythe, merchant banker, privately educated, true blue Conservative reads only truly Conservative newspapers. He believes people who live on the street choose to do so. They do not want to work or wash, just to beg, take drugs or drink alcohol. Algernon believes they should be removed from London to the wilds of say Scotland where he does not have to see them.

Algernon thinks they got it wrong when they handed out so many British passports to Commonwealth countries. There are so many foreigners in our country now. Also the whole Windrush thing was a great mistake, look how many of them are over here now! They don't have the same attitude to work as the British. It is time the government took proper control and sorted everything out!

Ethan Smith had lived his first fifteen years in an old bus, travelling round England, until the bus finally rusted away. Then he moved into a hippy type commune market garden in the wilds of Wales working on the land earning his keep with his own toil without being registered or paying any taxes.

Ethan believes people should love and care for each other not hate, to make the world a better place. He also worries about global warming; he does everything he can to live green.

Ethan knows that people sleeping rough on the streets are there for many different reasons: a relationship breaks up and a person no longer has a home; a business goes bankrupt; someone has no money for the mortgage; their home is repossessed. The capitalistic way of life does not suit everyone, they can't cope and no one notices until it is too late.

On the commune they provide one nourishing meal a day for anyone who needs it and they run a food bank too.

Ethan knows he can't help everyone and he also knows he must protect his own mental health. He finds the gardening helps.

There are people in the world who accept and help others for who they are, and there are those who judge, and do nothing. It is easy to see how discrimination can arise from these thoughts about the value of others.

Ruth Hughes

March 9

Working At Home-Two-Timing

Date: Monday, 8 January 2024
From: Diane Marston, Project Lead
Subject: security system
Brian, for the last time, we do not run node.js on our web server. :exasperated:
That said, your outline for the security system is a good one and I attach a copy with a few alterations for you to comment on.

Date: Monday, 8 January 2024
From: Diane Marton, Project Manager
Subject: proposed security system
Thank you for your comments on the draft plan for the security system. We will now proceed with the implementation as specified. I know how much you dislike node.js, but it's what we have to work with.

    The review meeting on Friday is moved from 2pm to 3pm. Ian has a leaving do to go to.

    No, I don't know what's going on between Molly and Dave. As long as my team members get their work done, their romantic entanglements are not my concern. We all have full-time jobs, after all.

    Also, my name is Marton, not Marston.

Date: Tuesday, 9 January 2024
From: Diane Marston, Project Lead
Subject: dependency injection
Does anyone know of a good explanation of dependency injection,

with examples? Steve needs to be brought up to speed. :hard_work:

Date: Tuesday, 9 January 2024
From: Diane Marton, Project Manager
Subject: Re: Dependency Injection
Molly says the best explanation of dependency injection she knows of is this video clip (attached, but you can find it on YouTube).

Date: Tuesday, 9 January 2024
From: Diane Marston, Project Lead
Subject: Re: dependency injection
Thanks a lot -- Steve found the video clip very helpful. :good_job:
With only 37 and a half hours in the week, we need all the help we can get.
:work:
P.S. The progress meeting on Friday has been moved from 4pm to 3pm. I think Charles wants to leave for the bowls club early. :sigh:

Date: Wednesday, 10 January 2024
From: Diane Marston, Project Lead
Subject: Re: progress meeting
Sorry, the change of time of Friday's meeting is absolutely irreversible. Charles is in charge and what he says goes. :fingerwag:
The meeting will be held on Zoom with the same credentials as last time. If you don't have them please let me know ASAP and I'll send them again.

Date: Thursday, 11 January 2024
From: Diane Marton, Project Manager
Subject: review meeting
Just a reminder that Friday's meeting will be held at *3pm* on Google Meet as usual. Please don't be late.

Date: Friday, 12 January 2024
From: Diane Marston, Project Lead
Subject: Progress Meeting
I hope you get the problems you were having with your camera fixed. It's always annoying when we can't see each other.
:crazy_eyes:
I attach a summary of the main points of discussion and decisions made. I know it's a tight deadline, but we can meet it if we stick at it.
:puff:

Date: Monday, 15 January 2024
From: Ian Walsh, Section Head
Subject: Review Meeting
Brian, I realise that you were having problems with your computer's camera at the meeting on Friday, but I gained the impression from what I could see that you weren't paying attention. I try not to pry into people's personal circumstances, but I expect meetings to have members' undivided attention, however boring they might be.
    Your appraisal starts next week.

Jim Hicks

March 10

The Rightful Heiress

I was working on August 25th 2005, when my boss Julia came to me on my afternoon shift to talk to me. She looked tired, with dark rings around her eyes. She clearly had had no sleep.

"Camila, can we talk in my office?" Julia said with a very southern accent.

She knocked on the counter, and I looked up at her. I was serving cake to a customer when she encountered me. I turned my head to my friend and colleague Alexander who was serving another customer next to me.

"Hey, Alex, can you cover for me? Boss wants me in her office," I said casually. Alex glanced up from the coffee machine.

"Sure, no probs, hun, you've definitely got a promotion!" Alex said with a laugh as he put up his thumb to me.

I nodded my head in agreement, fixed my dress, and then headed for Julia's office. It was only small, but it held a lot. I knocked on the door and entered swiftly. As I closed the door, I looked around at the office, trying to find Julia within the crowded office. I spotted her amongst files of all different heights and sitting at her desk. She didn't say anything at first. She just slid over a box of tissues to me.

"Camila! I am sorry to tell you this but your uncle in England has passed away. Apparently, you are needed to sort out his affairs," Julia said. I looked confused and shocked.

Suddenly, a man appeared from behind some shelves within the office. "You must be Camila, I am Neville, the driver, here to take you to the airport," the strange man said.

He held out his hand for me to shake. I reached out and shook it, lost for words, I made a swift exit out of the office and rushed to tell Alex everything.

"So, you're saying you must leave because your uncle died, who you never knew, by the way, and you have to be taken to England to sort out his affairs, today!?" Alex said, in a high tone.

"Yes, that's exactly what I'm saying. What shall I do, Alex? What do I even say to them?" I said, puzzled.

I poured coffee into a man's cup as Alex tapped me on the shoulder.

"All I see is a free trip to England and shopping," Alex said, laughing a little.

He leant up on the counter and started rocking, forwards to backwards, mumbling the word, "Shopping". I laughed.

"You can come Alex, if... you provide the entertainment along the way," I said, as I handed a man a cookie. Alex lifted up from the counter. He looked worried.

"Did I hear the word 'entertainment?' Girl, that's totally my thing," Alex said. This time, he wasn't looking at me. He was serving a customer.

I handed my duties to Alex, again, and headed back to Julia's office. This time, she was in heavy conversation with the man who called himself Neville. I entered the office, this time without knocking, and I faced both of them.

"I have decided to come to England with you, but I have one condition - that my friend, Alex, comes with me," I demanded. Both of them looked shocked that I spoke to them that way. Julia just looked at me and then towards Neville.

"Neville, do you agree to these terms Camila has stated?" Julia asked. She rose from her chair and then stepped away from her desk. Neville looked stunned. He didn't expect to be pressured into anything, yet he glanced at me and smiled.

"Yes, your friend is welcome to come. The more, the merrier! I will come back tomorrow at noon to pick you guys up. Pack a suitcase. You guys will be in England for a while," Neville said. He headed for the door and then left the office.

A while? What did he mean by this? I thought. I left the office too and headed to Alex to tell him the news.

Alex and I had taken the afternoon off work to pack for the trip. I only packed one suitcase, and not many clothes. I expected to go shopping for British designers once I had arrived. Alex packed one suitcase and two travel bags. He insisted on a full bag of makeup and loads of shoes. Obviously, it was his choice what he brought with him. We headed to the car and got in. We were directed to plug in our seat belts, and we could help ourselves to refreshments if we wanted them. I sat still and quiet. I felt uncomfortable in the car surrounded by the one person I knew, Alex, and strangers, who claimed to be workers employed by my uncle. The radio played, and I sat in silence for the whole ride to the airport.

The airport was huge. I grabbed my bag and headed to a woman at the desk. She asked for my ticket and ID, and I handed it to her. She wished me well on my trip and smiled. Alex and I boarded the plane, and we sat down in our seats. We spoke and admired our view from the plane. Alex talked about the fashion magazine for a while. I was worried about the trip. I hadn't really had a connection with my uncle, and we weren't close. To me, being his heir, that shocked me. Seventeen years ago, rumours spread about my uncle having a son. No one had found any proof of this, though.

The flight was over. I was in England. We had to take a white taxi to my uncle's manor home. Alex was excited to see the British culture and fashion. I took lots of pictures and recorded my time here. Alex and I giggled and laughed over the silliest things.

"We're here," the taxi driver said. We paid him, and we then left the taxi. We stepped onto freshly mown grass; I knew this because Alex had his hay-fever going nuts. A pebbled driveway came next. Our suitcases were bumping around on the ground as we turned a corner to the front of the house. This house was colossal. It had white walls and vines growing up and around it. Its windows were mouldy, mossy, and almost completely shattered. There were walls around the building. This house was lonely.

We headed inside. There were paintings of all shapes and sizes and tables made of oak. The setting was very regal. I met the lawyer, and we discussed my uncle's affairs. He took me into a private room to talk and sign a few documents.

"So, are you prepared to take on the estate and everything that your uncle left to you?" the lawyer said.

I nodded my head, and we began to process the forms. The lawyer handed me some papers to sign - about three. I lifted the pen and was prepared to scribble my signature down on the dotted lines when we were interrupted.

"Wait!" a man shouted loudly. The door swung open with haste, and two men entered the room.

"You can't go ahead with this," one man shouted again.

My lawyer looked at me clearly, thinking I knew something, but I had no idea what was going on.

"And why can't we go ahead with this? Camila is the rightful heiress to this estate and everything connected to her uncle's affairs," my lawyer said as he stood up and took off his glasses.

One of the men reached into his pocket, opened a wallet and took out a photograph and handed it to my lawyer. "It's me and my father when I was three," the taller man said.

My lawyer took the photo from him, observed it for a moment, and then headed to his desk. He opened the top drawer and took my papers from in front of me.

"What's going on?" I said. I began to look around at the men and then to my lawyer. The lawyer took out a green folder from his desk.

"Please take a seat, gentlemen. We all have a very important matter to discuss," the lawyer said, as he took a seat opposite me.

Everyone took their seats. I was really confused.

"Please can someone tell me what's going on?" I said again, but this time my voice was no longer the kind tone it was before. I wanted answers, and I wanted them now.

"This boy claims to be your cousin, Camila. Meaning that now a new approach must be taken, " the lawyer said.

He began placing new documents in front of us all. My eyes skimmed through the documents. I saw the words 'competition', 'two weeks' and 'estate'. I then read through all of the documentation.

"There were rumours that your uncle had a son, Camila. Of course, none of that was ever proven, but just in case anyone decided to claim the estate after your uncle died, he had a plan for it," the lawyer said and handed me one document about a competition that was written in my Uncle's handwriting:

"Throughout my years of being alive, I have had many lovers, and many have claimed that I have had a child with them, but nothing was actually proven. I suspect that, somewhere, I probably do have a child, and, someday, that child may decide to claim my family's fortunes. However, I am aware that at this time I have a niece, Camila, who I want to give everything to. But if a child claims to be mine, then I decree that Camila and this child, will have two weeks and have many tasks to prove themselves worthy of my estate and fortunes. If evidence comes to light that they aren't biologically related to me, after the competition has started, it is then too late, and they can still claim everything. If my Camila doesn't win the competition I have set, she doesn't need to worry because I have left her £45,000 cash and my bookcase with her favourite books in as her inheritance but she will lose the estate and everything within it. I wish everyone good luck and the winner at the end of the competition with the most points (and a few other things, details to come) will win everything. Good luck!"

I read through this and almost cried. My uncle knew I hated competitions, so why would he put me through this one?

"I will do it," I said. The words came out of my mouth so fast that I couldn't argue with myself or change my mind. I was in this for the long run, and I did not want to give up now. I took the pen and scratched my name above the dotted line 'Camila Lydwell'. I was now part of my uncle's test. I could not let him or my family down.

Chloe Huntington

March 11

My Life Of Crime

After an incident in town recently, we were driven home in a police car. As they drove us home, I told the two policemen about when, many years ago, the Police Training Centre invited theatre members to take part in crime situations, and improvise as victims or criminals, which the trainees had to deal with. I volunteered with other members and on the Saturday we turned up at the centre.

In the first scenario I was in the driving seat of a car, having committed an unspecified crime, so I grabbed the ignition key, got out and threatened to poke it in the cop's eye. He was scared stiff, ran off and hid behind a building.

The two policemen driving us home thought it was hilarious and said, 'I bet they said, "Don't have her again".'

But I had forgotten about the next scene that I was designated. I was a dead body and had to lie still on a cold concrete floor in what looked like an open-fronted bike store somewhere near the perimeter fence.

I lay there for ages but nobody came. I kept lifting my head up and peering round into the far distance, but no-one was about, until, at last, someone came and said, 'You can get up now. We're not doing this scene after all.'

It did not dawn on me, until we were back at home, after the two policemen had dropped us off, that I had been a genuine victim. That police trainee I had scared to death with the car key had fixed it and this was his revenge.

Still, it was a great day, including free lunch in the canteen with the cops, but I'm not sure where it fits in my CV.

Wendy Goulstone

March 12

A Metropolitan Day Out

Our university was not far from London but far enough to be comfortable. Me, Mark and Mike were looking forward to the festivities in the City of London including a visit to Saint Paul's which was going to be anything but sightseeing.

We hurried into London by train and many of the usual commuters clustered round as did holidaymakers, with suitcases and clutching passports. I never believed travel broadened the mind but that day I was going to have my consciousness expanded forever with a fifteen-mile trip.

We arrived looking for others like us and commenced with the traditional leaping over the tube train barriers. As expected there was no one point of focus but many small disruptive events protesting the City's involvement with the arms industry in 1983.

The late start meant we were already getting hungry. I shouted to Mike, "I've only brought five pound for the whole day."

He said, "If you like vegetarian food we'll go to the free stand outside Saint Paul's."

Sure enough a friendly woman in striped pantaloons was handing out lentil burgers and oat milk. It didn't sound too appetising to me but for nothing I couldn't complain.

We rounded a corner to see stockbrokers, that is suited office workers, using the pedestrian crossing again and again, effectively holding up the traffic with the sign saying *Stockbrokers against the bomb*.

But we were hurrying towards the Tower of London. Our appetite for free stuff was not sated as we headed for the free concert. How had Mark heard about all this in an era before email and internet? Arriving at the Tower, disappointingly few protesters were waiting for the concert to begin. This was due to a misapprehension on our part because the concert venue was mobile!

An ear-splitting chorus of *Stop the city, Stop the city* came down Tower Hill carried by a bus or coach; one side removed to make a stage. One of the most amazing memories of my early life was dashing around London with a crazy band bashing out *Stop the city* to anyone nearby unfortunate enough to have ears.

We blitzed the centre of London causing a racket and effecting zero change to zero opinions. Eventually we went around the back to the White Tower and the waiting arms of the Metropolitan Police.

However, my friends and I benefited from the appearance of average students without crazy haircuts or punk rock badges on our rather plain jackets. We jumped around about five feet to the pavement and avoided the police not for the last time that day.

Euphoric at escaping, we rushed to St Paul's. Almost one hundred people, sat on St Paul steps claiming an ancient right of sanctuary, were being corralled or 'kettled' by police officers while a colleague walked his horse towards the seated demonstrators. This was not in Brazil or Bolivia but in Margaret Thatcher's UK.

Fortunately for the demonstrators, horses are good-natured and there was the appearance of desperate dressage to avoid the human cobblestones and traumatising the horse almost as much as the demonstrators and myself.

With some of the joy taken out of the day, we met Matthew in Threadneedle Street. He had been in heated discussion with police officers for several minutes. Suddenly, a phalanx of nine constables walked around the corner to sweep up the protesters like skittles. It was a tennis match. I was turning to Matthew for instructions and then back to the scene and suddenly Mark and Mike were on the other side of the phalanx.

I was baffled. With the constables bearing down on me, Mark and Mike encouraged me, "Come on Chris. Edge through. They won't do anything!" Sure enough I simply turned sideways, walked through the gap and joined my friends. Unfortunately when Matthew tried the same trick, he was arrested, shouting, "Tell my mom!"

Only the stockbrokers caused any serious inconvenience to Londoners going about their business and even they only gave slight pause for thought, and soon we slipped away back to university in time for *Top of the Pops* and baked beans on toast.

Chris Wright

March 13

Learning To Swim

It all began when I went for swimming lessons and learnt to swim. I was nine years old, in the old swimming baths on the Northampton Road in Market Harborough.

I've always loved swimming wherever I've lived and been on holiday, in hotel swimming pools or occasionally in the sea, across various parts of the world.

The Harborough baths, four miles from the village where I lived, were designed by Herbert George Coales, who was the surveyor and engineer and partner of the architect, Henry Winter Johnson. The Baths were officially opened in 1896. I discovered they also designed the new Grammar School on Burnmill Road in 1909 which I attended in the early 1960s and is now known as the Robert Smyth Academy,

Mr Grimond was my swimming teacher. He was a short, grumpy older man with grey hair and frown lines and I was too frightened of him not to swim, as I didn't want him to tell me off.

Mother took my younger sister Diana and me for weekly swimming lessons. Warm humid air would hit us as we went into the building, especially on a cold winter's day. After we'd paid for our lessons, through a window in the ticket office on the right, the strong smell of chlorine pervaded our nostrils as we continued to walk through the turnstile at the far side of the entrance. I had another fear, of getting stuck, as it was difficult to push the stiff turnstile round and move forward, but it always did.

The changing rooms were on two levels - the upstairs with curtains to pull across for Ladies and downstairs just a half wooden stable door for Gents. We could see their heads over the top and feet below the doors. In each ladies' cubicle there was a bench to sit on when changing and clothes hooks on the wall. There weren't any locks and everyone trusted everyone else not to peek at us when we were changing nor steal our clothes.

It was embarrassing if we were changing and someone pulled the curtain back looking for their clothes or hoping for an empty cubicle, and a little awkward when some of the curtains didn't quite fit across the cubicle, the curtain hooks were broken and the curtain dropped off its hanging rail. For modesty's sake, somehow, the curtain needed to be held at the same time as getting dry and dressed!

When going into the changing room I threw off my clothes, as I'd put on my plain black, probably nylon and Lycra all-in-one swimsuit underneath my clothes at home, to save time changing and be in the pool as soon as possible. I wrapped a towel around me and ran down the steps as I didn't want to be last in the pool, and put my towel by the side wall and then jumped in. We had to learn to be restrained and not run along the side of the pool as it was wet and slippery. We often had to be reminded to walk, not run.

At last I was splashing in the warmish water, holding onto the side, hands gripping tightly on the bar that ran around the pool. Our elbows bent next to the tiles lining the baths, my hands gripping for dear life as we splashed our legs. 'Keep legs straight, and splash,' Mr Grimond instructed. And we obeyed his instructions and learnt to swim.

It took some time to learn to dive and this was not something I enjoyed. I didn't like to swim under water and didn't like to be splashed or have water in my eyes as the strong chlorine, used to kill bacteria, stung my eyes making them a little red and sore. Those first few lessons I remember worrying what would happen if I let go. Would my head go under water? Would I drown?

Mr Grimond told us to put our feet down. We were in the shallow end. Then we had to do the 'doggy paddle' with legs behind us splashing up and down and paddling with our hands, as a dog would swim. I soon mastered the art and 'swam' a few strokes. We went to lessons for many weeks to perfect our style. I needed to know how to swim before going to secondary school.

We went every week and moved up the baths towards the deep

end as our confidence and swimming progressed. I remember that I could swim before attending secondary school at the age of eleven.

The swimming pool was seventy-five feet long and twenty-five feet wide with a springboard and a ten-foot diving board. I jumped and dived off the springboard, only a few feet above the side of the pool. However, I took a sharp intake of breath when I jumped, not dived, off the ten-foot high board. It was unbelievably high and scary with many steps to climb to the top. I used to jump off the top which would not be allowed today, for health and safety reasons, as the pool was only six feet deep in the deepest end. It was a dangerous activity, but who knew back then that the water needed to be deeper, for it to be safe? We did not know and I don't remember anybody harming themselves.

I had learned how to jump in and how to dive to compete in the annual school galas. I remember that there was a slim space around the pool and anybody sitting by the side watching the swimming could be soaked, especially when there were swimming competitions!

Amongst items of memorabilia I've hoarded over the years is my County of Leicestershire Education Committee Swimming Certificate for passing Grade 11 of the committee's Swimming Tests signed by the Head Teacher J W Colley on May 29 1961. All competitors are listed, some I remember, most I don't, as they were older than me.

I was keen to participate in the swimming for our school house team. There were three houses: Bragg, who usually won; Wartnaby, my house; and Hammond. Unfortunately, I was always too nervous in competitions and splashed around too much in a panic. I should have calmed down and swam forwards fast enough to compete. I was so keen and excited that father, a busy man on the farm, would take time to watch me swim.

In the saved programme of the 1961 Gala, all the names of the swimmers are listed in all the heats and father wrote on the paper programme where competitors finished. I was probably the only pupil who has recorded results events from 1961! I competed in the 25 yards Very Junior Back Crawl and 50 yards Age Group 10 years.

Father wrote the names of competitors and their times, giving me a tick by my name for entering the competition although I did not finish in the top three places, which must have been disappointing for him. Maybe I was put into the heats, to make up the numbers.

I remember my friend Ann and I would compete against other swimmers in our heats and in one race I was fourth and she was fifth and vice versa in the other race. We both panicked and weren't successful in the swimming competitions.

As there wasn't any heating in the baths, besides the swimming pool water heating, we didn't hang around after we were dried and dressed and soon left the pool.

The baths eventually closed in 1991. They were demolished and a retirement complex, Marshall Court, was built in their place. There is a new leisure centre with a swimming pool about a mile up the Northampton Road, outside the town, with the original plaque of our old swimming baths on the wall outside the building.

Kate A Harris

March 14

Pip

First, there was just the warm, safe comfort of the womb and the steady beat of a mother's heart, surrounded by others just like him who then disappeared one by one. Then quite unexpectedly it was cold and he took his first breath surrounded by his six brothers and sisters and was vigorously licked by his mother.

This all seemed very strange but, tucked up snugly next to his mother and surrounded by siblings with food on tap, this new life wasn't half bad.

A week passed and another new experience: his eyes opened and after a while, he started to put names to things he only heard before. He also became aware he wasn't as strong as his brothers or sisters and quite often they would push him off the delightful food source even when there was no need. By about week four, even his mother was beginning to ignore him to the extent that the farmer's wife had to feed him with a bottle. He was beginning to realise he was not like the others, not as strong, and deprived of his mother's milk, wasn't developing as fast as his siblings. About week five, some strange humans came to visit, looking to give the pups new homes, and one by one all the others were selected except him. He heard the farmer saying he was the runt and would never find a home away from the farm, and had a mother who by now completely shunned him.

Perhaps this was how life was. The pup had no idea; he was still fed and had a nice bed of straw all to himself so things were not so uncomfortable.

His siblings were rolling around and playing with each other in play fights but none played with him or, if they did, it was usually very unpleasant and they would hurt him to the point that he didn't get involved any more.

Outside, the sun was climbing higher in the sky and getting

warmer, creating all sorts of interesting smells and sounds everywhere, with fantastic blue and yellow plants of all shapes and sizes springing up from nowhere. On such a day, three humans came and the farmer said this was all he had left. You can have him but be warned, he has a dicky heart so we can't give you any paperwork to qualify his breed even though he comes from a pedigree stock of Springer Spaniels that have won awards at Crufts. The farmer picked him up and put him in the arms of one of the younger visitors and as he looked up their eyes met. He felt his tiny heart beat a little faster. The older visitors took a photo of the moment and soon they were gone again.

At eight weeks, all his brothers and sisters went off to new homes and he was left alone. By now he was used to being by himself, wandering around the farm, discovering new smells, sights and sounds in the warming Spring air, and chasing the odd chicken or even being chased by them was fun. He also loved scaring the odd mouse he came upon though the rats were best left alone as they were nearly as big as he was.

Then during the eighth week of his life, the three visitors returned. He instantly recognised the smell of the younger one who had been so gentle with him and once again his heart beat faster. Was his future with these three nice people? The younger one picked him up and carried him to a car. As they both sat in the back seat he instantly knew he liked this place. It had many new smells but one stood out - the friendly younger human. When the vehicle began to move, it was a strange but not unpleasant sensation. There were lots of new things to smell, on the seats, in the air and the two older people in the front seats. All this was just so exciting it wore him out and, being completely exhausted, he curled up in the young man's lap and drifted off to sleep.

He never knew it but the older male never wanted another dog in the family, because having one was like having a child that never grew up and was a serious commitment altering many things including holidays, but as the years passed, he became more fond of this new family member than he ever thought possible.

The pup sensed the comforting vibration and noise that reminded him of his mother's womb stop. On waking he was being carried into a strange building unlike anything on the farm. It had soft bed-like material all over the ground and in one corner a cage with the most delightfully comfortable bed he had ever experienced. His new humans had made a special place for him to toilet but he was so used to being outside he never really took to it and would often do his business on the carpet. He also noted every time they talked to him they said Pip (for Pipsqueak).

After a few days it dawned on him that it was to be his name plus puppy, doggy, little man and, his favourite, good boy, The next experience was the garden that was part of his new home. There were fences all around this large bit of ground that was all his to roam freely in via the special doors fitted in the main house's back doors; the garden was full of the most exotic smells Pip had ever known and as spring was now well-established, it had flowers and insects everywhere.

All sorts of birds were encouraged onto special little tables and miniature houses. He recognised the tell-tale scents of mice at the top of the long garden that reminded him of his birthplace, probably encouraged by all the bird feed scattered around.

Pip soon settled in his new home that he regarded as his domain and although he was just a tiny ball of fur felt, it was his responsibility to protect it and his humans as his pack from anything that entered this property. He had great fun chasing the birds away but even more so those pesky grey squirrels that were encouraged by all the easy pickings of the bird food.

Of course, he had absolutely zero chance of actually catching anything but that never stopped him trying. One of his favourite pastimes was chasing balls thrown by his people in the long garden and returning them again and again and again. If they got tired of doing it, he would take the ball and drop it at their feet or put it in their lap as a hint he wanted some more.

Then something unpleasant happened. His people took him to a strange place that smelled of all sorts of other animals and he was left there. Other unfamiliar humans put him on a table and stuck a needle in him. He awoke in a great deal of pain in this funny-smelling place in a cage. Never had he experienced anything so frightening so he cried as loud and as long as he could, calling for his humans to take him home. The nice but scary people realised this was not good for him and brought back his people early who gently picked him up and took him to that safe womb-like car and brought him back to his own bed. Now he was back home and over the next few days the pain slowly went away.

The first year passed and then another. Developing much quicker than human children, he realised there were different times of year, some when he just liked to curl up by the fire and others when he and his people spent most of the time outside. The cage had long since been folded up and his bed now lay where it once had been. Pip's favourite time of day in spring, summer, autumn and winter was his walks to the park where he met others of his kind to play with. Some of these he soon learned were not friendly, reminding him of his infancy and to avoid them at all costs. The park had a stream running through it that was a delight beyond description, where he could find places where his feet couldn't touch the bottom and he could float; he discovered he could swim and dive, doing all sorts of things he couldn't on dry land.

One day Pip realised there was something wrong with his female human and she was very sick. She stayed in bed for days on end and was unable to walk him or indeed do hardly anything. At this point, he decided she needed him and his closeness would help her so he took to staying with her in her bedroom all day even though her male partner wasn't too keen; he understood that Pip's company was actually helping her condition.

Difficult times passed and his female person slowly recovered even to the point of a return to the walks in the park but he knew instinctively he needed to look after her and often barked at people who came too close. He also knew instinctively not to bite them but he could make a fair show of being really threatening. Often these people turned out to be friends of his human so, mid-threat, he had to resort to his friendly greeting barks often confusing the friend.

A couple of times a year he had to revisit the vets, who turned out to be nice people, but still so scary he found himself peeing on their floor when he saw that dreaded needle.

More years passed and now apparently he was middle-aged. Pip never felt his dicky heart was a problem though the nice vets kept an eye on it just in case.

His favourite person in all the world was the family's granddaughter who almost made him wet himself with pleasure every time she visited. Or he went to her house that had a garden so big it reminded him of the fields where he was born and a ball could be thrown as far as anyone could throw one; even better, it was on a slope that changed the way he had to run and stop.

Pip often lay on the bed at night next to his human and dreamt of the times he was bullied by his siblings and ignored by his mother, with his feet twitching, and he would cry out in the most blood-curdling wolf-like way till he felt that gentle hand stroke his back and heard her soft voice comfort him.

Eight more years passed and at the age of fifteen years, Pip was old beyond any estimates for his life. His muscles hurt, his bones ached and he spent most of his time sleeping. He could no longer jump on the bed to sleep with his human. In fact he couldn't even get up the stairs so he slept on his own bed where he started as a pup.

On a visit to the vets, his people were told to take him home and say their goodbyes and bring him back the next morning, stay with him and tell him he's a good boy as he gently drifted away.

Tucked up in his bed he could see his people crying with tears flowing down their faces and wished he could comfort them but he felt so, so tired. Looking up into their eyes he knew he was loved and his eyes closed for the last time. Then he felt warm all over and all the pains were gone. In a single heartbeat he was a pup again and as light as a feather, bounding up the garden, playing his favourite game, chasing the ball and bringing it back again and again and again forever.

Patrick Garrett

March 15

The Journey Home

I've been really happy here. Everyone thinks I'm daft when I say that but it's true. I've loved the hustle and bustle, the interruptions and constant noise, even the constant beeping of the machines. I've loved the way people say hello when they pass by, and how once a day for a couple of minutes a group of them gather around me and I'm the focus of their attention. It makes me feel like I'm part of the human race. But now I have to leave. They need the bed apparently and I'm well enough to go home.

They gathered up all my things at a record speed earlier. Now I'm sitting in a side room waiting for my transport home. I've been here for hours. They insisted I use a wheelchair. I told them I don't need one; if I did they wouldn't be sending me off to fend for myself. The nurse said it was just in case but I wasn't born yesterday.

I was amazed at the number of people who said goodbye to me this morning. I've tried to store it all up inside; to remember everyone's face and voice so I can relive it over and over once I'm home. Not that I'm going home as I used to know it. I'm going to a flat in a sheltered accommodation block, according to my daughter-in-law. They've decided that I'm not safe to live in my little house any more. I ask you! I told them anyone can have a fall. It's not like I make a habit out of it. But would they listen. No! Apparently this is for my own good and they've put my house on the market. No good dwelling on it, I suppose. It's not like I'm in a position to change anything.

+ +

A few hours later and I'm still sitting on my own. Maybe they've forgotten me. It wouldn't matter to me if they had; it's nice and warm and I can see the hustle and bustle in the corridor outside through the glass in the door. I wouldn't mind a cuppa though. It's been a while since lunch.

It don't half make me jump when the doors fly open. A young man and woman in green stride purposefully towards me and he grabs the wheelchair and spins me round, then breaks into, *Knees up Mother Brown.*

'Dora, is it? Good. Are you ready to go home then?' she asks.

'No.'

'No?' He stops. 'You are Dora? Mrs Brown?'

'Yes, I suppose I am.'

'We were told you were waiting to go home.' The woman comes round and bends down towards me.

'I don't want to. I'm not ready.'

'I'll go and check on the ward,' she says to him as if I'm not there. 'Won't be a minute.'

'No worries,' says he as he breaks into song again and starts dancing up and down the room. I don't know if he's trying to cheer me up or if he's a bit doolally. If it's the first then it won't work, and if it's the second then I can play silly buggers along with the best of them.

I don't get chance though because she's back within minutes with a nurse who stands in front of me looking put out. 'You're going home today, Dora. Can you remember us explaining everything to you earlier?'

'Of course I can. I'm not senile yet!'

'Then Susie and Matt will take you home and get you settled. There's a carer coming in to do your tea this evening and then twice a day after. Is that OK?'

'Not really, no.'

'Why ever not? Most people can't wait to leave us.'

'I don't want to.'

'Of course you do.' She nodded at Matt and Susie and dashed off.

'Come on then, Dora. Let's get you in the warm ambulance, it's cold outside. Do you want a blanket?'

'Not really.'

'OK, let's get you settled. There are three others travelling with you. I think you'll be the last drop-off, so you'll have a bit of a journey, I'm afraid.'

That perked me up a bit.

+ +

They were right; it was a bit nippy outside, especially after spending a few weeks in a warm hospital. I was glad I was in a wheelchair. I'd have frozen if I'd had to walk. They got me settled on the ambulance and Susie stayed with me while Matt went to get the others.

I say ambulance, but it wasn't so much an ambulance per se, not like you see tearing through the streets with lights flashing. It was more of a minibus thing really with space at the back for a wheelchair and nice big windows so I could see the world going by. I could have sat there for hours but Matt was soon back with the others.

They were all more mobile than me and got themselves into their seats. Matt introduced us all, then got in the driver's seat while Susie stayed in the back with us. Everyone was sitting apart, as if we were all frightened of catching something off each other. I reckoned it was going to be a long journey if we all just stared out of the window, so I thought I'd better break the ice.

'So, what were you all in for then?' I aimed my question at the backs of their heads.

'Bit personal there, Dora!' Matt piped up from the front.

'They don't have to say. I was just trying to get a conversation started.'

'I don't mind saying,' Mona replied, 'Me and Frank have been having dialysis, haven't we, Frank.'

'Humph,' came the reply from the front seat.

'Don't mind him, he's not so bad when you get to know him.' Mona winked at me. 'He just can't get his head around having dodgy kidneys. I told him, we're lucky we weren't around a hundred years ago. No dialysis then, was there, Frank?'

'Humph.'

'I've had another injection in my eye.' Pat lifted up her sunglasses to reveal a red, watery orb.

My knees went all wobbly at the thought of someone sticking a needle in my eye. They'd have to catch me first! This Pat was either very brave or a bit gullible in my opinion.

'So,' I quickly moved things on, 'I'm the only one who's been in for weeks then.'

'You must have been very bad,' Pat chuckled.

'Bad at staying upright! I fell and broke my collar bone and arm.'

'Oh dear,' said Mona. 'Are you going to be able to manage?'

'Heaven knows. My son's decided I'm a liability and is selling my house from under me and moving me to an old folks place.'

'That's a bit harsh after one fall.'

'I might have had a few. But that's not the point. I've never broken anything before. I've never even seen my new place but my daughter-in-law insists I'll love it. I won't though.'

Pat smiled sympathetically. 'Where will you be living, Dora?'

'I've no bloody idea.' I could feel the tears pushing against the back of my eyes and fumbled in my bag for a tissue.

'Richmond Court. That's where you're going, Dora,' Susie said.

'And I'm the last one to be dropped off,' I sniffed, 'so it must be miles from anywhere.'

'It's round the corner from me.' Pat handed me a bag of sweets. 'Here, have a Werther's. It's lovely at Richmond Court. I wanted to get in there, but there weren't any spaces, so I'm at Salisbury Court. Frank's there too. Maybe I can come and visit you.'

'Ooh. That would be nice.'

'Do you play bridge?' a gruff voice came from the front seat.

'I used to, years ago.'

'Good. I head up a bridge team at Richmond and we're a player down.'

'I thought you lived in Salisbury, Frank?'

'I do. None of them can play to save their lives. Tuesday mornings at ten. You can get Garth, the handyman to bring you over till you get mobile.'

'That would be great. Thank you Frank.' I smiled at the back of his head but he didn't reply.

I was basking in a warm glow as we pulled up at the entrance to a block of flats. Maybe things wouldn't be so bad after all.

'First stop!' Matt shouted, 'Are you ready, Mona? I'll see you into your flat. Won't be long folks.'

'Nice to meet you, dear,' Mona said as she got off. 'I'll no doubt see you again soon. We all meet up on a Thursday for coffee and I'm sure you'd be very welcome.'

'This is Chichester Court,' Pat said, 'in case you wondered. Ours is around the corner, then it's yours.'

+ +

By the time they'd all gone off to their respective homes and Matt and Susie had settled me in my new flat I was feeling quite hopeful. It's not too bad a place after all. It's on the ground floor so it will be easy for me to get in and out, and I can see a lovely grassy area from the bedroom window.

All my stuff from my old house is here apart from an old cabinet that belonged to my gran. I'd been planning on getting rid of it for ages but I'm not about to tell my son and daughter-in-law that. And if they've sold it, I'm going to make sure they give me the money. It will come in handy at Bridge. Unless they play with matches, of course. I hope they don't.

Every room has rails at strategic points on the walls, which will be handy until I'm mended. I don't intend using them after that. Someone's put a walker in too, which is a bit of a nerve in my opinion, but I won't kick up about it. I'll just get the carer to fold it up and put it in the cupboard. It's a trip hazard left there in the middle of the floor!

All in all this isn't a bad little place, and seeing as how I seem to have made some friends already, I reckon I'm going to be ok here. Once I can get this old arm working normally again, I'll be able to get back to normal with a vengeance. That'll show my son and that wife of his. There's life in the old gal yet. **Rosemary Marks**

March 16

A Bit Of A Shock

Edgar Wishaw, known as Septimus to his friends because of his almost saturnine appearance, sat dolefully staring out of the narrow side-window at the driving sleet.

'Why sleet?' he thought. 'Snow would have been more atmospheric for a funeral. But sleet just soaks all your clothing, and you get cold, and end up with the ague.'

A quick glance at the clock told him it was time he left the vestry, put out the hymn books, and took up his place by the font, to hand out the Order Of Service sheets. His six-foot-plus frame unfolded from the vicar's chair he'd occupied for the last hour, and he shook out the folds of his cassock, so that it no longer stuck to his bony backside.

In long, loping steps he moved down the side-aisle to the font, and just as he finished setting out the hymn books on the pews, he heard the vestry's outer door open, and close. The vicar had arrived. Edgar had moved himself just in time to avoid another condemnatory lecture. Seconds later Keith Walker's face appeared at the vestry door. He nodded and retreated.

Checking up on me. Again! thought Edgar, but then he applied a sympathetic look onto his long, naturally gloomy looking face as the first of the mourners arrived. He handed them an Order Of Service, and told them the first three rows, on both sides, were reserved for the immediate family. At shorter and shorter intervals more people arrived, and then the close relatives. The vicar had taken his place on the chancel step to greet the immediate family with silent nods, as they took the front pews. Finally the coffin entered, hefted up onto the shoulders of Major Hefflin's play-soldiers, as Edgar always referred to them.

A hush had descended, and once everyone was settled back down, and, as Keith Walker opened his mouth to speak his welcome and introduction, the big Western entrance doors flew open with a resounding bang, and a slim, female figure, swathed in clouds of black veiling strode in, marched up to the coffin, placed on it the single deep-purple rose she had brought with her, then turned to face Major Hefflin's wife sitting in the first pew, caught in the act of theatrically dabbing her eyes, her mouth hanging open in silent shock, and looking definitely panicked.

The veiled woman spoke.

"I am Percival Hefflin's wife, and I'm taking him back. Now!"

EE Blythe

March 17

Flower Power

Back in the days of free love, 'flower power', the world was our oyster, and anything was possible. I was the roadie for a rock band called Big Idea who eventually dropped me after many years for a bigger van as the kit was becoming bigger and bigger and my quite large vehicle was just too small. I had no hard feelings as I'd experienced some fantastic things and worked with big name bands and people, including some that were destined to become household names.

A few years after I left, I noticed the elderly parents of a band member and offered them a lift. Mum was friendly as ever but Dad was distinctly cold, unfriendly and hostile towards me. Taken aback somewhat, I dropped them off at home and went away pondering why the aggressive change of attitude towards me.

Months later, while chatting to another band member, it transpired the new roadie was more than a tad friendly with one of band's go-go dancers who were part of the act and just happened to be the daughter of the old fellow, and I was getting the flak for my replacement's amorous pursuits. I could say oops because, had I been the villain of the peace, I wouldn't have minded in the least as the young lady in question was not at all undesirable and quite an accomplished go-go dancer.

Many, many years later our paths crossed again and, reminiscing with her, it turned out we both had a crush on each other but were too shy to do anything about it. Oops again, but it's regrets and life's missed chances that lead us to where we are now and I'm not at all sorry for the way fate played her hand on my behalf. But, what if, just supposing, what if, I can't help but wonder in the wee small hours.

Patrick Garrett

March 18

Springtime

Spring has sprung, the grass is riz
I wonder where the flowers is?
The bird is on the wing I've heard
But that's absurd
I always thought the wing was on the bird!

So goes the zany rhyme that my mother used to recite, to announce the coming of Spring in our part of the world. It was always a bit of fun, and if her motivation for saying it every year was to shake us out of our winter torpor, well, it worked!

Every living thing on the planet looks forward to Spring: a time of renewal, so essential to the rhythm of life. This year, the season is even more special, as springtime 2020 never really happened, with the lockdowns that we've had to endure. The end of a twenty-four-month Winter is finally in sight, with many experiencing twice as much anticipation and twice the enlivening effect of the new season. We can all draw even greater pleasure from imbibing the warmth of the longer days!

Looking back, the drawn-out period of enforced isolation may have had a positive effect. Many have found that the things we took for granted weren't actually essential to our enjoyment of or engagement in life. The restaurant visits have been replaced with more home cooking.

The cinema trips have made way for playing family games and reading more often. Others have found that, rather than consuming media content, that they get more pleasure and fulfilment from creating it. All of this is to the good in boosting one's own self-reliance and ability to cope with whatever life might throw at us in the future.

So here's to springtime! May we all enjoy it to the full, as we cautiously tread our own paths into an uncertain but exciting future.

Simon Parker

March 19

Morning Chorus

When she opened the back door that Sunday morning, Spring stepped in, settled on her nose. She closed her eyes, felt the warmth on her cheeks and breathed in. She tasted the sweetness of violets, the cool scent of snowdrops, the heat of daffodils on her lips.

In the cherry tree a thrush was perched on its podium, practising its notes, over and over again until it was chirp-perfect. A robin hunted for grubs in the flower bed. A pair of sparrows sauntered across the lawn. A Jenny wren, tail up, hopped from twig to twig in the forsythia. Somewhere a blackbird sang.

Today she would take her lunch and a book into the garden and relax.

This was going to be a good day.

That was the plan.

She read two chapters, closed her eyes and dozed, to be woken by the sensation of someone close by.

It was Gary. Was it Gary? He was bronzed, had put on weight, not fat but athletic.

'Hello,' he said. 'I didn't want to wake you.'

'What are *you* doing here? '

'Fantastic welcome, thanks!'

'You are supposed to be in Australia.'

'Well, I am. I mean I'm here now, for a few weeks between jobs. Thought I'd pop over and see the folks.'

'Oh.'

'Well, are you pleased to see me or not?'

'Where's Geraldine?'

'Oh, you know.'

'No, I don't know. You went out with Geraldine, so where is she?'

'Erm, she had work, couldn't get leave. Do you mind if I have that sandwich? I'm a bit peckish. That's if you don't want it. Lousy meal on the plane.'

'Plane? Do you mean to say you came straight here from the airport? Where are your bags?'

'Left them in the porch. Rang the bell. Thought you might be round the back. So, here I am.'

'So, why didn't you go straight to your parents' house?'

'You were the nearest. I thought I would just drop in on my way. So, can I have it? The sandwich?'

'It's ham.'

'Great, I'm famished.'

'I thought you were a vegetarian.'

'I was,' he mumbled, mouth full, 'but you can't be a vegetarian in Australia. It's against the law.'

'Ha, ha! Very funny.' She wondered where this was leading.

'So, when are you going back?'

'Oh, great! I come twelve thousand miles to see you, and you want to get rid of me.'

'I thought you said you came to see your parents.'

'Well, yes, them as well.'

'Why don't you sit down? And try not to drop crumbs on my patio.'

'The birds will eat them. I miss the birds. The early settlers took some out with them, but they've become naturalised, granted Aussie citizenship. There's a kookaburra comes and makes a racket in a tree outside the house. Damn thing wakes me up every morning, Sundays included. Louder than an alarm clock. I can't catch up on my beauty sleep.'

'I'd noticed.'

'Now, now, Paula. That isn't very nice'

'Sorry. But you know, Gary, you can't just breeze in and expect me to be the same as when you left. I'd cut you off my radar.'

'Well, ship's in port now. Good to be back in dear old Blighty.'

'When are you going back?'

'That depends. You know, it depends on flights, and stuff, and the folks, and well, I thought I might stay for a month or two, or longer. I might get a job; settle down back in the old country.'

'Haven't you forgotten something?'

'Eh?'

'What about Geraldine?'

'Ah, yes. Erm. Well you see... well you see... Geraldine and me, we weren't really... well, you know.'

'Yes, I know.'

'So, well, the folks are getting older now. I don't want to make them extra work, so I was wondering...'

'Are you trying to tell me something? I mean, *ask* me something?'

'Please, Paula, erm... is your spare room free?'

'Well, it's full of stuff, but I may be able to find a space for you... somewhere.'

'Great! Great! I'm still good at washing up. And I can cook a great steak, especially on an open fire in the Outback. Good on ya, Paula. Love you, by the way. Do you want that piece of cake?'

Paula leant back, closed her eyes. It *was* a good day.

The birds sang in harmony.

Wendy Goulstone

March 20

Goodbye Miss Maudsley

The Coventry Metro conurbation, Rugby sub-unit, outside St Andrew's Community Nexus; a white building. Clearly, a converted church labelled with purple banners, saying things like *Library socialisation, nutrition and connection.*

A young woman wandered around looking at the centre walls, looking for something. A gardener approached; very white skin, purple hair and almost seven feet tall.

The woman said, "Android! I'm looking for my great uncle's memorial stone. It was placed here somewhere." The request was a little curt.

The gardener replied, "It will be one of the largest stones somewhere here but much of the inscriptions were sandblasted smooth at deconsecration. The process provides a good aesthetic but can be seen as somewhat anonymous."

"Robot. What is your designation?" she asked. The gardener didn't flinch at the R-word.

"My name is Pascal. A friend's joke as I talk so much. You?"

"Address me as Miss Maudsley. Look at those piles of leaves all perfectly arranged, computer accuracy!"

Pascal smiled. "Do you think they look more elegant this way, Miss Maudsley?"

"But how can you judge elegance, beauty or kindness? You're just a machine. My great uncle wrote about AI a long time ago and I have found his story."

"You're grown from different materials and use a different fuel source but aren't you a kind of machine too, Miss Maudsley? Your great uncle should not have been worried about artificial intelligence but about artificial diligence, the idea that... ahem... robots could come in and not just do everything better but care better and even pray better.

"Excuse me but I'm late to go home to my wife. She asks me often, 'Do you love me?' I tease and say, 'Until my memory banks corrode to dust, so for about six hundred years.' "

Joyce Maudesley had never heard a robot joke before. She smiled and realised she also needed to leave and asked Pascal for a weather report.

"What do I look like, Google? Ask your flexi Mac, I've got to go. Goodbye, Miss Maudsley."

Yet she could tell he was still joking.

Joyce marched toward the Clock Tower where the MicroUbers jostled like three-metre bees licensed in Wolverhampton.

The wind seemed to blow a little less coldly.

Chris Wright

March 21

First Day Of Spring

I could feel Spring coming a good few weeks ago. I could smell it, hear it in the urgency of the bird song, and the nights were drawing out. I noticed this because I have hens at the bottom of my garden and I shut them up when it goes dark.

Now we have passed the official first day of Spring. I love the sound of all the birds singing; I thought they sang from joy as I do but I learned from a nature programme that they have to sing to entice a mate, and to protect their territory. I was disappointed. I thought that God had made them sing for our pleasure, but no.

As I go for my daily walk down to the crossroads and back, I appreciate all the appearing spring flowers growing now - primroses, cowslips, violets, celandines. The wild cherry is covered with white blossom.

The hedges are beginning to shoot green now. I can almost see changes each day. Then there are swathes of daffodils that groups of villagers have planted over the years. I am told there is plenty of frog spawn down the Great Central Way too.

Ruth Hughes

March 22

Hot Cross Buns

Spring means Easter, and the start of Easter is Good Friday, which means Hot Cross Buns. I got married in 1977, in May, but that Easter, I came up from Essex to help get the house ready. Painting kitchen cupboards was the main job, but I had found a recipe. I would demonstrate my culinary credentials and make some hot cross buns.

As you can imagine, with a half-built kitchen, it was a difficult operation and I forgot to add the final ingredient – an egg. They still tasted fine.

Of course, having started a tradition, I had to continue. Every year, whatever happened, I made hot cross buns, and traditionally every year, my husband always asks, "Did you remember the egg?"

Several years we went camping in the New Forest; the hot cross buns came too. If we visited relatives, it was my job to provide them. Once, not that long ago, I had to look after my mother after an operation and my husband had to send a copy of my recipe for me to make them there.

Every year, until... Well, I expect you remember Lockdown One: the empty shelves, the shortage of toilet rolls and baked beans. And flour. And yeast. I was unprepared. I might have scraped together the flour, but hot cross buns without yeast? I looked everywhere, there was none to be had. I had to buy hot cross buns – it wasn't the same.

This year I'm prepared, and I will prepare the dough (not forgetting the egg) and let it rise. I will knock it back and it will rise again, add the crosses and bake. If my timing is right, we will have hot cross buns for tea, warm from the oven, sliced and thickly spread with butter.

Spring has arrived and all is well.

Christine Hancock

March 23

A Change of Location

March 23rd 2020: a plague engulfing the world like a sudden tsunami; governments scrabbling to adequately respond; the entire globe entering a period of uncertainty and fear.

March 23rd 2020: Jane and I were exiting: after a decade of serving coffee and cake to wide-eyed, foot-weary tourists, the sale of our high street cafe had completed. Sadly, it was also the day we said a final goodbye to each other; a matter I need not dwell on here, except to state that the decision was mine.

On that memorable day, Boris Johnson announced stringent travel restrictions and the requirement to stay at home, with the aim of minimising a rapid spread of the contagion and to avoid overwhelming the NHS. But I no longer had a home. It was now owned by someone else! I did, however, have a new abode, ready and floating on the Grand Union Canal. I had decided that my living needs would be best met on a canal boat. The idea had come from a friend who was retiring and moving onto her narrow-boat and after exploring this avenue further, I had purchased a fifty-foot vessel of my own. I hurriedly crammed my belongings into my car and set off to take up residence on board NB Pastures New.

The Spring of 2020 was idyllic. I set to, making adjustments to my boat that suited me and exploring my new surroundings on foot and bicycle. I kept myself to myself, waving cheerily to new neighbours and conversing with them across the width of the canal. When a day's work was done, I rested on my bow deck in the sunshine. I sipped tea, or perhaps wine, and served myself suppers as the sun set across the fields. I felt I had stepped off a ship, tossed upon troubled waters and buffeted by the gales of conflict and circumstance, to find peace and calm on the sheltered waters of the canals…

Time passed, we emerged from lockdown to regain some form of freedom and take tentative steps towards a half-remembered normality. At last I was able to cast off from my moorings and start cruising the cut at the helm of my own home!

And so, as my future course is now plotted, there is not much to add. But I will provide a brief progress report: new friends; beautiful countryside; tranquil waters; my life afloat again.

Is a change of location ever merely - solely - geographical? There are times when hearts and minds need to inhabit places fresh and new. When you leave a room, whether through choice or necessity, make sure to close the door, and then look ahead, for another will be sure to open.

Steve Redshaw

March 24

Real Life

'He's got a knife, Miss!' The shout rang out, high pitched.

As I turned, the sun caught the steel in a flash across the playground. Without hesitating, I found myself moving fast towards a group of teenage boys at the far end of the playground. Alarmist tabloid headlines were ringing in my ears. As calmly as I could, I marched straight up to the boy with the weapon in his hand. He was holding it out with a questioning expression on his face, looking at each of the boys challenging him, almost as if the knife were a tube of sweets. However, collectively, and slowly, the other boys were backing away from him in fear.

'Thank you, Peter,' I said firmly, taking the knife immediately out of his hand and slipping it into my handbag. He looked stunned and suddenly sheepish.

'OK chaps, show's over,' I said. 'Peter, to the Headteacher's office, now!'

To my utter relief, he turned and loped away towards the main building. I followed, watching a red blush creep up his neck from under his collar. Though only thirteen, he was a lot taller than me, with a loose-limbed, clumsy gait and the stoop to his shoulders which many teenage boys have as if they feel awkward in their own bodies. I felt myself trembling, but fortunately it didn't show, and to all outward appearances, I was just an efficient teacher doing my job.

When the boy had received his grilling from the Head and was safely installed back in the classroom, it was my turn to be grilled.

'You absolutely DO NOT act of your own accord in an emergency like that!' the Headteacher bellowed. 'In situations of extreme danger firstly: You seek assistance from another member of staff. Secondly, you...'

And so he went on. I hadn't stuck to the rules.

I must have drifted off because he ranted on endlessly. Suddenly I realised he was talking about suspending, or even excluding, the boy. But he couldn't. He wouldn't, would he? Yes, of course it didn't sound good, when you put it in black and white like that. Yes, he did have a knife in the playground. But he wouldn't have used it on anyone. This was Peter we were talking about. Peter wouldn't deliberately hurt anyone.

But the Head went on and on: How the school couldn't afford to overlook events like this; how it could give the school a bad name; bad publicity; bad for fundraising... bad for Ofsted... bad... bad.

I drove home too fast, with my mind definitely not on the road. A teacher's lot is not a happy one. Suspending the boy would have all sorts of repercussions for him. It would affect the rest of his life, and for what? I knew he hadn't meant anything by producing that knife. He had seen it on television. It was like a game to him. It was nothing. There must be an explanation. I was tired and needed a hot bath and a good meal.

It was at times like these I was glad I had met Mike, my new boyfriend. He was such a good listener and so considerate to talk to after the harsh realities of life in a comprehensive school. I liked him, I trusted him and I felt drawn into his world, bringing a whole orbit of consciousness into my rather mundane life. I loved his old and rather smelly springer spaniel and his teenage son. He lived not far from me and when I went there it felt like a real home should feel, with bits of stuff everywhere including all Mike's hobby paraphernalia. He was divorced and had been left with raising a quite troubled teenage boy on his own.

As soon as I was ready and recovered, I walked down through the town and knocked on his door. He greeted me with a hug but was surprised to see me. We hadn't arranged to meet during the week; we were both working full-time and very busy. He made me a cup of tea, glancing at me occasionally, rather anxiously, it seemed. It was almost Easter and nearing the end of term. The evenings were growing lighter. A blackbird was singing in the trees. I relaxed into an armchair. Peace at last. Wrapping my hands around my mug of tea, I gazed out to the quietness of the garden. Mike had been mowing the lawn and the heady scent of fresh cut grass mingled with narcissus and daffodils, floated in through the window.

But Mike knew something was wrong. He sat down beside me and put his arm around my shoulders. So I told him, from the beginning, all that had happened, the drama in the playground, how I had dealt with it, the reprimand I had received from the Head and the threat of the boy being suspended from school. I told him how worried I had been all the way home. And finally, how glad I was to have him to talk to.

As I poured out the whole story, he nodded understandingly, although at times he looked at me anxiously, more anxiously than I expected. Perhaps the Head was right, that I shouldn't put myself in danger. It was only a job, after all. I would get no reward for bravery. All I had was my adrenaline running high and my heart racing to keep up. Unable to hold back any longer, I reached down and took the knife from my handbag. Placing it gently on the table and looking sadly up at Mike's face, I said, 'This was the knife.'

He looked incredulous. 'But that's my old fishing knife!' he exclaimed. He picked it up, weighing it in his hands, presumably pleased with the old feel of it until realisation dawned. 'Oh, no,' he murmured. Our eyes met.

'Where is he now?' I asked.

'He's upstairs on his computer, as usual.' Standing up, he left me and went to stare out at the garden with his hands in his pockets. 'Peter never said a word to me,' he said. Looking shocked, as if unable to comprehend the situation, he raised his hands in despair. 'But I don't understand. Peter is as harmless as an old spaniel!'

'That's almost exactly what I said to the Head,' I replied. 'A pity he didn't quite see it that way.'

As if in response to our words, the spaniel got up from his rug and nuzzled against my hand.

'Peter's missing his mother; he's going through a rough patch, but he's not violent. I'll go and talk to him now, and tomorrow I'll go and explain to the Head.' He turned to me with a reassuring smile. 'Don't worry, it'll be OK.' He winked at me then, as he went out of the door.

And after he went, I realised something. The so-called harsh realities of my working life weren't real at all. Only this life, a family life with all its difficulties and ups and downs, with all its love and trust and warmth, with all its complexities, this was real life.

Theresa Le Flem

March 25

Two Spring Days

Saturday March 25th 2023
I'm sitting in the Budgens petrol station as Lizzy fills up. We had to wait behind a guy who then went into the shop for his copy of *The Sun*. What can you do? We went to Nero for a pleasant coffee. Plenty of punters are in, including a long-haired young woman sitting alone, doing puzzles and mashing her phone. Rather elegant. I wonder about her story.

I email five dog breeders from the kennel club website without much hope of finding a Dachshund. Surprisingly, two respond almost immediately with news of litters fairly soon. I am quite shocked by how sudden it could be. Birth in ten days for one responder which is too soon for us to do anything. Lizzy talks quite positively about it but we need to talk about every aspect of our lives and how they would be affected.

Gabriel sends a message tonight. He's in a bar and Freddy Steward, the England fullback, is in there as well. I tell him not to mention the red card which Freddy was given last week.

Today I mow the lawn for the first time this year. Complications arise over the power leads but Lizzy manages to change a fuse. I don't seem interested in making videos at the moment and Elton's music is leaving me a bit cold. I'm not sure why I feel this. I'm spending more time with Paul McCartney or just not listening to anything specific.

Monday March 27th 2023
I check the NHS app to book my clinic appointment. Finally there are some choices and I book one for the end of April in Coventry. What a relief. But when I am transferring the date to the kitchen calendar, I notice a discrepancy in the day of the booking. I check back on the app to find the appointment is for next year. What a joke the

Conservatives are. Is this really the best we can do? I cancel the booking and will keep looking out for something within my natural lifetime.

We have coffee at Costa. I am a bit glum but gradually thaw out with a couple of puzzles to solve together. Our walk turns into something fairly joyful as the spring sunshine appears and we look closely at some buds on various trees near the new pond, watched carefully by a neighbourhood robin. I drop Lizzy off at mother's at 4pm as she is going to a prize-giving at her school for year eleven. She says she is anxious and I am sorry about this. I hope she reconnects with her chums and is made to feel welcome. Getting home, I am bereft as usual and not looking forward to teaching and then going to choir alone.

I leave early to pick up Lizzy from Sainsbury's. She has walked there from school after the speech day presentation. As always, it is lovely to see her waiting, and her smile, when I draw up, is the moment of the day.

John Howes

March 26

The Dancer On The Green

Mrs Martin played the final notes, thumbed the pages to find the next hymn and leaned back on the piano stool.

Mrs Carter stood and said, 'Thank you, Mrs Martin,' as she did every school morning. I wriggled a bit on the hard floor and wished I could stretch my legs.

'Now, children,' said Mrs Carter, after the usual reminder to hang up our coats on the pegs. 'Now, remember, tomorrow is our fête on the village green, so I hope you are all going to bring your parents, as we hope to raise a lot of money to help the boys and girls who lost everything in the terrible earthquake. Please thank your parents for contributing so many lovely things to sell on our gardening and bric-à-brac stalls, and for prizes for the games, and I know that all the boys and girls, who have given up their playtimes to learn to dance round the maypole, are so excited that at last they will be dancing to the whole village. Could I see who you are?'

My hand shot up with the others.

'Mrs Martin, could we have our second hymn, please.'

After school I went home with Sarah and her mum and we played in their garden until my dad arrived from work to take me home. I helped him get the tea then hung up my best dress for the dancing so the creases would fall out and I'd look smart. Dad washed up a great mound of pots because we hadn't done it all week. I put it all away 'cus Dad still hasn't learnt where it all goes. He opened a bottle of beer, sat on the sofa and switched on the telly to watch the news.

'You'd better go to bed early,' he said. 'So you won't be tired tomorrow.'

So I had a good wash, well, the bits that showed, put on my pyjamas and read a bit of my book in bed, then I whispered to Mum that I wished she could come to watch me dancing round the maypole tomorrow, and blew her a kiss and said goodnight, very quietly in my head because my eyes were a bit runny. So I snuggled under the covers and hugged Teddy.

Next morning Dad gave me a drink of milk and some crispies.

'Big day today, Jenny. Pity I shall miss you. Gotta go into town.'

'What for?'

'Oh, this and that.'

He never said what he wanted in town, and he never took me with him. So I got myself ready with my best frock and my black pumps and brushed my hair, and at one o'clock I locked the door and hid the key and went to school with Sarah and her mum to be ready for the dancing.

'Now, boys and girls,' said Mrs Carter. 'I know you are all going to have a wonderful day at the fête. All the stalls are set up and everyone will be arriving soon to watch you dancing round the maypole. Mrs Martin is going to put the music on a piece of equipment called an amplifier so you will hear it. Remember to hold your ribbons tightly, think only of the steps and enjoy it. Your teachers and all your parents will be so proud of you.'

I wondered what my dad was doing in town and I wished my Mum could be there.

At two o'clock the vicar made a speech and we all took our places round the maypole, but there was one ribbon, a purple one, without a dancer. That was strange because no-one was missing. Mrs Carter didn't notice the purple ribbon when she checked to see if we were all in the right places. Mrs Martin put the music on and we started to dance. We had to concentrate because we mustn't go wrong.

But then the music went quiet and everyone was dancing slowly, as if they were dreaming. I looked across the circle. And there was a girl there, a girl I hadn't seen before, holding the purple ribbon. She was looking at me and smiling. I smiled back and danced and danced for joy.

Wendy Goulstone

March 27

Falling Down

Mother would not, under any circumstances, travel by Skyways. No matter how we begged and pleaded, cajoled and coerced, teased, taunted, threatened, or offered to travel with her, Mother steadfastly refused to try. Which rather limited her choice of shops, services, and days out for fun. On a positive note, for us offspring, it meant no unexpected visitations!

Of course the downside was that whenever she needed help, one of us had to travel to her, lugging toolkits or whatever was required for this month's absolute emergency.

She was possessed by the notion that she might fall, and do herself a mischief, such as breaking her hip, smashing her head open, or, worst of all, land on her bum, displaying her capacious drawers to all and sundry passing by. So strong was her belief, or fear, that she would fall, that she'd had us move her bed into the small sitting room, and we'd also had to turn the outside toilet, an old coal shed, into a second bathroom, with shower.

I travel by Skyways, well I have to. I live way out beyond the other side of town, but it's no fun trying to get on with a heavy toolbox (new lock and bolt for the inner porch door) or my big sewing machine (new curtains for the main sitting room), and sometimes I feel Mother has a point!

There's no way I can fall off, I know, the system has controlled air all around it. 'The see-through walls that have greater strength than the strongest brick or metal constructions.' That's the Skyways slogan. But I still can't bring myself to look down as I walk on nothing across the sky. And it does make me shudder to see hundreds of commuters seemingly walking through thin air, fifty feet above the ground.

My brothers have joked for years that when Mother dies they will shift her coffin by Skyways, just to make sure she is truly dead, as, if not, she will surely sit up in her box and scream. And swear at us all. But we can afford to move her by hearse, on the precious roads. Well, we can just about afford it. And yes, I have seen coffins, and whole funeral processions, cross the sky, to the Necropolis. It is considered shameful though. It marks out the poorer classes.

Anyway, I'd better go, or Mother will accuse me of falling down on the job. Today I'm painting the new bathroom a different colour. The opalescent shell-pink that Mother chose was apparently too pink, so now I'm going to spend my one free weekend, a month, repainting the girlie pink bathroom a lurid shade of purple (she chose this colour too), and I've got to leap onto the Skyways with these two five litre cans of paint.

Pray for me!

EE Blythe

March 28

The Diaries of Sylvia Starr

'It was a glorious first night,' Maggie whispered to her partner, theatre director David McAllister, in the back of a hackney cab. As the elderly cabbie expertly negotiated a small gathering of late-night partygoers, Maggie laid her head on David's shoulder.

The taxi moved smoothly through the London traffic, down the Strand and over Westminster Bridge, before turning to follow the River Thames southwest to Richmond. Maggie yawned. She was tired, but she was too excited to sleep. Sitting up, she watched the moon's reflection dancing on the dark river. She reflected on her past and how different her life might have been.

+   +

It had been three years, though it felt light years ago that she had been sacked as producer of the most popular current affairs programme on television. The hierarchy said it was because of cutbacks, but Maggie knew the real reason was her boss's daughter.

John Stanford, CEO of the television station, had asked Maggie to take his daughter Demi under her wing, which Maggie was happy to do. It took Demi two years of making herself indispensable and ingratiating herself with people who mattered before she persuaded her father to give her Maggie's job. Maggie shivered as the memories of that unhappy time flooded her mind.

Fred, the station's head of security, looked embarrassed while he waited for Maggie to clear her desk. 'Would you prefer to leave by the back stairs, Miss Moran?' he asked with affection.

'No, thank you, Fred. I'll go out the way I came in, through the front office,' Maggie said, with her head held high.

Maggie hugged her PA and best friend Jan, assuring her that she had lost a boss, but not a friend – and promised to see her soon.

Jan burst into tears saying, 'I'm sorry,' and ran out of the office.

Maggie walked through the production office to a round of applause and calls of good luck. Passing the boardroom, she saw Demi Stanford sitting at the head of the conference table. The ping of the lift arriving took her out of her reverie, and when the doors opened, she stepped in without looking back.

The journey home in the cab didn't take long. She would have walked, but for the brown box containing her working life on the seat next to her.

Being home in the day was alien to Maggie, and she was bored. She picked up the telephone to ring her fiancé, Ken. Then, remembering he was on an outside broadcast and knowing how irritating it is to be disturbed in the middle of filming, she put down the receiver. Out of habit, she went into the kitchen to make a coffee. She switched on the kettle and sat at the small pine table to wait for it to boil. She thought about food, but although she hadn't eaten yet, she wasn't hungry.

The click of the kettle switching off made Maggie jump. She was miles away, as if in a dream. Ignoring the coffee, she went upstairs, lay on the bed and closed her eyes. As tears of injustice, frustration and anger began to fall, she buried her head in the pillow and wished Ken was there to hold her.

Woken by the telephone ringing next to her bed, Maggie reached out and lifted the receiver from its cradle to hear the voice of her ex-PA, Jan, crying hysterically and begging Maggie to forgive her for having an affair with Ken. When she said she loved him, Maggie hung up the telephone.

Trembling, Maggie waited for the computer to whirr into action. The day had started like any other, but in a few short hours, her safe, happy, comfortable life had come crashing down around her ears. Losing her job was bad enough, but to be told her best friend was sleeping with her fiancé was unbearable.

Maggie logged into the television station's computer and accessed Jan's email account. The last email she sent was to Ken. She opened it and read a somewhat crude and explicit love letter. With one click of the mouse, Maggie CCd the email to everyone at the station.

To lose the job she loved was a blow, but to read about the sexual exploits of the man she loved, the man she was going to marry, with the friend she had confided in about her fears that Ken was having an affair, broke Maggie's heart.

'What has that stupid bitch done?' Ken bellowed, after reading the email, which Maggie had purposely left open on her computer. 'She's mad! She lives in a fantasy world,' he said, finding Maggie in the bedroom putting his clothes into black bin-liners. 'It was a one off, darling. It meant nothing; she means nothing.'

'Ken,' Maggie said calmly, 'Just pack the rest of your belongings and go!'

'But I love you, Maggie,' Ken pleaded.

'You should have thought of that before jumping into bed with... with my PA,' Maggie said, unable to say her rival's name.

'Please darling, let's sleep on it. I'll explain everything in the morning.'

'Going to bed won't help, Ken. This time you've gone too far.'

'I'm so sorry, Maggie.'

'You're only sorry you got found out!' Maggie shouted.

'I'll make it up to you, I promise,' Ken pleaded. 'Come on, darling, you can't throw away four years of happiness, because of one stupid mistake.'

'I haven't thrown it away, Ken - you have! Now, please, leave.'

+   +

The letter from her aunt's solicitor came out of the blue. It said that her Aunt Sylvia had died and, as the sole beneficiary of her aunt's estate, Maggie was required to attend a meeting at Simons and Simons the following week. Maggie had loved Aunt Sylvia and, although she knew her aunt was frail, she was shocked and saddened by the news of her death.

The day after she received the letter, a trunk arrived, containing scripts and programmes dating back to the turn of the twentieth century. It was a treasure-trove of priceless memorabilia, which great-aunt Sylvia had collected over a lifetime, spanning more than ninety years. Maggie could hardly believe her eyes as she gazed at almost a century of theatrical history.

'Dear Aunt Sylvia!' Maggie said, unrolling a theatre poster, advertising, *Pygmalion* with Sylvia Starr playing Eliza Dolittle, at The Vaudeville Theatre, June 1932.

Maggie knew her great-aunt's stage name was Sylvia Starr. She was christened Ellen but changed her Christian name to Sylvia in 1931 after reading *The Suffragette Movement* by Sylvia Pankhurst. What Maggie didn't know was her aunt had changed her surname from Moran to Starr by deed poll. It seemed there was a lot Maggie didn't know about her remarkable great-aunt.

Exploring further, Maggie found a curious black and gilt, lacquered box. She lifted the gold clasp on the extraordinary box to reveal twelve beautifully bound red leather books. Carefully opening the first, a handwritten note weaved its way to the floor. It read:

Dear Maggie.

As the only member of my family who genuinely cared for me and, as an actress, shared my love of the theatre and the belief that our theatrical history must be preserved, I Sylvia Starr, leave you my diaries. Make use of them my dear.

Your loving aunt, Sylvia.

+ +

Great-aunt Sylvia would have been in her element if she could see one of our most famous actresses in London portraying her so truthfully in the theatre she loved so much.

'Thank you, Aunt Sylvia. Thank you for having the faith in me to write your story,' Maggie said, as she made her way backstage to the first night party. 'I hope I did you credit.'

'You did,' a familiar voice said.

Startled, Maggie turned to see a young woman standing next to her wearing a 1930s costume. 'Excuse me, did you say something?'

'Yes! You asked me if I thought the production of *The Life of Sylvia Starr* did your aunt credit, and I said yes.'

'Thank you for saying so. Sylvia Starr was my favourite aunt and my mentor.'

'She would be very proud of you,' the young woman said.

At that moment, the door to the stage opened, and David, leading a welcoming party of actors and backstage crew, cheered her in. Maggie looked over her shoulder, expecting to see the young woman in the 1930s costume, but she had gone.

Madalyn Morgan

March 29

The Woodland Wedding

Tara shut her black eyeshadow-covered eyelids as she heard the sound of rustling spring trees all around her. This was the moment she had been anticipating for almost a year. She was getting married to her fiancée in the woods under the cherry blossom trees. Her father was standing to her left, holding her arm in patience but also for support. Tara looked down at her emo black wedding dress and her knee-length boots.

Is marriage really what I want? she thought for a small moment before nodding to herself and ignoring her doubt.

Then, she glanced up ahead as the light spring breeze started to brush her basic black hair around her face. She saw her fiancée, Lorna, waiting for her at the end of the aisle, smiling in her direction. Tara smiled back at her. "I'm ready."

Tara whispered to her father anxiously before signalling for the procession to begin. Her best friends, Madelaine and Faith, walked down the aisle before her. Their bridesmaids' outfits consisted of dark leather boots, black and blood red dresses with laced corsets and a small garnet-red flower in their hair.

Then suddenly Tara's favourite song started playing *The Only Exception* by Paramore. Tara knew it was her time to walk down the aisle. Her hand gripped her father's arm as they began to walk slowly to the rhythm of the music.

As she walked down the aisle, Tara turned her gaze to the setting around her. It was April. Flowers were blossoming and the animals were out. The warm breeze of nature fluttered Tara's dress slightly. Tara's gaze then landed on Lorna. Her dress was the opposite of Tara's. It was full of bright colours. It was a shorter dress with frills and multicoloured flowers all around it. Lorna also wore a crown of flowers in her strawberry-blonde hair, which matched her outfit.

Lorna watched in awe as her emo bride walked towards her. Tara smiled at Lorna as they met at the flower-covered altar. The crowd was silent and the only thing heard was the sound of the swaying trees.

Chloe Huntington

March 30

No Good Deed

Janet looked at her watch. She wasn't late, even though she'd decided to change the sheets on her bed at the last minute. The previous week she'd cleaned both sides of the living room glass doors and then the patio doors, arriving ten minutes late with hands smelling of Windolene. The week before she'd emptied her kitchen cupboards and checked all the sell-by dates, filling her dustbin with five year old cans of sugar-free baked beans and expired bottles of wine vinegar. That had made her twenty minutes late. Today, though, she would have time to sit down and compose herself, maybe have a glass of water or a cup of coffee. She would not arrive hot and flustered and full of excuses.

As she walked slowly and carefully towards the car park, she saw a woman in a wheelchair by the entrance. Several CO-OP carrier bags hung from the back of the chair, like fungus on a dead tree. The occupant was slumped forward, baseball cap pulled low over her face. Waiting to be collected, Janet assumed, unless she'd been abandoned by a burnt-out carer, unable to cope any more, but that wasn't her problem. She had an appointment to keep and she was on time. There would be no delaying tactics this week, and no disappointed sighs at her lateness.

As Janet came closer, the woman turned her wheelchair to face her. The cap covered her eyes, but she appeared young, in her late twenties. She'd expected to see someone old and grey-haired, not a young woman wearing jeans and a sleeveless denim jacket, with tattoos on both arms.

She's going to speak to me, Janet thought in a moment of panic. What shall I do? She closed her eyes, even though they were hidden behind her dark glasses, and counted to ten. When she opened them, the woman was still there.

"Excuse me, could you give me a hand, please?"

Janet took off her sunglasses and glanced at the rough surface of the car park. How they had the nerve to charge you for parking on potholes and in puddles, Janet didn't know.

"It's just that the shopping makes my wheelchair so heavy and I find it hard to get up and down the kerb."

"Of course," Janet said and took hold of the handles.

She started to push. The woman was right. The wheelchair was heavy and the bags banged against her legs. Her sunglasses were crushed between one hand and the handle, but if she let go, she would lose control. Janet carefully steered the wheelchair between two potholes, across the cracked, muddy tarmac and onto the pavement, which narrowed as it turned the corner towards the pedestrian crossing.

"The footpath's too narrow. You'll have to go on to the road," her passenger said.

With some difficulty Janet heaved the wheelchair over the kerb into the road. This thing has all the manoeuvrability of a supermarket trolley, Janet thought. If some idiot in a four-wheel drive takes that corner too fast, we'll both be flattened. The pavement widened again and Janet turned the wheelchair to pull it backwards up the kerb, its passenger grasping the wheels to help. They continued towards the pedestrian crossing. The road was always busy here, cars whizzing through the one-way system, switching lanes at the last moment and jumping the lights, always too impatient to queue.

They stopped and waited for the lights to change. Janet shoved her sunglasses into her pocket and looked at her watch. Now she was going to be late when for once she had been early, but this time she had a proper excuse. She was doing a good deed. The heavy wheelchair pulled at Janet's hands. Her palms were so sweaty that she was afraid the handles would slip through her grasp and then her passenger would be off across the road, a denim-clad Boadicea lacking only the scythes as she wreaked havoc with the traffic, bags spilling groceries everywhere.

The lights changed and the bleeps prodded Janet into action. She pushed the wheelchair across the road, picking up speed as they reached the pavement so that she struggled to come to a halt.

"There we are," Janet said to the woman, who said something Janet didn't quite catch. "I beg your pardon?"

"I'm going to The Engine. I like a drink in the afternoon. That way." She pointed to the left. "I'm not keeping you, am I?"

"No, no, of course not," Janet said, mentally crossing her fingers. She could hardly abandon her now, could she?

She carried on pushing. The wheelchair and its occupant were getting heavier. The sun was shining straight in her face. Janet was sweating and her sandals were rubbing her heels. The shoes had only been worn once before, to the funeral, and since then they had languished at the back of her wardrobe, along with the black suit now several sizes too big, gathering dust for the last five years. This morning she had felt ready to wear them. It was a mistake. She could feel the blisters forming and she didn't have any sticking plasters with her.

"Turn right here."

Her passenger pointed to a narrow alley that ran along the side of a tall office block. At the end was a car park and beyond that a building site. Workmen in hard hats and tool belts clambered about the scaffolding, laying bricks and hammering things. The air was full of dust and her eyes were watering. Why hadn't she put her sunglasses back on? Sweat was dripping down her back and her armpits were wet. She knew there would be dark patches forming under her jacket. A cement mixer churned away, making it hard for Janet to hear what the woman was saying and she had to bend down.

"That's going to be a doctor's," she informed Janet. "Should have been finished by now. It's going to be really convenient for me."

Across a narrow street stood The Engine, a small pub at the corner of two rows of terraced houses. The sign depicting exactly what type of engine was hidden under the layers of dirt. The paint work was flaking and the windows were grubby, although the gold letters spelling out the name were bright and clean, as if they'd just been painted.

"I do like a drink after I've been to the doctor's. And before if I'm lucky." She laughed. "A couple of drinks and a packet of fags and I'm happy."

Janet felt uncomfortable. She, herself, rarely drank, and she'd never spent much time in pubs. And she was worried that her feelings of disapproval were prompted by the woman being disabled, although she couldn't think of a good reason why disabled people shouldn't go to pubs and get drunk, like anyone else.

The door to the pub didn't have a step, for which Janet was grateful. The passenger reached out and shoved the door open. Inside the small room was empty, an L-shaped bar taking up half the space. There were a couple of bar stools and a table and bench under each of the two windows. Janet was surprised how clean it was. Even the floorboards had been swept recently. There was only a faint odour of tobacco instead of the expected stench of stale beer and cigarettes. And it was quiet, no voices or loud music. A pool table was visible through an open door, but no-one was using it. The pub was empty.

"Are you OK now?" Janet asked.

"Yes, thank you very much. Stay and have a drink."

"I'm sorry, I can't," Janet began to say, and then she stopped.

Her appointment, every Wednesday afternoon from two till four. She'd never missed one. But did it help? No. Then bugger it! This woman was the first person she'd spoken to for months who wasn't being paid to listen. She hadn't looked at Janet and seen a victim or a loser. It had been a long time since someone had asked Janet for help.

"Yes, I will have a drink," Janet said decisively.

A barman appeared, silently for such a large man. He was balding and wore an eye-patch. His other eye was a clear blue.

"All right, Dawn love," he said. "What'll you be having?"

"A pint of bitter, please, and whatever my friend's having."

"A mineral water, please," Janet said.

"No, no, no, have a proper drink," Dawn said. "You deserve it after all your hard work."

"OK, then. A glass of white wine, please."

"That's still not a proper drink. Have a Scotch or a vodka, go on."

The barman poured some whisky into a glass and put it down in front of her. Janet took a sip. It tasted like antiseptic, but it warmed as it went down. And she felt wonderful. She took another sip. Dawn was smiling at her, raising her own glass in encouragement. Janet laughed. She wanted to sing and dance and laugh and cry. Everything was brighter and sharper, in focus for the first time. Dawn was younger, more vivid, her tattoos vibrant against her pale skin, pulsating with life, writhing up her arms, crimson roses, Chinese characters, green ivy and an eagle, each feather outlined, wings flexing gently.

Janet's glass was empty. She held it up to the light and watched the little rainbows splintering and flying off into the corners of the room. Dave leant on the bar, his one eye watchful, and Dawn signalled to him to refill Janet's drink.

And the pub was full of people, brightly dressed, happy people. Janet talked to them all, and they listened to her and bought her drinks. She was brilliant, witty and amusing, the right words leaping out of her mouth. They liked her. Dawn was by her side, a smile on her face and a light dancing in her eyes.

In the back room the jukebox was playing and each tune was Janet's favourite. She danced, gracefully swirling about the floor in harmony with the music until her feet ached. Then she sang and everyone listened spellbound at her beautiful songs, and she marvelled that she could remember so many words in languages she had never spoken. And Dawn watched her and smiled.

But everything ends and suddenly Janet was tired. She drank a little more and the room began to dissolve, colours blending into mist, everything merging, edges blurred as the people melted away and the music faded into smoke, and Janet too faded into nothing.

+ +

The sunlight woke her. She felt strange, disconnected from her body. She tried to sit up, but she couldn't. Her legs resisted her and she had no strength in them. She lay on her back, hands clutching as the rails at the side of her bed. Rails? She didn't have rails. Why had her bed shrunk? The walls were the wrong colour and the window was on the other side. Where were her curtains? And her wardrobe? And her dressing table? Everything was wrong.

The door opened in the wrong wall and a woman walked into her bedroom as if she had every right to be there. She had frizzy blonde hair and too much lipstick and wore a blue overall over her jeans.

"Who are you?" Janet mumbled.

"Time to get up, dear." The woman came over to the bed and cranked it up, so that Janet was sitting almost upright.

"What?" Janet croaked.

"Oh dear, you've been out drinking again, haven't you? We've told you about that before, haven't we? People like you shouldn't drink, not in your state of health, with your medication."

"Where am I?"

"Don't be such a silly girl," the woman said and fetched the wheelchair from the corner of the room. "Hurry up now, or you'll be late for breakfast."

And Janet looked into the mirror and screamed when she saw Dawn's face looking back at her.

+ +

In the park, in the bright sunshine of a new day, Dawn ran barefoot across the wet grass.

Fran Neatherway

March 31

Gryphon

After the event, everyone was sure it had been Robin's idea originally, but she wasn't so sure. She freely admitted that the twilight paddle out to the island had been her idea, but not the second part. She was fairly sure she knew who had seeded the idea into the mix. But it wasn't her.

Roscoe, older and wiser than the others, brought his inflatable raft in his backpack, and Davy, a 'bit of a lad', brought the cider. Robin and Caroline, being practical, carried big towels, Penny thought chocolate would be good, and the other two boys, Siadwel the Softy, and Wyvern, who was supposed to have been registered as Griffin, but ended up as Wyvern when his dad got his mythological creatures muddled, had cigarettes, matches, and a torch. As the sun touched the horizon the little group set off through the shallow water for the island, where they set up camp, failed to get a fire going, and generally just messed about, as teenagers are wont to do, until it was quite dark, and the stars shone out clear and bright. It was then that someone suggested skinny dipping. Robin heard the words rise above the general drunken murblings and totally crazy pronouncements from Wyvern. They stood out as if written in neon against the dark sky.

In minutes they were all running to the far side of the little island, where the water was much deeper, throwing off clothing as they went. Shrieks and whoops accompanied the splashes of bodies hitting cold water.

Not long afterwards, once everyone was dry again, having used or not used a towel, the group decided it was time to go, and Roscoe and Davy took turns to inflate the raft. Wyvern scoffed.

"We paddled over, and I'm going to paddle back."

Robin opened her mouth to say something, but Roscoe gave her a warning look. So she just sidled over to Wyvern, and tried to persuade him to come on the raft.

"We need all the feet we can get to propel it," she smiled.

"No fear! I fell in last year," and he began rolling his trousers up, "I'm not going to get soaked again."

The raft set off, in a slightly tipsy way, with everyone seated facing out. Roscoe steered with a board, and the raft swung this way and that, shipping and shedding water as it lurched. Everyone held on with one hand while the others held their clothes aloft, to keep them dry.

Robin saw Wyvern set off behind them, then he stopped to watch their jerky progress, and she soon lost him in the dark. She was worried; Wyvern had forgotten to allow for the incoming tide in the estuary. The water was now much too deep to paddle. She felt ashamed that she hadn't warned him, that she'd let Roscoe intimidate her. She heard him shout, maybe he'd stepped into a deep spot, but the others were too busy being silly to hear him, or listen to her. She sent up a fervent wish for him to be OK.

When they reached dry land, they dressed, then descended on the late night café for coffee, or hot chocolate, and wait for Wyvern. They were planning their next big, or silly, adventure, when the heavy door swung open, revealing a terrifying sight. An alien creature stood there, trying to enter the café. Bedraggled, dripping and festooned with tufts of bright green seaweed, eel-grass garlands, and dark belts of sugar-kelp, Wyvern stepped forward, shedding clumps of wet sand, eyes blazing with barely concealed anger.

The crowd around the table, stunned into silence, looked at each other for one more moment, then everybody fell about laughing.

EE Blythe

A Story for Every Day of Spring

April

April 1

The Glorious First of April

The very best April Fool joke of all time was the BBC's *Panorama* documentary in 1957 of the spaghetti harvest in a Swiss village.

Television was in glorious black and white then and not every household owned one. You could rent one for an annual fee, and watch the Fry's Turkish Delight girls as they reclined on cushions in the harem. A girl I once knew, in the tiny tots' class at ballet school, was one of them, her fair curly hair echoing that of Shirley Temple. No, of course I wasn't even a teeny-weeny bit jealous of her hair, her pliés or her prospects. I hope she went on to greater things, and probably did, if her mother had anything to do with it.

Our rented TV went up in smoke one evening. Radio Rentals, the hire company, was not at all pleased that we had put it outside in the rain to cool off. At least they didn't have the effrontery to charge us for damages, it being a cheaper option than them forking out for rebuilding costs and funeral expenses.

But I digress. The spaghetti harvest. There it hung in long strips from the branches of the spaghetti tree, while the female pickers picked the dangling strings and carefully laid them to dry to a deadpan commentary.

Was anyone fooled? Apparently. The BBC even received letters asking where a spaghetti tree could be bought. Spaghetti came in tins in those days, drowned in tomato sauce. Hoops came later. I, for one, had certainly never seen a packet of the real thing, let alone travelled to Italy to dine on the genuine article.

The next day the hoax was the talk of the office, the shop floor and the pub, and black and white images of this fine harvest are still imprinted on the minds of the generation brought up on steam radio's Mr Growser and *Larry the Lamb*, raised their children on TV's *Muffin the Mule, Bill and Ben the Flower Pot Men, Andy Pandy* and the delightful *Magic Roundabout*, which grown men rushed home to watch.

Turkish Delight, anyone?

Wendy Goulstone

April 2

The Bells of St Mary's

It was Friday the last week of April. It seemed that overnight Boston had shaken off its winter coat and had donned a light flowery spring dress. This had filled Edith Strauss with so much joy that she had decided that afternoon to take a walk across the city to her favourite coffee shop, The Blue Rose. And to match Boston's warm beauty she decided to dig out her own summer dress. She put it on and smoothed down the front with her palms as she looked out across the park to the Church of St Mary's. She could smell the freshness of the park and hear the birds singing in praise of springtime. Oh I wish they would ring the bells, she thought; that would make my morning complete.

Edith was sixty-three years old, she worked part-time as a lecturer at the Wentworth Institute. After a relationship had gone wildly bad in her teens, she vowed that she could just do without people for the foreseeable future. That foreseeable future was now forty four years old and counting. Edith had enjoyed her life alone and was never resentful or bitter. She thought that if the right opportunity came up, she'd just take it, but so far nothing. Most of the women she'd been attracted to over the years were either spoken for or heterosexual.

Still, the morning had lifted Edith's spirits, and she spent it spring-cleaning her tiny apartment. She always loved the dawning of spring, every year it filled her with optimism, even if so far, it had always been misplaced. Perhaps this year will be the one, she thought, just a little love, it's not much to ask.

Although the sun was shining and the sky was clear, there was just the slightest nip in the air so Edith put on a light summer coat. The Blue Rose Coffee Shop was just over a mile from Edith's apartment and her walk took her through Boston Common, the city's most beautiful garden and America's oldest park. It seemed that this spring morning had infected the whole city. There were flower sellers and ice-cream vendors in the park and folk just seemed to be full of the joys of Spring. Edith was so consumed with joy that she did not notice that from the west, dark clouds were forming and threatening to take over the sky.

Once inside the café, Edith secured an empty table near the window. She sat with her back to the window so she could observe the people in the café. Presently, a waitress came to take her order and place a lit candle on the table. Edith ordered a bowl of mushroom soup, and while she was waiting a woman came to the table and asked if Edith would mind if she sat there as The Blue Rose was quite full.

'Not at all, be my guest,' said Edith

'Do you come to this coffee shop often then?' enquired the woman.

'Oh yes,' said Edith, 'I do like this part of town and come down most Saturdays, but today the weather was so gorgeous I thought I'd come down a day early.' She continued, 'It's very nice, don't you think? And I love the name, though I don't think there is such a thing as a blue rose, is there?'

'I'm not sure,' replied the woman, 'it's my first time in here. I'm from just outside of Boston and very rarely make it into town.'

Edith looked across at the woman and they both smiled.

'Oh, isn't this just lovely?' said Edith.

'Yes it is,' said the woman, still smiling. 'What's your name by the way?'

'My name is Edith,' said Edith, 'Edith Strauss.'

'Well, my name is Peggy Applebee,' said Peggy Applebee. 'It's very nice to meet you, Edith.' Both women simultaneously reached out across the table and shook hands, and when they did so Edith felt something. Peggy's hand felt warm and comforting. Her skin was neither dry nor damp, but silky smooth. Then it dawned on Edith exactly what this sensation was. It was physical human contact. It was intimacy, and Edith couldn't remember the last time she'd felt it. She looked into Peggy's eyes as she released her hand and both women smiled. Again.

A few moments later the waitress came again and Peggy ordered a sandwich.

'This little coffee shop seems to be getting a lot busier.' remarked Edith.

'I'm not surprised,' replied Peggy.

'Why's that then?' asked Edith. Peggy, who was facing the window and had an excellent view of the street, said 'Why, it's absolutely pouring with rain, everyone's coming in out of the wet.'

Edith turned and looked over her shoulder and said 'Why, so it is. I wonder when that started.'

'It started just before I came in here,' said Peggy, 'that's why I came in here.'

'Oh well, drip drip drop little April showers I guess,' said Edith.

Their order was brought to the table and there was a halt to any conversation while soup and sandwiches were consumed. When they'd finished and both dabbed at their mouths with napkins, Edith said, 'I didn't bring an umbrella. I'm going to be soaked by the time I get home.'

'There's a department store right across the street that sells umbrellas. You got far to go?' asked Peggy.

'Well, I live north of the river by St Mary's Church, but I could just take a cab all the way home.'

'And is there anybody at home?' asked Peggy changing the subject.

This question was asked in the most polite way and didn't seem in the least prying, so Edith answered truthfully. 'No, there's nobody at home.'

Edith was aware that she could feel her shoe was touching something under the table, probably Peggy's foot. Peggy was aware of the same sensation. It was a comforting sensation. For either woman to remove their foot from this slightest of contact would be to acknowledge that contact was taking place, so they both sat there refusing to do so, both aware that their feet were touching but uncertain as to whether the other was aware also.

A couple of hours and a few glasses of wine later, Edith was in her element. Peggy was the most wonderful person she'd met in years. They laughed and told stories just like old friends. The light outside was beginning to fade from the day, accelerated by the dark clouds which had brought the rain. As the daylight faded, the glow from the table candle increased giving a romantic aura to proceedings. After the last of the wine was consumed, Peggy started putting on her coat and she thanked Edith for a lovely afternoon. Edith was suddenly struck by the thought that she may never see this woman again.

'Would you like to meet again?' Edith blurted out.

'How do you mean?' said Peggy.

'Well, I just thought, you know, if you're in town next weekend, maybe we could meet here, it's been such a lovely afternoon.'

'Well, I'm away for three weeks, but I tell you what, I'll give you my number and you can call me, say the end of May. Yes, I'd love to meet up again. It's been really nice meeting you, Edith.' Peggy produced a notebook from her purse and wrote her name and telephone number on it.

+ +

Half an hour later Edith was in the department store buying an umbrella. She had no trouble finding them among the ladies' hats and shoes. There were quite a few opened umbrellas hanging upside down from the ceiling so the different patterns were visible. There was one that Edith was quite taken with; it was light blue in colour and around the edge was a print of a mother duck and continuing behind her around the umbrella were several of her chicks. Edith thought this so sweet and decided straight away that this was the umbrella for her.

She pointed it out to the assistant behind the counter and the assistant said, 'That's a very good choice ma'am, it's very popular.' The young assistant then turned to her colleague and said. 'Carole, would please get this lady one of the duck umbrellas from out of the rack.' Carole went to get the umbrella and when she returned Edith asked how much it was.

'That'll be four dollars fifty with tax, please ma'am.'

Edith fumbled around in her pocketbook whilst still holding the umbrella and produced a ten dollar bill. As she did this the note that Peggy had written for her fell unnoticed from her pocketbook and landed at her feet.

'There's five-fifty change ma'am. Thank you very much,' said the assistant.

'Thank you very much,' said Edith. 'I hope you girls have a nice evening.' And pleased with her purchase she walked out of the store and into the Massachusetts rain.

A few moments later Carole noticed the folded piece of paper on the floor and, picking it up, said to her colleague, 'Hey Elisabeth, do you think that old lady dropped this? It wasn't here before.'

'What is it?' asked Elisabeth.

'It's just a piece of paper, looks like it's got a woman's phone number on it.'

'Do you wanna call her?' asked Elisabeth sarcastically.

'Nope,' said Carole.

Elisabeth was checking her lipstick in a compact mirror. 'Well, put it in the trash then,' she said, 'and come on, let's shut up shop and get out of here, it's Friday night.'

+ +

When Edith got home she was quite wet in spite of the new umbrella. She was also starting to feel quite chilly after an hour walking in the pouring rain. But it didn't matter, she'd never felt warmer inside. She'd just spent the most exquisite afternoon she could remember, in years, possibly decades.

She showered and got into some warm dry clothes. She could feel the effects of the wine but thought she'd pour herself another one nevertheless. She suddenly remembered she must transfer Peggy's number to her address book. She walked over to the window and opened it so she could hear the pitter-patter of the rain falling on the trees in the park. She picked up her pocketbook from the dresser.

I'm so glad it's spring she thought, winter's yoke seemed to drag on so long this year. She walked back to the window. This year will be different. This will be my year. She fished her billfold from her pocketbook and started to pull out the contents. There was a twenty dollar bill, a five dollar bill, a receipt for the umbrella, and a receipt from the Blue Rose Coffee Shop, and nothing else.

She checked again then threw the billfold on the floor. She emptied the contents of her pocketbook onto the bed; as she did so she could feel her heart sinking low. Oh Edith, what have you done? She felt as though she was getting short of breath. She went to the open window and gazed across the darkness towards the Church of St Mary's. Faintly coming through the sound of the rain Edith could hear something else. Across the park, through the rain and the darkness Edith could hear the bells of St Mary's.

Martin Curley

April 3
Say It With Flowers

The fact that the chrysanthemum seemed to be speaking unsettled Mark, but it was when the bunch of red carnations burst into song that he began to worry. The carnations were singing *Oh, What a Beautiful Morning* from *Oklahoma*.

The chrysanthemum spoke again.

'Excuse me,' it said, 'but could you possibly explain to me what an elephant is? I've often wondered.'

'What?' said Mark.

'You know,' said the chrysanthemum, 'that bit in the song about elephants.'

The carnations were now singing *Surrey With a Fringe on the Top*. Wasn't *Oklahoma* on television last week? thought Mark. He hadn't watched it, but his mum had. She liked musicals and it was one of her favourites.

'An elephant is a large greyish-brown mammal. It's about twelve foot high and weighs about two tons. It has a very long nose called a trunk and big floppy ears. It has a small tail and two long front teeth called tusks. Elephants live mainly in Africa and India and are often killed for their tusks by poachers.'

'So the corn would be about twelve foot high, then,' said the chrysanthemum. 'I've never seen corn growing much higher than four foot-ish.'

Mark tried to pull himself together - he couldn't possibly be discussing corn and elephants with a chrysanthemum whilst listening to a bunch of carnations singing greatest hits from 1950s musicals. They had moved onto *Some Enchanted Evening* from *South Pacific*. Another of his mum's favourites.

He said to the chrysanthemum, 'Where have you seen corn growing? I only bought you from the florist's yesterday. I can't believe you go off on trips to the countryside when the shop is shut.'

'Where do you think flowers come from? We don't grow in the florist's. I grew up in a very nice nursery next to a field of corn and I didn't see any elephants or corn twelve feet high.'

'It's not meant to be taken literally,' said Mark. 'It's a metaphor, or do I mean a simile? Anyway, the song is just expressing what a lovely day it is and how well the crops are doing.'

He stood up.

'What the hell am I doing? I'm discussing song lyrics with a chrysanthemum. My God, Lisa was right. I have turned into a cabbage. How else would I be able to understand these bloody flowers?'

He walked into the kitchen, opened the fridge and took out a beer.

'Wotcha, Mark,' said the geranium on the kitchen window sill. 'Got any of that for me?'

Mark managed to spill most over the beer all over himself as he took a large swig.

'I suppose you're into the meaning of song lyrics as well?'

'Oh, no, we geraniums are tone deaf. We prefer rap music. But you could tell me the score in the football match.'

Mark glanced through the open door at the television. It was 0-0 at half time.

'Are you a Spurs or Manchester City supporter?' he asked the geranium.

'No, I'm an Arsenal supporter,' said the geranium. 'Mind you, that City striker is a bit useful.'

Mark went back into the living room. 'This is getting worse. Now I'm discussing football with a geranium.'

The carnations had now moved onto Maria from *West Side Story*. Now that was by Leonard Bernstein. He knew that because the biopic had just been released.

He said to the chrysanthemum, 'Do carnations always sing? And is it always musicals?'

'Yes, they all sing. The red ones like musicals. The white ones prefer opera and the pink ones like R'n'B. The yellow ones mostly sing Beatles songs and the purple ones are really into heavy metal.'

Mark sat down on the settee and took another swig of his beer. Behind him the carnations began to sing *I Feel Pretty*, swaying in time to the music.

Mark felt relieved - it could have been a lot worse, he could have bought that mixed bunch.

Fran Neatherway

April 4

April In Harwich

Derek asked Doris if she could spare some time for a meeting. He'd indicated it was to do with work but would prefer if they had the meeting away from the office. He asked Doris if she could make a Wednesday lunchtime in the Green Apple coffee shop in the town. He figured Doris would be able to make this as she only worked half days on Wednesdays. Doris agreed but told Derek they would have to be done by two as she actually had another appointment that very afternoon.

'A job interview?' enquired Derek.

'Well no,' said Doris. 'Why would you think that?'

'Oh I just wondered,' said Derek. 'You're perfectly happy here?'

'Why yes, perfectly.'

'Ok, then, I'll see you next Wednesday.' said Derek.

Doris's other appointment next Wednesday was actually a blind date arranged by a dating agency she had recently subscribed to. She had been single since Matthew ran off with their cleaner five years ago. Childless and single, Doris just got stuck into work to take her mind off everything, and this continued until now when she realised that if she didn't do something positive, she would end up at the back of the very top shelf.

It was the first Wednesday of April and Spring had announced itself emphatically. The sun was not only out and shining, it felt positively hot. Men were walking around in shirt-sleeves and there was an ice-cream seller set up in the market square. Doris treated herself to a 99 with a flake and sat on a bench waiting for a quarter to one.

She looked at her dating profile on her phone.

Name: Jillian Mayer (although she was called Doris, she'd always

preferred using her middle name, Jillian).
Age: 34.
Marital status: single (divorced).
Number of children: none.
Likes: Theatre, walking, listening to music.
Dislikes: Noisy pubs. T.V. commercials. Currants and raisins.

She read Brian's profile.

Name: Brian Henderson.
Age: 47.
Marital status: single (divorced)
Number of children: two.
Likes: sports-cars, rock concerts, watching snooker and darts on TV.

Underneath was a typed message:

Hi Jillian we've arranged for you to meet Brian (see above) in the White Horse in Market Street on Wednesday April 7th at 2.10pm. Brian will be carrying a copy of *The Daily Mail*, and will be wearing a red silk scarf.

Hhmm, it's a bit warm for a scarf, thought Doris, but we'll see.
Doris finished her ice-cream and made her way to the Green Apple coffee shop. She could see through the glass Derek was already seated, his messenger bag lay on the table next to a small bottle of beer. She entered and joined him.
'Oh, hello, Doris,' he said looking up. 'Glad you could make it. I thought you weren't coming, I've been here ten minutes and had just about given up.'
'But you arranged the meeting for one Derek, and it's only five to.'
'Well let's not get hung up on detail,' said Derek. 'You're here now, so would you like a drink? Tea? Coffee?'
'I wouldn't mind a cup of tea actually,' said Doris.

'Very good,' said Derek. 'You have to order and pay at the counter.' He hesitated then picked up the small beer bottle off the table. 'Oh, would you mind getting me another one of these?' Doris looked at the label on the bottle.

'Yeah, sure,' she said, then waited for just a moment in the expectation that Derek might offer a five pound note or something. Anything. He did not.

'Okay, I'll be back in a mo,' said Doris. And off she tripped.

Presently, she returned and placed Derek's beer down on the table.

'Ah, lovely,' said Derek. He made no attempt to say thank you to Doris. Doris sat down opposite Derek and took a sip of her tea.

'So what did you want to see me about, Derek?' she asked.

'Well, I'll get straight to it, Doris. There's no point in beating about the bush. I've been somewhat disappointed in your performance of late. It hasn't gone unnoticed.'

'Really?' said Doris. She felt her heart beating faster. She really wasn't expecting this.

'In what way exactly, Derek?'

'Well, in every way really, Doris. Some days you turn up on time, which is fine, and then other days it's like you can't be bothered, especially in the last couple of months. With no rhyme or reason, no explanation. You just seem to waltz in and out as you please...'

Doris cut him off.

'But there is a rhyme and reason,' said Doris.

'Which is?'

'Well it's the train strikes, Derek, and the appalling state of the Great Eastern Mainline.'

'What train strikes?'

'Oh Christ,' said Doris. 'There are a series of train strikes going on at the moment, Derek. It's all over the news.'

'Well, I don't use the trains,' said Derek, unhelpfully.

'Well, I do,' she continued, 'and some days I turn up at the station, there are no trains to be had, so I have to get a taxi to and from work, which costs almost as much as I earn in a day, so I'm working for a pittance.'

'Okay, okay,' said Derek, 'I will take that on board, going forward.' Doris hated it when people said going forward, as if there was any another direction we could go.

'Anything else, Derek?' she asked.

'Well it's just that the other girls in the office seem to get through more work, Doris, you know, on a general level. Take Tina for example. She's already handed in last quarter's VAT returns, and the deadline's not till next week.' Tina was a lovely girl but she was in an abusive relationship. She'd opened up in despair to Doris and was worried that she wasn't even capable of starting the VAT returns, let alone finish them. Doris had told her not to worry, Doris knew VAT inside out and she would take care of it.

'I mean, is everything okay at home Doris?' said Derek, 'you know, with the kids, your husband?'

'I don't have any children, Derek, I'm not even married. Did you not read the CV I filled out before I started?'

'Well maybe I forgot that bit. Sorry, Doris?'

'Are you married?' she asked. Derek hesitated.

'Mmm, well technically yes.' he said, 'but probably going to be divorced within the next year or so?'

'Oh, well, I'm sorry to hear that, Derek. I've been through a divorce and I can say first hand, it's not pleasant. How's your wife taking it?'

'Well I haven't actually told her yet,' said Derek. 'I'm kind of building up to it.'

'You mean she doesn't know?'

'Well, no.'

'So is there somebody else?'

'Not really.'

'So why on earth are you thinking of getting divorced?'

'Well, you know. I could do with a change and all that, I'm not in the first flower of youth, but I'm not too old. What do you think?'

Doris stared at Derek. She was incredulous.

'What do I think about what, Derek?' Derek didn't seem to understand the question.

'What?' he said, 'you're divorced, you must know how it is.'

'Derek, I got divorced because my husband couldn't keep his dick in his pocket. If I didn't get divorced legally I would have lost my home.'

'Well I'm hoping Anne is gonna move out, I don't fancy moving, a lot of agro you know,' he said matter-of-factly. Doris finished her tea and asked if the meeting was over.

'Well, yeah pretty much,' said Derek, 'I just wanted to raise those couple of points with you, and hope that you'll take them on board, going forward.' Doris could feel her toes curling up inside her shoes.

Derek continued, 'It's nothing personal Doris, and I hope you don't take it the wrong way. It's just that as head of department I need to be seen as though I'm doing my job properly,' he paused, then added 'not least because my bonus depends on it. I actually quite like you as a person.'

As opposed to what exactly? thought Doris.

'You know, I actually think you're quite attractive,' he said.

Doris took a long and deep breath.

'Well, thank you for saying so, Derek, that's very kind of you.'

'Ah, that's okay,' said Derek in a jovial manner. 'I like to think of myself as someone who's not afraid to speak his mind.'

'Well, I admire that in people,' said Doris 'and I shall take on board everything you've said this afternoon and I shall implement it going forward. But if we're all done, I really need to get going.'

'Not at all Doris, in fact I need to get a move on myself.'

As Doris walked back to the Market Square she found herself gasping for breath. She'd made her mind up to hand in her notice the very next day. She knew there were people on the planet like Derek, but she'd never actually met one in the flesh. She went and sat at the same bench where she had eaten her ice-cream earlier. There were even more people about than an hour ago. All seemed to be drinking in the spring sunshine. Everyone looked happy and glad to be alive. Why can't I just be like them? thought Doris. She had fifteen minutes or so before her date, so she just sat on the bench and let the sun warm her face.

About five past two, she made her way to The White Horse along Market Street. A few yards before the entrance she suddenly stopped dead in her tracks. Walking in front of her she noticed Derek. He stopped directly outside the entrance, then after a quick nod of his head he went inside. You have got to be joking, thought Doris. She walked slowly and snuck a peek through the window. The White Horse was the poshest pub in the town; they only did table service. Doris watched as Derek found a table. He tossed his messenger bag on the table and slumped into a leather tub chair. After a few moments, he reached over to his bag and extracted a newspaper which he lay on the table. Then he took out a red silk scarf which he nonchalantly draped around his neck.

Doris couldn't quite believe what she was seeing. A waiter came over and took Derek's order, returning a few minutes later with a glass of white wine. Doris paced up and down the pavement outside the White Horse wondering exactly what she should do. Eventually she had an epiphany. She entered the White Horse and walked briskly past the seating area to the bar.

'Good afternoon madam,' said the barman. 'If you'd like to take a seat I'll be right over,' then added, 'it's table service.'

'Yes, I know that,' said Doris, 'it's just that I'm with that gentleman, over there, and I'd like to surprise him.'

'Okay,' said the barman.

'So what's the most expensive Champagne you have?' asked Doris.

'Well, that'll be the Dom Perignon Vintage,' he said. 'It's £230 a bottle.'

'That'll be fine,' said Doris, 'can you put it on our tab?'

'Absolutely,' said the barman. When he returned with the bottle Doris asked if she could take it over to the table as she'd like to open it in front of her guest.

'Of course madam,' said the barman, 'you take it over and I'll pop downstairs and get two of our special Champagne flutes.'

'You're a treasure,' said Doris. When the barman disappeared Doris grabbed the Champagne and walked toward the exit. As she walked past the seating area she called out, 'Brian?"

Derek span round in his chair, and as he did so, he replied, 'Yes?' but then stopped stony-faced when he saw who it was who'd addressed him. Doris kept walking out into the refreshing warm sunshine, clutching tightly the bottle of Dom Perignon.

Martin Curley

April 5

Menage A Trois

Every autumn she spent the majority of her free time clearing leaves, trimming shrubs and deadheading the perennials, exhausting work after the glory of colour had faded.

She loved winter, when the network of branches enmeshed the sky, but best of all was the dawning of Spring, when buds opened to dress the trees in new frocks, trimmed with delicate frills and flounces, transparent in the morning sunshine.

Each year three wood-pigeons, one male and two females, returned to rebuild their flimsy nest. At six o'clock every evening, all three landed side by side on the back of the garden bench and took turns to flop down to a stone beside a small pond to quench their thirst. There was no squabbling. This was a perfectly harmonious marriage.

She watched with interest. Ideas began to glide through her mind like phantoms. What would it be like? Would it be a success? Would it even be possible? Two women in the same kitchen pandering to the needs of one man? Would they be rivals, each striving to outdo the other, desperate to be the favourite? Would they be continually arguing over who did the least chores, had the most fun, the more tender embraces? Would he treat both alike? Could two wives remain friends under those circumstances?

Or two men with one woman? Now, that was a better proposition. Spoilt by both, feet up on the sofa while one went round with the vacuum cleaner and the other worked in the garden. Yes, both striving to be the favourite with the best reward! The more these ideas lingered in her head, the more she longed to put them into practice.

There were several candidates for her affections, but which to choose? She began to accept the advances of two young men, their invitations to events, office parties, tennis club teas. Outings to town, country, concerts, the theatre, were no longer rejected with some excuse or other. She engineered a meeting, ensuring that both were present, leaving them together to become acquainted. Before long the two men were great friends, and when an opportunity arose, she seized her chance to put her ideas into practice.

It happened that both were searching, without success, for more convenient accommodation.

'Gentlemen,' she said, 'I have two spare bedrooms. You are both welcome to stay with me in exchange for a few jobs around the house and garden. There is some decorating to do and the garden is in need of some tender loving care now that we are into spring.'

And so it was that her experiment was put into practice.

They all lived as harmoniously as the pigeons. Her garden was admired by all the local residents. Her house sparkled with fresh paint and polish. She was served delicious meals every day. And a rota was pinned on her bedroom door.

Wendy Goulstone

April 6

The Nest

A bigger project than one based on primary school labour was a new playing field for the village, a new Nest for its football team the Outwell Swifts. I went just once to their former home, somewhere by the Basin not far from Grandad's. One of the team's heroes of the day, a Hanslip (John or Derek, names have become confused with those of subsequent generations) was pointed out to me. Some branch of his family may have owned the field.

Crossing the Sluice footbridge from the chapel to where Aunt Gert lived, turning left along the Wisbech Road on your right is a flat space – aren't they all in East Anglia? – big enough for fifty cars or so. A waist-high one-rail metal barrier ensures vehicle access is only by the paved road on the town side. A girl lived in the bungalow there, of roughly our age but curiously not at our school. She must have gone to the Convent.

As the field became playable, we quickly wore a path to it from the other end of the barrier, easily vaultable but in any case with a gap big enough to walk through between it and the clapboard fence of the neighbouring property. The boy who lived there, a year or two younger than me, had never been so popular. He had a football. We would always call on him to fetch them out to play.

I don't imagine Grandad minded no longer having to supervise Barrie and me, now my cousin. He could come to stay with us in Isle Bridge Road. Indoors at Maileborne there was a gramophone, which I never knew Nana or Grandad to use. Barrie had some records, of which I would beg him to play Frankie Vaughan's *Tower of Strength* time and time again. Grandad could escape this. When we invaded his land, he had more reason to be careful.

The boundary between Grandad's land and his neighbour's orchards (from which we took the odd apple without any qualms), was a dyke nearer to the house, and then Robb's Lane with a dyke on either side. From pigsties to the halfway shed, which held little of interest for us even when it was not padlocked, the distance must have been about a hundred and fifty yards. At the shed the dyke broadened and deepened somewhat, to the point where it was worth throwing stones in. One day Barrie and I began a more ambitious project.

The land was freshly rotavated. There were plenty of fresh, sizeable clods for us to hurl into the dyke just below the shed. Although some landed on the banks, it did not take long before we were markedly impeding the flow of water.

In family legend, tragedy was only narrowly averted. Grandad's anger seemed disproportionate even at the time. Surely he did not really believe we would block the dyke, backing up the water to flood all his land. He sounded as if he believed it. Sending us scurrying for cover with curses and threats of a thrashing, he was not quite concerned enough to scramble down in his wellies and overalls to bust our dam. The whole family heard about our criminal vandalism, nevertheless.

Barrie was fondly imagined as an ideal playmate for me, a suitable male role model, the older brother I never had, etc etc. I agreed wholeheartedly. He never bullied me, always showed tremendous patience though I accept that may not have endured if we were real brothers. In return I was happy to follow him loyally in all his passing enthusiasms. Football was the next of these.

It was a slow-burning fuse at first. The playing-field had not only the Swifts' pitch, its full-sized goals with round metal posts and stanchions plus wooden backboards, leaving only the nets to be strung up for games. Crossways to it, the council had kindly put up smaller wooden goalposts suitable for us kids. A boy from Upwell soon broke one of these, swinging from the crossbar. It was removed but never replaced, and that lad was not seen again in our village for some time.

We were too old to play on the swings and roundabout, not old enough to hang around them with girls. The commendable initiative of two hard-surface tennis courts would not interest me until later. Otherwise within the field boundaries of dykes on three sides there were only the pavilion, where the players would change and take their half-time cuppas, and a smaller wooden shed by the halfway line. With an earth floor and without seats of any kind, this offered some little shelter from the elements for the hardy Swifts' fans.

Barrie and I took a ball to the big goal nearer to the road (consequently much more worn than the other, since informal games would rarely cover the whole pitch). I suppose I was hopeless. At school, while the girls were occupied at something indoors, there would be an afternoon game once a week for the boys in Mrs Booley and Mrs Lawrence's classes. Still at the younger end of the age range from eight to eleven, I counted my participation in this by the number of kicks I had, a number usually between zero and five. Headmaster Stan was nominally in charge. Beyond seeing the sides selected in the corridor outside his office, he took little interest. If he came out to watch at all, it would be for only a few minutes. There was no coaching, and at that stage I wasn't even watching football on television. I was not a good player. Perhaps I didn't realise it at the time, but neither was Barrie. We didn't make it a regular thing, shooting at each other three-and-in.

Football fever was still some months away in the spring of 1966. But the field was built, and we would come.

David G Bailey

April 7

Judge Not

People don't usually bother to speak to me when I'm out and about; and I'm out and about a lot. You would be too. It's no fun being cooped up in a flat on your own, especially when your neighbours are a funny bunch and don't mix. In my old place we all got on great. I was always popping in to see one of them or another and they were always there to lend a hand. But then I started to get a bit wobbly, had a few falls, and before I knew it I was here, with a button round my neck, pull-cords in every room and a warden who thinks she knows better than I do. And my old neighbours haven't been near me since I moved, even though a few of them promised faithfully to visit. Well, sod 'em I say. I don't need them.

It's no fun being old, but we don't find that out until we get there do we? I suppose I was as guilty as the next person when I was young. Always dashing about; juggling family and work and getting cross when my old mum wanted me to do something I didn't think I had time for. I thought I'd be able to run around forever, but one morning you wake up and think, 'What happened? How did I get here?' I suppose the alternative is worse though.

I can manage quite well, despite what everyone thinks. My flat is near the centre of town so it's handy for everything. The warden told me not to go too far on my own and to make sure I always took my walker, just in case. She can bugger off. I hate being stuck in on my own, staring at four walls while life carries on around me, so every day I take myself off down the high street and sit in a café or, if the weather's fine, on a bench. And, I don't take a walker, thank you very much!

At least when I'm out and about I feel part of things, even though no one acknowledges me or even looks my way. When you get to my age you're not a useful part of society anymore, so you're pushed into a corner and ignored, like those old animals in the wild that are kicked out of the herd and left to wander the plains alone until they die or get eaten alive. The circle of life they call it. It's a long, hard climb to the top of the wheel but once you get there it's a much quicker journey on the way down.

+ +

Today, I decided I'd have a change and go to the park. It's near where I used to live and I haven't been for ages. I thought I might see someone from my old street while I was in the area too. Mind you, I'd probably end up giving them a piece of my mind but it would be no more than they deserve. Thoughtless lot.

The park is lovely at this time of year with the daffodils and tulips out; it looks a picture.

I found myself a nice bench in front of one of the bigger flower beds and settled down to enjoy the spring sunshine. Within minutes a young couple with three kiddies turned up and they came straight over to speak to me. I was made up I can tell you. It gave me a warm glow inside.

They settled on the grass a bit away from me and started laying out a picnic. It took me back to when mine were little. We loved a picnic. I always made sure they had something nutritious but I'd bring cake too as a treat if they were good. I had a little plastic picnic set I bought specially; I wonder what happened to that. I loved sitting in the sunshine, enjoying the peace and quiet while the kids played chase or read their books.

I was so lost in my memories that I didn't notice another two couples had turned up with their little ones, until one of the dads put a music thingy on and blasted me out of my reverie. I say music. It wasn't what I'd call music, all bumping and banging and wailing. Then one of the men got cans of beer out of his bag and handed them round while one of the mums started throwing packets of crisps and sandwiches wrapped in tin foil to everyone. Why she couldn't put them on a nice plate and let everyone help themselves I don't know. Meanwhile the kids were running wild through the flower beds and chucking crisp packets and empty pop bottles everywhere.

Out of the corner of my eye, I could see the mum who'd spoken to me earlier trying to get my attention. She was waving a packet of biscuits and gesturing if I wanted one. As if I'd want their food! Cheeky beggars. Scum of the earth, that's what my mum would have called them, spoiling a lovely place, and intruding on people's peace and quiet. I pretended I was asleep, I'm good at that.

In the end I couldn't stand it anymore and I went home. The youth of today have a lot to learn I can tell you. In my day we respected people and places. We didn't have much, we certainly didn't have fancy phones and music machines, and fifty-inch tellies and the like. Our life was hard but I wouldn't swap with those young madams and their families for all the tea in China. They proper ruined my day, they did. I won't be rushing back there again in a hurry.

Rosemary Marks

April 8

A Change Of Air

He stood at the entrance of his home, as he'd done every day for the last three weeks. But today was different. He'd known it before he'd stepped out. The air was different. Lighter? Damper? Fresher, certainly. Greener? Yes, that was it. Greener,

Too early for three-cornered leek? Maybe. Certainly a bit too early for wild garlic, but the thought of fresh greenery had his mouth watering, and his stomach rumbled hopefully, in concert.

It was very quiet. Did that mean he was one of the first to notice the change, or had he been a bit slow and others had been out foraging and had finished already? Or was everything hiding, wary of a big predator; an owl, or a fox? Especially a vixen with cubs. She'd be mighty hungry.

But he too was hungry. Hungry for fresh greenery; hungry for a good run that would get his heart racing and his muscles working. Hungry for a bit of adventure?

Yet still he didn't move, wary of what might drop from the skies, or leap out from the undergrowth. He sniffed again, sniffed carefully, but all he could detect was the change in the air. Tentatively he stepped away from the grassy bank beneath the trees, first one step, then three, then a quick scurry to the open end of a fallen hollow branch. Moss. Fresh moss. He nibbled delicately, relishing it. His eye caught sight of more fresh green, out towards the stream. He didn't just run to it, he listened, he scented the air, and then he shot over, a blur of reddish-brown, to the short green stalks. No sign that anyone had already marked this stand as theirs; he didn't want a fight, just something nice to eat.

Just as he bit into the first succulent green stem, another red-brown blur of fur arrived. They both froze, berry-bright black eyes fastened on the other. Then slowly they started to eat, one at either end of the patch. Careful not to eat too much after such a long time on minimal rations, he slowly withdrew, and made his way back to his hole in the bank.

He heard the whoosh of wings just as he reached safety, but a truncated squeak, and a single small feather drifting slowly down, told him that his breakfast companion had not been so lucky. Shivering with relief he retreated into the dark tunnel, and the comfort of his nest-bed.

EE Blythe

April 9

Firey Fenzoy

Firey Fenzoy's notable pedigree foretold a successful career. He was a born winner in the Miss Fable family kennels, bred in the famous Eastern Whistles, Nevida. Firey was the Fable's favourite for his first outing of the spring season and needed to prove worthy of the money spent on his purchase.

His sleek coat was shiny and healthy under his bright red racing jacket. He was perfectly race ready for Friday's 2.15 race. It was the long-awaited first race and the day his handler, Jimmy Jacks, and trainer had planned for all their racing lives. Jimmy knew he'd chosen well, endorsed by Firey's trainer Sadie Franks, but needed a good win to prove his worth.

Rain had soaked the race track. Firey was drawn in Trap 1, known to be the luckiest trap. His muscular, heavier weight was perfect for speeding through the mud and the track had been passed fit by the racetrack officials. They were the experts.

Conditions were ideal for Firey's maiden race, run over four hundred metres. The stadium was full. Keen spectators were queuing, ready to place their bets. As it was the first race of the season, hundreds of spectators were out in force to watch the races. Tension was building before the race.

Jimmy Jacks couldn't wait for Firey's first win of the season. He was his most expensive greyhound and Jimmy, excited with the twenty to one odds, desperately needed a return for his massive outlay. Betting had gone well and Firey was calm before the start of his first race.

The starting pistol began the race with Firey flying out of his trap; a racing snake of a muscular dog. Tension was at fever pitch as he was overtaken by Mercy and Jumping Crumb, the favourite. They were no match for Firey, a streak of lightning as he ran faster and overtook both dogs to take first place for the remainder of the race.

The six dogs in the race didn't come near to Firey, a clear winner by twenty-five seconds down the home straight and an incredible five lengths ahead.

What a fantastic beginning to a wonderful future career for Firey. Firey Fenzoy by name and fiery by nature. Jimmy Jacks smiled all the way to the bank, clutching his massive winnings.

Kate A Harris

April 10

A Number

"What's the number?" he muttered. Then louder, "If I can just work out the number."

From across the room, Alice, intent on counting stitches on her knitting needles, absent-mindedly said, "Yes dear," and thought nothing more about it. Half an hour later they had a last cup of tea, and went up to bed. Alice read the next chapter in her book, Reginald was scribbling something on a notepad. She turned her bedside lamp off. He didn't. She fell asleep. He didn't.

Alice awoke, instantly knowing that someone was creeping on the stairs. She tried nudging Reginald, but he wasn't there! Alarm quickly morphed into relief as she heard Reg muttering to himself. Then came the click of the living room light being switched on. Smiling, Alice closed her eyes and drifted off again.

Something brushed against Alice's face, and, still asleep, she brushed it away. Waking reluctantly she rolled onto her side, and the quilt crunched. Bleary eyes focused on a mass of papers, torn from the notepad, each one covered in scribbled numbers; workings out that made no sense. And there was no Reg beside her. She went downstairs.

The living room light was still on, the curtains closed, and in a thick layer across the floor were more pieces of paper covered in scribbled calculations. Not just the floor, all the furniture was covered in scrunched papers. And sat in the middle, still frantically writing numbers, his eyes wild and crazy, was Reg. It was obvious he hadn't slept at all. Alice took it all in, and her heart sank.

"If I can just find the right number," he said, "I can make everything right again. For the whole world." He kept repeating himself, getting more and more agitated.

Alice thought here we go again, and brought him a lorazepam and a glass of water. Twenty minutes later Reg was quiet, and curled up on the floor, drawing in all the screwed up papers, as if making a nest.

Once he was asleep she carefully collected all the papers, and threw them in the bin, then she made herself a pot of weak tea, throwing the used teabags into the bin. She watched as the paper at the top changed colour, and a thought struck her. Slowly, carefully, she poured half of the pot of tea onto the papers, obliterating the numbers.

She didn't know that the sheet on top, the last one that Reg had written out, combined with the next sheet, had there been one, would have been the number Reg had been pursuing. The number that would make everything in the world right again. A truly cosmic number. Ah well...

EE Blythe

April 11

Fighting The Black Dog

During the middle of 1998, I became aware of a growing feeling of sinking. A terrible sorrow seemed to overwhelm me unexpectedly. I got home from a family visit or a meeting and collapsed into tears, fearing that everything I held dear was about to be taken from me. I thought it was some kind of psychological problem, and it seemed to coincide with prolonged headaches and bad thoughts. I was not suicidal, though I had every sympathy with those who have been through that nightmare. But the desperate gloom didn't lift.

I found I was not interested in all my favourite pastimes - music, books, art, even cricket. I felt this dreadful horror of being alone. I shared this feeling with friends who were supportive and eventually took myself to the doctor who diagnosed depression. This came as something of a shock to me, but also, strangely, it made everything seem sense. Perhaps I had always been a depressive, or at least a potential depressive. While the diagnosis was not a solution, it was an explanation and would provide me with an awareness of when it was creeping back and give me possible tools to tackle it.

I tried fighting it with medication to begin with but found this made me so drowsy it was counterproductive. After a couple of weeks, I came off the tablets and settled for a series of counselling sessions with a community psychiatric nurse. This taught me various techniques to try to deal with depressive thoughts. I had a tendency to catastrophise - always expecting the worst to happen, and I was encouraged to challenge each of these negative thoughts and replace them with positive ones. It was not always effective, but it brought me an awareness of when I was succumbing to negative thinking. The difficulty was in trying to break the cycle. You could realise that one negative thought was being followed by another; it was less easy to make a replacement.

Chains of negative thinking clearly happen in the brain and they can lead to dark places. Sometimes they were prompted by life events but sometimes they were just a different way of thinking about the same topic. For instance, if you awoke feeling unwell, one day you might shrug this off and get on with the day. Another time you might think this is something terrible happening to you and link it with other miserable thoughts and have a terrible time of it.

With some people, medication is necessary to try to change this. As a work colleague said to me, "It's a chemical imbalance. Why should you have to put up with it when it can be sorted?"

People are naturally reluctant to go on antidepressant medication. I was - but a few months later, I decided to give it a go on advice from the doctor. I was on medication for about a year and found it really helpful. It was as if there was a safety net holding me up, not letting me drop beneath a certain level. The medication got me through some challenging times but the other side of it was that there was also an upper level in mind beyond which I could not go. There was little euphoria and sometimes a flatness which could not be improved upon. The tablets kept me somewhere in between and that was a safe place for me to be at that moment.

My heart goes out to all who suffered from this terrible condition. Many have encountered far more serious symptoms than me. All I have to say is that there is help out there. The difficult first step is to ask for it. Without doubt, socialising with others is one of the best ways of support but that is not always open to everyone. In many ways, I was fortunate though I would much rather not have encountered the black dog, as Winston Churchill referred to it.

Depression is a horrible condition to have because it lacks any clear cause. It can creep up on you without you knowing, and you can suffer from it in the most bizarre ways. For instance, you can be in a beautiful place with the people you most love, in the most relaxed of situations, yet still feel utter gloom; such gloom that you don't want to speak and you would rather crouch in a corner with a blanket over you until it goes away.

Everything you have ever been interested in can have no meaning. Nothing can lift you out of the pit in which you have found yourself. Something has pulled away the ladder which takes you back to reality. Fortunately for me, my periods of depression are mercifully short; often not lasting more than twenty-four hours. They are usually prompted by minor disagreements or just things not running my way. At certain times, my mind seems predisposed to react in a bad way. A simple disagreement does not always set off a depressing episode; but, on certain days and at certain times, that silly conflict can flick a switch which all but shuts down my communication skills.

Everything is dark and I withdraw, often only allowing myself to act out certain roles that are expected of me, such as teaching a lesson 'in character' and then returning to the gloom. It is not easy living with a person suffering from depression. There is absolutely no point in suggesting they 'cheer up'. That implies they have some sort of choice in being depressed. Believe me, no one would actively choose to feel like that.

Occasionally, I can spot a fellow sufferer. They might be the life and soul of a particular party, but I can sense they are not like that all of the time. Sometimes I want to say, you suffer too, I know. I just hope they have someone to be alongside them when it strikes.

What is my suggestion to those who live with or are friends with someone suffering from depression? Well, I think I would urge them to be aware of the symptoms and not to think they are to blame. We all have disagreements but we do not intend them to devastate the other person. The friend should not take it personally: it's not their fault, and they should not feel aggrieved by it. Instead, they should stay alongside the depressed person. They can try to talk and to listen, try to draw out of the depressed person what they are feeling. If necessary, they can stay silent alongside their friend, hold their hand, just be there until it passes. If appropriate, they can offer to go for a walk or for a coffee or a change of scenery. Even the smallest thing could make a difference and begin to turn the lights back on.

John Howes

April 12

Missing My Wife

From: richard@springmail.com
To: louise@springmail.com
Date: 1st May
Subject: Missing You

Hi Lulu

How is your book tour going? I know it's only been a few days, but it seems ages since you left. It's so quiet here without you. Nothing much has happened here except that it hasn't stopped raining. And this unseasonably warm weather is making the grass grow very long. It's up to my knees already! Missing you. Rich xxxx

From: richard@springmail.com
To: louise@springmail.com
Date: 3rd May
Subject: RE: Missing You

Hi Lulu

Glad to hear all is going well, except for that one man. I can't believe he asked for your number. I don't care if he does look like Tom Cruise, it's still really cheeky. And yes, you're right. I know I should have cut the lawn when you told me to do it before you left. But I didn't know we were about to go through monsoon season. It hasn't stopped raining now for five days. But as soon as it dries up, I'll get the lawnmower out. Keep in touch. xxxx

From: richard@springmail.com
To: louise@springmail.com
Date: 5th May
Subject: RE: Missing You

Hi Lulu

That meal last night sounds amazing. Wouldn't a three star Michelin restaurant be expensive? I hope someone else paid. Who did you go with again? Good news and bad news here. The good news is that it stopped raining yesterday. The bad news is that the lawnmower is broken. But I have a new one on order that is due tomorrow. I'm on the case! xxxx

From: richard@springmail.com
To: louise@springmail.com
Date: 6th May
Subject: RE: Missing You

Hi Lulu

What do you mean you went for a meal with no one I know? I know all the people you're with. Who did you go with??? The new lawnmower arrived today. But there's a problem. The box was all bashed in, and the handle's all bent. I don't know what happened in transit. So I'm sending it back and a new one is on its way. I'm going to hack back the grass today to get it to a length where I can mow it. It's only up to my waist. Nothing too dramatic. xxxx

From: richard@springmail.com
To: louise@springmail.com
Date: 7th May
Subject: RE: Missing You

Hi Lulu
I'm a short man. When I said waist, it really isn't that bad. Trust me.

Attached is that photo you asked for. I have tried to hack it up, but I've realised I've lost the cat. I think she's trapped out there somewhere. But I'll find her. It does not look like a wilderness. It's actually quite pretty. You mentioned someone new was travelling with you now. Who's that? xxxx

From: richard@springmail.com
To: louise@springmail.com
Date: 10th May
Subject: RE: Missing You

Hi Lulu
I can't believe you accused me of photoshopping that picture! As if I'd spend three hours faffing around on photoshop so you wouldn't believe that the grass is now up to my chin. I have work to do, you know. And if I wasn't busy enough, the new lawnmower has now got lost in the post. It says it's been delivered on my account, but I definitely haven't got it. Don't worry about Tiddles. I haven't found her, but I can hear her meowing, so she's definitely out there somewere. So that's good news. Who's the friend you're now staying with? Sounds fun! xxxx

From: richard@springmail.com
To: louise@springmail.com
Date: 11th May
Subject: RE: Missing You

Hi
I didn't appreciate the tone in your last email. I have now done as requested and got off my lazy backside and I've bought a lawnmower from the local garden centre. I hope you're happy now. Glad you're having the time of your life, despite the fact that I'm annoying you.
Rich

From: richard@springmail.com
To: louise@springmail.com
Date: 17th May
Subject: RE: Missing You

Hi

I haven't heard from you now in a few days. Are you okay? The grass has been trimmed, you'll be pleased to hear. I couldn't cut it all because by the time I figured out how to use the new lawnmower, it started to rain again. But I went out with some shears and gave it a haircut, if you like. I could hear Tiddles howling. She's a survivor, so I'm sure I'll see her soon. Rich x

From: richard@springmail.com
To: louise@springmail.com
Date: 20th May
Subject: RE: Missing You

Hi

What do you mean you're going to be delayed coming home? Who is this new friend that you're going to the Caribbean with? Good news at this end. I found Tiddles! It would seem that she was knotted up in the grass, but in the end she chewed herself free. So she's not even that hungry. Could you ask for a better end result? It's stopped raining today, so I'm tackling the lawn tomorrow. Definitely. Before it goes dark. xxxx

From: richard@springmail.com
To: louise@springmail.com
Date: 21st May
Subject: RE: Missing You

Hi Lulu
Sorry for my really late reply. I've been binge watching that series on

Netflix you said your new friend really likes. She's right, it's amazing! Oh God. I've just realised. I never mowed the lawn! Sorry! I'll do it first thing tomorrow. Well, as soon as I wake up. It's going to be a late one as I have four more episodes to watch. This is your fault for getting me hooked on that series. Rich xxxx

From: richard@springmail.com
To: louise@springmail.com
Date: 23rd May
Subject: RE: Missing You

Hi

What do you mean your new friend is a man? Do I have something to be worried about? Right, I'm getting on the next flight to Aruba. You'll be pleased to hear that the grass is now cut. Sort of. It's the best I can do as I'm now all stressed that you're running off with another man. Okay, it's not cut at all, but it's all your fault. I'm coming to Aruba, and when we get back you're paying for AstroTurf. See you tomorrow. Rich xxxx

Lindsay Woodward

April 13

The Tree Branch

Times have changed and there is more acceptance, but it is not absolute.

Kit was walking down London Road. He was in a joyous mood. Life was starting to look up. He was bringing Will to his home for the first time. He could feel the excitement building up like electricity passing between them where they were holding hands.

They were almost skipping when a male cyclist rode past them. They would not have paid it much attention; however, he stopped halfway up the road next to a tree. The cyclist looked back at them, and Kit instantly sensed that something was wrong, and he held Will's hand a little tighter for reassurance.

They would have to pass the cyclist to get home. They moved cautiously forward as the cyclist sat there on his bike by the tree, watching them.

As they came within earshot, the cyclist called out, 'Why are you holding hands? Are you queers?'

Several retorts passed through Kit's mind, but they all died on his throat as it went dry. The cyclist dismounted from the bike, and both Kit and Will took a step back, letting go of each other's hands. The bike clattered onto the pavement. Kit looked desperately at the cars whizzing by on this main road. Surely this man wouldn't do anything with so much traffic going by? Kit stepped slightly in front of Will, putting himself between his new boyfriend and this potential of malice and pain.

'It's f***ing wrong!'

Kit had never heard hate like this before. It was heavy like stone and sharp as steel. Kit's muscles tightened, and his heart was beating fast. Then the man turned around and walked back to his bicycle. He must have realized doing violence here on this busy road would attract unwanted attention.

But instead of mounting his ride, he stooped down to pick up a branch that lay on the path by the tree. Panic flooded Kit's body, and every instinct told him to run. However, he tapped into a well of courage he didn't even know he had. He just knew he had to protect Will.

'Run,' Kit cried as he stepped towards the branch-wielding cyclist.

Kit was focused on the man in front of him.

'Sorry if we've offended you, we didn't mean to.'

'My son plays on this street, I don't want him seeing your filth and being turned!'

'It doesn't work like that!' Kit started but realised there was no reasoning against this hateful ignorance. He just hoped Will was already halfway down the road.

He didn't hear what the cyclist said next as the man swung the tree branch like a rounders bat and connected with Kit's head. The world went white briefly. He thought no yellow canaries, the cartoons got it wrong. He could taste blood in his mouth and realised he had staggered backward from the blow, but remarkably was still standing.

The enraged cyclist was shouting something, but Kit couldn't even hear the traffic, just a high-pitched whine.

Why hasn't anyone stopped to help us?

Then Kit noticed the cyclist was going to head for Will. Why hasn't he run? Kit's only thought was to protect Will. He rushed forward and pushed the cyclist away. The man-shaped embodiment of hate turned on Kit with an unintelligible snarl and swung the branch again.

BAM.

Kit was on the floor this time, and he could feel pain surging through every part of him. He noticed the cyclist had discarded the tree branch, which had snapped in two on the last hit. His fists were just as bad as they pummeled into Will.

Why didn't he run?

Adrenaline was surging through Kit's body, and he somehow

managed to get to his feet. Anger and fear in equal measure coursed throughout his body, and he walked up to the bully and pushed him away again.

'You want more, queer?' shouted hate.

At least my hearing's coming back.

Two punches to the face.

Pushed hard into the fence. Thank god not into the road.

Then Will was standing next to him, loving concern on his face. The cyclist was riding away.

'Why didn't you run?' Kit asked.

'Because I love you,' Will said.

So why is this story about discrimination?

Because if Kit had been holding a woman's hand, then the day would have played out very differently.

Christopher Trezise

April 14

Oops

It was late when Oscar arrived at the cemetery and he had to ask for directions to the chapel. He wanted to pay his respects to his favourite aunt, Cecilia. There was a man with a high-viz jacket walking briskly along the road and Oscar stopped to ask him the way to the chapel.

The man was in a hurry and didn't appear to have listened to the full name of his aunt before giving directions. 'It's the third turning on the left, down about twenty yards, turn right, that's Hopkins Chapel. Have to go. Bye.' He rushed off down the nearest turning and Oscar followed the man's instructions.

There wasn't anybody around to check it was Hopkins Chapel and he rushed in, quietly sat at the back and listened to the proceedings. It wasn't long before he realised he hadn't really known his aunt and didn't recognize the wonderful things said about her.

The service didn't last long, without any hymns, just a few pieces of her favourite pieces of classical music. He didn't even know Aunt C liked classical music. He got up and walked towards the door. A tall slim young man held out his hand and Oscar shook it.

'Did you know Julie Driscoll? She was taken too young, don't you think? It's complicated finding the location of the wake. Follow our car, it's parked outside the front, a blue Mercedes estate. I'm taking four members of the family.'

Oops, a mistake; it wasn't Aunt C's funeral. He couldn't admit he didn't know Julie and had missed the funeral of his aunt. Not saying anything he fetched his car and followed the Mercedes. On arrival, all the mourners were directed into a plushly-decorated room with fabulous massive glass chandeliers, dark burgundy velvet curtains and luxurious gold-coloured seating. He had found himself in a five-star hotel somewhere in the Cotswolds. Oscar sat in the nearest large winged chair with two white cushions and beautiful peacocks emblazoned across them.

He had chosen to plonk himself down on his own, terrified anybody would ask him an awkward question about the Julie person who had died. Sitting silently surveying the beautiful painting of a red poppies on the wall nearby, he wondered what the young man, owner of the Mercedes, was about to say.

'Well, folks, we are here to celebrate the life of Julie. We had only been married three years and shared a wonderful life together and working in industrial electronics. Anyway, Julie left a pot of money that she decided to share with all the people who came to her wake. She had made plans and details of her funeral. There are thirty-five of us and that equates to £3,000 each. Enjoy."

Oscar took the money and made a hasty retreat feeling rather guilty!

Kate A Harris

April 15

Creative Thinking

Stella stared at the pile of badly written papers with resignation. Why had she set her Year Sevens a poem about Spring for their homework? Why hadn't she learned from the Autumn poem fiasco of the previous term? Keats would have been turning in his grave.

She pulled the first one towards her. Danny. Of course. How could he produce anything worse than his *Ode to Autumn*?

> *Autumn. Season of boring TV.*
> *Strictly all Saturday evening. Boring.*
> *Not allowed to watch anything else. Boring,*
> *Do your homework. Boring.*
> *What about the match of the day?*
> *No, you've got to go to bed now. Boring.*

And yet, he'd succeeded.

> *I walked around a bit, bored out of my head.*
> *And it rained a bit.*
> *I saw a pile of tulips, lots of different colours,*
> *Mostly red.*
> *Why aren't there green ones?*
> *I went home.*

Followed by Tyler's offering.

> *Don't want to be here now that spring is sprung.*
> *Who cares about flowers anyway.*
> *Rather be anywhere else.*
> *Especially at the Cup Final.*
> *Anyone got a spare ticket?*

She read on. Many daffodils, many clouds, cuckoos. And birds and the weather. Many, many daffodils. Stella liked daffodils, but now she was sick of them. And she was sick of poetry. If she never read another poem, it'd be too soon.

Finally, the last poem. Patsy-Edina's poem. Poor kid – her parents were big fans of *Absolutely Fabulous,* the father had told Stella at parents' evening. The mother's face had said different, especially as he didn't stop talking about how beautiful and charming Joanna Lumley was, how lovely she was when he met her, luminous he'd said. He'd never asked once how his daughter was doing, didn't even mention her. No wonder Patsy-Edina chose to be called by her surname, Brooke, and refused to answer to anything else.

> *Boing, boing, boing,*
> *The slinky tumbles down the stairs,*
> *Step by step,*
> *Boing by boing,*
> *Until it lands on the hardwood floor,*
> *With a clatter of metal,*
> *And subsides in a trembling heap.*
> *The coiled spring finally rests.*

Creative use of the word spring, Stella scrawled at the bottom of the page. *Excellent. A+.*

Fran Neatherway

April 16

Cucumber Fields Forever

Let me give you a piece of advice: never take a short cut through the cucumber fields on the island of Crete. You could be in there forever.

It was Easter, the best time to go to Crete. Warm clear days, snow sparkling on the mountain tops, and everyone in festive mood after the winter. A perfect time for a walk from Malia on the north coast to Kato Zakros, clinging to the beach, in the south.

We left the flesh pots behind, passed the foundations of a Minoan palace, and deviated from the route to take in more ancient sites and splendid Byzantine churches.

Perched on a rock at the top of a hill, we were looking back to see the route we'd travelled, when we were startled by a male voice wishing us 'Kalimera'. He beckoned us over the brow of the hill to a little conical stone-built hut, where he and his wife were making cheese in a pan over a fire. It was delicious.

Back on the route, high up on the gorse-covered heath, tired and desperate for a sit-down, we came to a junction of tracks. Our planned route led right, but, hey, there was a lane straight ahead which promised to be more direct.

The staple meal-starter in Greece is choriatiki, a village salad comprised of cucumbers, tomatoes, a lump of feta cheese, a chunk of crusty bread, and, if you are lucky, black Kalamata olives. My friends, we soon found ourselves completely lost in a forest of cucumbers, a jungle of cucumbers with paths that led off in all directions, for this was the birthplace of the cucumber, the nursery of the cucumber, the university and the care home for the aged of the cucumber, and we were being sucked into the tomb of the cucumber.

Until, until, in the distance, the far distance, sunshine bounced off glass and white framework. Could it be...? Yes, it could, a greenhouse standing proud amongst the cucumbers, and beside it stood a white-coated figure watching our approach. It was, yes, you have guessed - a human being, a human being who greeted us with an armful of cucumbers and a fistful of tomatoes as big as my head.

He pointed out the path that led down to the coast and off we trotted, juggling with the pile of slithery tomatoes and cucumbers, until we emerged from the plantation and arrived in a village, which had a church we wanted to see.

It was locked. But we were greeted by a woman, who went into her house and came out with a bundle of traditional, twisted, Easter bread-sticks, and directed us to the papa's house for the key. On returning it, he gave us two hard-boiled eggs, dyed red with cochineal.

Now, if you have been paying attention, you will have worked out that we had enough ingredients of a Greek salata to satisfy the five thousand, and still a few more miles to go down to the coast, in a wind powerful enough to blow a motorcyclist off his bike and halfway down a mountainside. But that is another story.

Wendy Goulstone

April 17

The Power of the Pen

There's frog spawn in the garden pond
And blossom on the tree
The daffodils are stood up straight
Smiling yellow for all to see
The birds are waking early now
Singing out their song
But I feel miserable as hell
Why did it all go wrong.

Blimey! That started well and ended badly. Before you start thinking I'm a miserable old so and so, let me explain. I decided to have a go at writing a poem because I'm going to a poetry group later. I haven't been near a poem since I was at school and I didn't go near them then if I could help it. I could never see the point of them to be honest.

I'm only going because the doctor recommended it. She seems to think it will help me because apparently, it's been proven that writing down your innermost thoughts and feelings helps you to deal with them. I thought I was dealing with things actually, but she's so nice I didn't like to say no. She also said that if I can get to a better place, I might be able to come off the tablets. I can't see that happening. I've been on them too many years to live without them now, but I told her I'd give it a go.

I'm getting quite nervous actually. I'm not very good at new things but I said I'd do it so I thought I'd better have a go before I get there and make a twit of myself. I was really getting into it until those last two lines appeared. If I keep writing things like that people will think I'm weird.

I might not go actually. I'll see how I feel later.

+ +

I nearly didn't go to poetry group, but I gave myself a proper talking to and ended up arriving half an hour before anyone else. At least I got a seat on the back row and I'm glad I pushed myself because it wasn't that bad. There's nine of us in the group. I'd never seen any of them before but they seem OK. I'm the oldest there. I knew I would be.

The lady who runs it is called Julie and she seems nice. She read us a couple of poems first; to get us in the zone she said. One was about daffodils by some fella called Wordsmith or something. It was ok. The other was called *The Gardening Man* by Pam Ayres. I'd heard her on the radio and I liked her poem. It reminded me of my grandad when I was a child.

Julie said that poetry doesn't have to be deep and high falutin'. It can be serious or funny and it doesn't have to rhyme. Who knew!

Because it's April she said we should all write a poem about April and we'll discuss them next week. She said we don't have to write much, which is just as well because I'm not sure I'm going to be able to do it.

+   +

April. April. Where are you?
You stayed for such a short time.
I'd barely got to know you
I thought you'd always be here, be mine.

That nearly broke me. I couldn't write any more. At our second meeting Julie invited us to read our poems out. One person didn't write anything at all but everyone else wrote about April showers and Easter and the coming of Spring. I thought I'd completely missed the mark, especially when I saw the sea of blank faces when Julie read my poem out (I couldn't do it myself). I heard one of the women whisper that it was a bit daft thinking a month could belong to you. If only she knew.

After class I had a word with Julie because I was worried that I'd bitten off more than I can chew, but she said mine was very good and clearly from a deeper place within me. Thinking about it, I think she's right, but I didn't elaborate. I'm glad I pushed myself to do it actually.

+ +

I can't believe I've been going to the poetry group for over six months now. I've loved every minute of it and I've made some good friends there and a special one in Bob.

It turns out I'm not the oldest after all because Bob's a whole month older. He sat on the back row at the beginning too and I think he was more worried about being there than I was, although you couldn't tell. He struggled to put pen to paper at first but you should hear his poems now. He's brilliant. He says he's found it really cathartic. I'll admit I had to look that word up but now I know what it means I have to agree with him.

Most weeks we all go out for a drink after our meeting and sometimes Julie comes too. Me and Bob have discovered that we both love the theatre and we try to go as often as we can. We've also found a little pub that does poetry nights and we love to go and listen to people reading poems. Who knows, one day we might read ours out too.

After all these years I'm nearly off my tablets. Can you believe that! The doc says in a couple of months I should be completely free of them. I'm so proud of myself. I've got quite a busy life now, compared to before anyway, and I feel so much better about things. I'll never forget, but I think I can forgive and I know now that I'm strong enough to hold my head up high and smile at the world.

+ +

Dark days in Spring, Summer, Autumn, Winter too
Dark days forever since I lost you
I fought for you, kept you, held you for a while
You gave meaning to my days, with your cheeky, toothless smile
You were too good for this world, you weren't meant to stay
I thought my life had ended when you went away
There I was, a fallen woman, no future, a tainted past
Life held nothing for me, just pain. I had no mast

To cling to. No hope, no help to weather the storm
Just criticism, derision, blame, pain, heavily born
But I was saved by the pen and a doctor who cared
And a teacher who was patient and by friends who dared
To face their demons along with me
To write them all out for all to see
Now, darling April, when I think of you
I smile and remember when it was just us two
I feel blessed to have held you, I was luckier than some
We'll meet again one day. Until then I'll keep you in my heart
From your ever loving mum.

Rosemary Marks

April 18

More, More, More

Carol-Ann sat on the oversized steps of the cathedral, drinking in the sunlight, and absorbing the stored heat in the stone through her back and legs. Next to her on the steps was a brown paper bag containing a somewhat damaged spiced bean pastie; a big green jumper, rolled tightly; and a small plastic box in which she kept various pieces of paper, both legal and sentimental.

She squinted up at passers-by, fretting someone might recognise her, but she needn't have worried; five years of extreme deprivation and random medicines had changed her appearance beyond all imaginings. Five years of living rough: living by foraging, bin-diving, and on occasional welcome hand-outs from the Salvation Army. Five years moving away, to any place where she was unknown, and now back again because she didn't have long, and there were two people she had to apologise to. If they would let her.

Six years ago they were always happy to see her, hear her news. Hug her. That was before the money, the need to make more money, had got between them. Her need for more, more, more. More money, more recognition, more acclaim, more of everything she could think of. It had become an obsession. And then she'd lost control of it, over-reached her financial reserves, left others to deal with the business in her name while she had more fun and excitement. And then everything had imploded. She lost it all. Including her mind, for a while.

She ran. No more buying anything she wanted. No more lavish gowns, and food, or parties with the glitterati. Even charity shops were beyond her means when the winters came and she needed a warm and waterproof coat. Reduced to living in such a desperate way she thought it was no wonder she was now terminally ill.

So now was the time to make her peace with her mother, and her son. She staggered to her feet, and collected her few belongings. The cathedral swayed and the world twirled about her. She did not have long.

EE Blythe

April 19

Talent Spotting

The new volunteer in the charity shop was impressive; moving without slowness or stiffness, she was alert. Her speech revealed the clarity of her mind. I was even more surprised when I learned later that she was eighty. She was, however, still a woman white-haired and wrinkled of skin and so destined to be labelled as 'sprightly' by those younger and less discerning.

But I had learned from someone else's experience to be wary of patronising: not everyone fits a stereotype. A friend's father, a dental consultant, had taken us to Skomer Island, a wild-life sanctuary off the Welsh coast, renowned for puffins. He spoke of his former visit when he'd found himself alongside a stranger on the cliffs watching seals below. His sense of wonder had led him to share enthusiastically, and in some detail, numerous seal-related facts. The two temporary soul-mates chatted about themselves. He revealed his profession and soon found he'd been instructing the Head Seal-keeper at London Zoo...

I resolved to learn from his oops moment and recalled it when I was browsing in the charity shop and heard a customer calling the volunteer sweetheart in an "ah, bless" voice. I probably rolled my eyes to the ceiling and sighed. All this took place decades ago. I'd been attending free computer courses that were held at the end of town beyond the shop. It was for beginners: you followed, at your own pace, a booklet of instructions, with tutors you could ask if you got stuck. There were various courses. I did them all: word-processing, desk-top publishing, databases, spreadsheets, power point, even web-page design and then I did the advanced courses. I did try. I could paper a small room with my certificates but every time I learned something, computing changed, and at home there was no helpful tutor at hand for questioning. I still - years later – can't understand computers but those courses took me past the charity shop and I would enter searching for bargains or donating stuff and enjoy a chat with the assistants. And then one day I tried to recruit this age-defying assistant onto a course. She'd just been complaining about the till.

'It's for beginners. You'd manage it.'

She dismissed the idea.

'It's free, and they help you.'

'Pah! Computers. Never again. Had enough of them at Bletchley Park.'

Oops.

She'd known Alan Turing. 'A strange man.' She'd been recruited at fourteen, in a nationwide war-time search for the mathematically gifted. I was left to console myself, I suppose, on my talent-spotting.

Chris Rowe

April 20

Yorkshire Holidays

Mary and Peter spent their Easter holidays in Yorkshire with their family. Just the children and Mother went; Father had to work. They went by coach from Birmingham to Pontefract, where Uncle Alf met them with the van and drove them home to Stapleton to be warmly greeted by Aunty Nellie. They brought their Easter eggs with them.

It was a marvellous place to holiday, an organic market garden. There were goats, bees, hens, and large greenhouses full of tomatoes. Also raspberry bushes with red and white raspberries. Nellie cooked in a pressure cooker: broad beans, carrots, potatoes, and much more.

A man called Sydney looked after the goats. They were white and friendly; the children liked to watch him milk them with his three-legged stool close into their side, the milk making a lovely shushing noise as it plopped into the bucket. It tasted delicious.

When the family arrived at Stapleton, their first job was to say hello to the bees, their mother insisted. There were two old quarries in the area, and when they walked in them, there were many wildflowers growing in the bottom, including six-foot-high yellow Verbascum with grey furry leaves and yellow flowers. Then there were wooded places, part of Stapleton estate, wild garlic littered the ground and smelled of garlic when stood on, wood anemones white and delicate, and yellow primroses. They would gather armfuls of sticks to feed the fire.

Auntie Nellie was small, round, and cuddly; she wore her long hair plaited up and curled over her ears like earphones. She would sing happily while she worked; she was tone deaf, but the children did not know or care.

There was no better place for holidays. There was a barn full of sweet hay to play in; there were hens to collect eggs from. They were allowed to travel in the van to take bee hives to the Yorkshire moors, where they gathered pollen from the heathers for heather honey.

They liked to go into the honey room that smelled gorgeous; this was where the honey was extracted from the combs. Sometimes they were given a piece of comb to eat.

The holiday seemed to stretch a long time, but eventually, they came home on the coach to be greeted by their father, happy, healthy, and ready for school.

Ruth Hughes

April 21

White Rabbits, White Rabbits

We said it on the first of March, a family tradition, but why we said it was a mystery to us, for luck, perhaps, a ritual we kept thoughout our childhood, that lapsed as we grew up. It was just something we did, accompanied by giggles as we competed to be first to say it, and then just as quickly it was forgotten over the cornflakes, or, more often, jelly dripping on toast.

Making the toast was Dad's job, but Mum carved the loaf as I watched, nerves twitching, for Mum was left-handed and carving the loaf seemed to me to be a hazardous experience. The grandmother I never knew, and my sister, were left-keggy, too. I always was the odd one out.

When the doorsteps were carved, Dad took a slice and pierced it with the prongs of a wire toasting fork, a wonky, home-made heirloom that hung on a hook by the black-leaded grate in our kitchen-cum-living room. He would take the poker, carefully remove any 'strangers', the sooty deposits that hung from the bars of the grate, and hold the bread to the glowing coals beyond the bars. A cup of cocoa or Ovaltine completed our weekday breakfast before we set off for school. I still have the toasting fork. It hangs on a hook by our kitchen fireplace. In memory.

On Sundays, Dad cooked bacon and eggs and, sometimes, tomatoes, a treat eagerly anticipated. That was after the war, of course, when bacon and eggs became available and we no longer had to eat tinned bacon, which I loved, and reconstituted powdered egg, which I hated.

Much later, after I married and left home, I usually called in to see my parents on my way home from work on Wednesday afternoons.

Mum would rustle up something to eat, then Dad would get out an ancient pack of cards, the pegging board and four matchsticks, the ends carefully pared so that they would fit into the holes.

We played with great concentration, because the loser did the washing up, a daunting task, for, by the time we had played two games and one for his hat, the plates and pans were covered with congealed fat. Dad was a dab-hand at cribbage, and usually won, white rabbits or not, and, when he moved his peg to the final hole on the board, he would rock with a great roar of laughter. But, nine times out of ten, he would take pity on me and do the washing up anyway. Poor old Dad, World War One survivor, who regularly revisited the traumas of the battlefield in his nightmares, and fought them on the pegging board.

Wendy Goulstone

April 22

Incident In Berlin

Checkpoint Charlie had been fascinating, the Brandenburg Gate majestic, and the Reichstag - standing where Hitler had stood seventy-five years before - memorable in a not-so-brilliant sort of way. Berlin was moody, trendy and very, very graffitied, but I hadn't quite got to grips with its charm, possibly because of the incessant, driving rain which had greeted us just about everywhere.

That day we walked along what was left of the Berlin Wall, now an art gallery for a myriad of murals and alternative interpretations of what freedom was all about. It was quite interesting without matching up to the first half of our holiday in beautiful, glorious Prague.

I crossed the street at some traffic lights, heading for the nearby station. When I got to the other side of the road, I reached for my shoulder bag. Reassuringly it was still there, on my shoulder, but I didn't remember the zip being undone. Feeling inside for my phone, I soon realised it wasn't there. Some swine had stolen it, in its wallet, together with my bank cards. I was crushed and sank to the floor, not because I had lost my phone and spending power - they could soon be replaced - but because I'd taken about a hundred pictures of Prague and hadn't uploaded any of them. They were all gone and I was so, so sad.

I blamed myself for not taking enough care, for allowing myself to be the victim of some seasoned thief who was able to unzip my bag whilst it was still on my shoulder, and carefully remove my phone. They must have been watching me to know the phone was there.

My son sprang into action, retracing my steps and discovering my donor card which had been thrown to the ground as the thief made his escape. But the pictures and video were gone and there was a big gap in my album of memories.

When we got back, I related the incident to my parents who said, "That must have spoiled the whole holiday."

No, I said, it didn't. I wouldn't be that melodramatic. Nobody was hurt. Nobody died. It was just a phone and some cards. But where are those pictures now... my wife, my son, my stepson and me in the city of Prague, on the Vlatava River. Who is looking at those pictures now, and what are they thinking?

John Howes

April 23

That's What Friends Are For

Me and Gemma met when we were in high school. I was in my usual seat at the back of a maths class, trying not to get noticed, when I heard someone whisper in my ear, 'Bet you can't hit old Hughsie with your rubber.'

I got him right on the back of the head. Maria Jenkins, who was a proper teacher's pet, dobbed me in. I got into big trouble. I didn't tell him it was Gemma's idea though. We've been firm friends ever since.

Despite what you might think, I've always been quite shy. I've never really liked to draw attention to myself, whereas Gemma's a bit of a wild card. You never know what she's going to do next.

Since that incident with Hughsie I've tried to keep out of trouble. I don't like the way it makes me feel. But even though we're complete opposites, Gemma has never judged me or left me in the lurch. She just carries on being Gem. I can't imagine life without her.

+ +

We got our own place a couple of years ago. It's only small but it suits us fine, and more importantly it's a good bit away from my mum. She can't let me go though; she keeps harping on that she doesn't understand how I can afford the rent, and how it would be cheaper for me to move home. I've told her that Gemma pays her fair share but she just looks at me like I'm crazy.

'If she's been your best friend since school, how come I've never met her?' is all she says.

The truth is, Gemma doesn't want to meet her. She's got no time for clingy parents, or anyone in authority really. And Mum's seen Gemma's artwork all over the flat, which should be enough proof that she exists. I've told her if she wants more proof she should go to the local gallery on the High Street. They've got lots of her work, including two pieces she's just sold - for a good price too. The only response I get is, 'You're really good at art too, Jen.'

I'm not, but you just can't win with my mother.

+ +

All my mum has ever wanted is for me to meet a nice man and settle down. She has no idea how hard it is. It's not like I haven't tried.

I wish I was like Gemma. She's always out at clubs and bringing blokes home "for a bit of fun". She says life's too short to settle down.

A couple of years ago, she signed me up for internet dating. She said it would be a laugh but it wasn't. Everyone I met turned out to be a nutter; Gem will back me up on that. It didn't matter how nice they seemed when I swiped, after a couple of dates they always turned out weird. The last bloke I met said he was a teacher. He turned out to be a bloody paedo! I found out he spent his time hanging around schools trying to "make friends" with the kids. After we broke up, it was all over the papers that he'd been found in a playground one morning with a serious head injury. He was in a coma for weeks, and word is he'll never be the same again. They never caught who did it either. Gem said he got what was coming to him.

That was kind of the last straw for me. I decided I was going to pack dating in. Gemma wasn't too impressed with me at first; she said I have to make the effort to get out a bit more. I told her she sounds more like my mum every day. We didn't speak to each other for a couple of days, but we soon made up again. We're too close to fall out for long.

+ +

Fate had other ideas though. One day I was walking through town with a coffee, head down and reading my book when I bumped into someone. My coffee went all over him and his went all over me. After we'd cleaned ourselves up and apologised, he bought me another coffee, and that, as they say, was that. I was smitten.

His name was Richard and he was six years older than me. We shared a hatred of crowded spaces and a love of reading and quiet nights in; we hit it off straight away. Mum would say he was nothing to write home about, but he was just my type. I knew he was special because, when I got home, I didn't want to tell Gemma about him. I felt that if I talked about him too much I'd be tempting fate and things wouldn't work out. She knew though; she's known me too long not to recognise a difference in me.

She started quizzing me the minute I walked in and I had to lock myself in the bathroom to get away from her. I love her to bits, but she can be a bit jealous and possessive. There was no way I was letting her ruin what I hoped was going to be a good thing.

+ +

Six months on and things with Richard were going strong. Gemma wasn't happy that I was in a serious relationship and she refused to even meet him. She stopped bringing people home and started staying out all night. She wasn't around much in the day either and even stopped painting.

Finally I'd had enough and decided to confront her. She refused to discuss it at first, insisting that nothing was wrong and I was imagining things.

'You've got your life, I've got mine,' she said banging the pots around as she dried them. 'There's no rule to say we have to be together all the time.'

I told her I knew that, but I missed her and I was worried that she was hardly ever home any more.

'And what about your painting?' I asked her. 'How can you make a living if you stop that?'

'Is that all you're worried about? Whether I can pay the rent? I'm sure your precious Richard will help you out.' She slumped to the floor, sobbing. 'I don't want to lose you Jen. I'm scared he's going to take you away from me.'

It took a long time to calm her down but she finally settled. We spent the evening drinking wine and reminiscing over good times, and in the morning I felt we were back on track again. But she still refused to meet Richard.

+ +

On our first anniversary, Richard said he was taking me somewhere special.

As he drove into the countryside, I could feel my heart fluttering nervously. I've never been good with surprises.

After a while we stopped at the bottom of a hill which had an old stone tower at the top. Richard led me up the slope and through the wooden door. There were tea lights on the stone steps to guide our way up. At the top we stepped out onto a balcony which was strung with fairy lights. The sun was slowly going down in the distance and it was stunning.

'This is gorgeous,' I said.

'I did it for you, Jen.' He took hold of my hands. 'You must know by now what you mean to me.' He got down on one knee, put a hand in a pocket and pulled out a small box.

I could feel a familiar whoosh of blood in my ears.

'Jen. Will you...'

The scream came out of nowhere. 'NO!'

'Gemma!' I gasped. 'What are you doing? Go away!'

'No!' she screamed at me. 'This isn't what you want.'

'Yes, it is!'

Richard stood up, looking shocked. He backed up against the balcony wall, watching us with a horrified look on his face.

Before I could stop her, Gemma launched herself at him and pushed. I watched as he struggled frantically to regain his balance, then he disappeared. There was an eerie silence, followed by a faint thud.

'What have you done?' My legs had turned to jelly, I couldn't move.

'Stopped you making the worst mistake of your life, that's what. Did you really think we could stay friends if you married him, Jen? We'd lose each other forever. He'd never understand you like I do.'

'But he loved me.'

'Not like I do, Jen. No one loves you like I do.'

'You didn't have to kill him, Gemma.'

'I did though. It was the only way.'

Strange as it may seem I knew she was right. Me and Gem are like identical twins. No one could ever come between us.

She let me cry for a while, then told me gently we needed to go. We went quickly down the stairs to where Richard lay on the concrete path. I made my way over to him.

'Come away, Jen, we need to go.'

'Not yet. I just want to look.' A pool of blood was slowly spreading out from his head. I bent down to look at it, beckoning her over, 'Look Gem. Look at the pattern it's making. It's like one of those inkblot tests that Dr Fleming keeps showing us. I think I can see a butterfly. What can you see?'

'I can see trouble if we don't get out of here, Jen. Come on.'

We ran as fast as we could across the field. Gemma started whooping and laughing, flinging her arms out and shouting, 'We're free as birds.' We ran and laughed and danced all the way home. It was miles, but neither of us was tired or cold. We were on a high, the sort of high you get when you know you so nearly made a really bad mistake but your best friend in the world saved you at the last minute.

'Gem,' I said when we were finally curled up at home with a nice bottle of wine and a Chinese takeaway. 'I'm sorry I let myself be fooled by him. I'm so lucky to have you to keep me on track.'

'No worries.' She raised her glass and took a big gulp. 'I'll always watch out for you, Jen. I've done it before and I'll do it again. That's what friends are for.'

Rosemary Marks

April 24

Seven Deadly Sins

Merrick Ganz, tech billionaire extraordinaire, had an ego the size of the Great Wall of China. And he was bored. Like Alexander the Great, he had nothing left to conquer.

An idea occurred: what about the Seven Deadly Sins?

He called his team of PAs into his office. Seven apprehensive people filed in.

'New challenge. I have decided to…' he paused, trying to think of the appropriate verb,'…commit all Seven Deadly Sins. Suggestions?'

There was silence, punctuated by seven people all biting their tongues.

"Go away and come back with a plan tomorrow.' He waved a hand in dismissal.

They'd be going to the conference room – which he had bugged several years ago. Some very illuminating conversations had taken place there.

+ +

'Anyone know what they are?' Melinda, Chief PA, asked.

'Yes,' Trudie said to the astonished group. 'Religious upbringing. Pride, Greed, Lust, Envy, Gluttony, Wrath and Sloth.'

'He's got Pride nailed,' Charlie said. 'We've all heard him boasting about his "achievements".' He made air quotes with his fingers.

Everyone nodded in agreement

Ganz decided he really must install cameras as well as microphones. All those silences were annoying. They could be doing anything.

'And Lust,' Melinda said. All four women had expressions of disgust. 'I told him I'm gay.'

One good session with the Merrick Love Machine would soon fix that, Ganz thought.

'That's why Jenny and I always walk out holding hands. But I'm not.'

Lying cow. Ganz was not pleased.

'But I am,' Jenny said.

'Melinda, would you like to come out for dinner with me on Saturday?' Charlie crossed his fingers.

'Love to.' Melinda smiled. 'Thought you'd never ask.'

Charlie punched the air to the applause of his colleagues.

That's two people who'll be getting their P45s on Monday, Ganz thought.

'I'm gay too,' Patrick said. 'But he doesn't like poofs, so I'm still in the closet at work. My boyfriend's getting pissed off. All those after work trips to strip clubs.' He shuddered. 'Is one of the Sins bigotry?'

'Plus misogyny,' Jenny said.

'They should be,' Melinda said.

'Wrath,' Anna said. 'You know how he gets when he's crossed. Remember Lena?'

Bloody women. He knew he should never employ them. Too sensitive. Only hiring men next time.

There was a moment's silence for Lena, the PA who'd had to tell Ganz he'd been outbid for the *Mona Lisa*. She'd never recovered.

Honestly, you dangle one woman out of a tenth storey window. And he'd paid for her stay at The Priory. On his lawyers' advice.

'Does that cover Envy as well?' Richard asked.

'Ooh, I think so,' Melinda said, ticking it off on her list. 'If someone else has something, he wants it.'

'And Greed,' Trudie added. 'He always wants more – faster cars, bigger yachts, more expensive houses. How many can one man want?'

Ganz snorted in derision. Who didn't want bigger, better, more expensive stuff? And getting one over his rivals – how else did you keep score? He'd already set plans in motion to get the Mona Lisa back.

'What's left?' Patrick asked.

'Gluttony and Sloth,' Melinda said, consulting her list.

'He does eat a lot,' Jenny said. They sniggered. 'And it has to be expensive – caviar, Kobe beef, expensive wines.'

'He wastes a lot of it,' Patrick said. 'Chef takes it as a personal affront when his plate comes back untouched.'

'He paid Chef a fortune to leave his five-star restaurant and work exclusively for him,' Melinda said. 'Another example of Greed and Envy.'

Why wait till Monday? P45 for her tomorrow.

'I'd leave if I could,' Charlie said, 'but he's got us all sewn up with those contracts. I'd be lucky to get a job with MacDonald's.'

He'll be finding out on Monday! In fact, why not fire them all? Ganz rubbed his hands. Haven't had a good mass sacking for months.

'Sloth's a bit tricky, though,' Richard said.

'It means lack of interest or ignoring your responsibilities,' Anna said, looking up from her phone.

'He's definitely got that covered then,' Charlie said. 'He doesn't even know how many kids he's got, let alone take responsibility for them.'

'Not to mention his total lack of interest in any of his wives,' Trudie said. 'For which, no doubt, they are all truly grateful.'

You are definitely sacked.

'Right then,' Melinda said. 'We're agreed? We tell him we've carefully researched the Sins and there's no way someone as wonderful as him could ever do such things.'

'He'll definitely believe that,' Patrick said, smirking.

The laughter went on for some time, then a door closed and there was silence.

Maybe they weren't so bad after all? Just letting off steam. But Melinda and Charlie still had to go, plus the gays Patrick and Jenny. There'd be four P45s on Monday.

Ganz smiled, shark-like. He loved firing people – he took Pride in it.

Fran Neatherway

April 25

Dear Luke

10th October
Worcester

Email: Dear Luke

I hope you are well. Your mother phoned last week and told me you had an accident at the weekend due to a cracked pipe. I hope you have got it sorted. We had a cracked pipe, when your grandad and I lived in Swindon. Water came through the kitchen ceiling and shorted the cooker. I still can't see how a cracked pipe could cause you to become that sick. Your mom mentioned something about marshmallows, can that be right? Mind you, I am due for a new hearing aid. Anyway, I hope you are feeling better and I've enclosed a twenty-pound note so you can treat yourself to something (don't tell your mother I've given you some money).

Your mum also tells me you've started courting again. I'm sorry things didn't work out with Emma. I really thought she was going to be the one. We had some really lovely conversations when I was down in the summer. Well, I hope you have better luck with Edie; she sounds wonderful, as long as she doesn't end up like Edie Sedgwick. I'm sure she won't. I must say your grandad wasn't my first love, though he did turn out to be the best. I actually courted quite a few boys back in the day, but when things went wrong, as they inevitably did, I'd just shout 'Plot Twist!' and move on.

Well it's only about two months till Christmas, and I shall see you all then. I'll probably come down on the train as usual, and now you've passed your test perhaps you could pick me up from the station. I shall feel so proud. So take care, Luke.

Love and Kisses, Gran X X

21st October
Swindon

Dear Gran,

Hope you are well. Thank you very much for your lovely letter and thank you so much for the twenty pounds. You really shouldn't send me money, I mean really, you shouldn't. I'm on £28,000 a year, Gran, and I know you're only on a widow's pension. I shall keep it safe and give it back when I pick you up at Christmas.

With regard to this accident, Gran, because you're my favourite person in the world, I can't lie to you and this is kind of difficult for me to explain, but what Mum was trying to tell you, was that a friend and I had come in after a night out in Swindon, and, well, he had this crack pipe, and crack to boot. So anyway, we tried it, mainly because we were curious and we are at the age of maximum stupidity. So after we'd tried it I went to the all-night supermarket and bought two large bags of marshmallows, and ate them on the way home. I was quite sick, but thankfully nothing serious. It was all my stupid fault, I've never taken drugs before, Gran. I feel rather foolish.

Changing the topic, Mum was quite right. I have started courting again, but the name's Eddie not Edie. He's a man, Gran. And you're the first person I've come out to. Mom doesn't even know yet, I just can't bring myself to tell her. Emma was great, she really was, she's the most wonderful woman I've ever met, but there's the rub, she's a woman.

Well, there it is, Gran, you now know your only grandson is a crack-pipe-smoking poof. I'm sorry if I've let you down. You're still my favourite person in the world. Can't wait to see you at Christmas

Lots of love, Luke.

29th October
Worcester.

Dear Luke,
Thank you for your letter. Yes, you are correct to feel foolish, and yes, your so-called accident was all your stupid fault. Even I know if you've never taken drugs before, you don't start with a crack pipe. That's insane. Crack isn't a gateway drug, Luke, crack is where you end up after you've opened the gate and gone to the furthest corner of the field. What were you thinking? You should have tried a few spliffs or at least some of them happy pills. Back in my day we could only get hold of marijuana, and that was pretty rare in Swindon, and it wasn't that strong either. Life's not a fairy-tale, Luke. Back then, if we lost a shoe at midnight, it's probably because we were bat-shit crazy on something.

With regard to your boyfriend Eddie, good for you, Luke, I look forward to meeting him. And, if I may take you into my confidence, there was more than one occasion when us girls would end up bunking-up together, if you get my drift. Well Swindon wasn't exactly teeming with available men back in the seventies. It's just what we did. Don't worry about coming out to your mum, I know her better than she knows herself. If there is one thing I'm capable of, it's telling my only daughter that my only grandson is gay. So you take care, and take care of Eddie and I'll see you at Christmas.

Love and kisses, Gran.
P.S. I've enclosed thirty quid. Get yourself over to Eastcott Hill, and treat yourself to some weed. They do the best rates in Swindon.

Martin Curley

April 26

Springtime

It was springtime and my favourite season to make improvements in the house.

The year was 2021, three years since we had moved in, and time to modernise with necessary changes, major changes. Several home renovations had already been completed: a new kitchen, en suite shower room and redecoration of most rooms over those first three years.

Crash, bang, wallop. The plumbers had moved in. The porcelain wall tiles had been attacked, then the bath, toilet and flooring removed. The plumbers were having a smashing time. There were two workmen on the job, Chris and Ray.

Everything was taken out of our old bathroom. Our more elderly knees did not allow an easy climb into or out of the old bath. The rubbish had been removed and the new bathroom totally empty, ready to install our more practical shower along the whole length of the room, a new sink in its vanity unit and the toilet to be fitted.

It was and still is much more suitable, as we look into our future and older age!

Eventually the wall tiles were fitted around the sink, toilet and the shower, with its new shower tray and screen. It was tidied, cleaned and decorated, almost finished.

It looked great, apart from the flooring which we were assured would be delivered within the next few days. It was après Covid and lockdown, when there were horrendous problems with sourcing items, including our new flooring into the local tiling shop. Quicker than anticipated we were informed by phone that the vinyl flooring had arrived. After a short but tense wait for the fitters, it was fitted and I was pleased with the look of the seaside and its planks of driftwood.

It was eventually finished. Our new bathroom, now shower room, looked better than I imagined and two years later it is still looking great.

Next we decided that the floors in our 1989-built house needed attention. They are boarded, not with floor boards as previous 1930s houses where we lived, but with boards that squeaked when we walked on them making an annoying sound when in the rooms below. New floorboards were placed on top dulling the sound.

The next job was decorating the hall. We were on a roll and needed to update and brighten the tired-looking walls. Newer houses have their problems which are similar problems to the older houses that we were used to updating. There is always something else needs doing.

I love our newer home with smaller rooms and easier cleaning.

Desperate to escape from the loud and noisy radio, workers and choking dust I decided a walk was essential for my sanity. I enjoyed the fresh air at a quiet time of the day.

When I returned from my walkies to the noise and chaos, it was time for another coffee and I decided to make bacon sandwiches for the hardworking workmen. It was a special one-off occasion, I pointed out, as it was my birthday. Birthdays are sent to try us. I was another year older, couldn't avoid it, and looked forward to the evening when the family were due to visit and share my birthday cake.

The hall was improved with its newly-painted, lighter yellow and the following Monday the old carpet was ruthlessly ripped up from the landing ready for the new boards and later new carpets. The floor squeaking was sent to try us and quietened a couple of days later when the carpet fitters arrived and fitted the new lighter grey, more plush carpets.

Updating and renovating the house never ends. Next springtime, I wonder what changes our house will undergo.

Kate A Harris

April 27

A Ghost Of Golden Daffodils

The sun shone down brightly onto the carpet of naturalised daffodils. Peta regarded them with pride. Her great-grandmother's work, her Grandmother's work, her mother's work, and now her work: encouraging the carpet to spread, and protecting it from predators, both animal and human. Great-grandad's Hill, that's what her father had called the gentle slope where his grandmother had planted the first clump, when she had been a small girl of seven years.

Now, her great-grandmother was gone, her father was gone, and Peta herself was getting on in years, but that clump of daffodils had spread all across the slope, and down to the flat ground through which the brook ran. The daffodils wouldn't be able to cross the brook, so sometime in the near future someone would have to start thinning-out the field of yellow, as there was nowhere else to go.

When Peta had taken over running the farm, she had been anxious about the daffodils crossing the brook and being eaten by the cows. She knew daffodil bulbs were poisonous to humans, but had no idea if the cattle would be affected. Unlike her brothers, Ray and Frankie, she hadn't been to agricultural college, and what knowledge she had came from the remaining farmhand, the locals, and from snippets of past conversations with her father.

It wasn't just the daffodils; Peta didn't know a thing about running a farm. She could keep hens, run a dairy, and make butter, but nothing else. Why would she? She'd spent her teenage weekends and evenings working with Dolly and Eva in their little shop, selling fabrics, and notions, and making children's clothes to sell in the market. After that it had been college, and then abroad to work in a series of small fashion houses.

She'd have been there still if it hadn't been for Foot and Mouth, Ray's death, and Frankie's head injury, rendering him incapable of virtually everything. It had been a steep learning curve, but somehow the farm had eventually pulled through all the trouble and was now functioning well, providing organic milk, butter, and beef, as well as gate sales of the surplus from the kitchen garden. It had been hard work, but worth it, she supposed, if only to keep this beautiful field of daffodils. The blaze of gold was breathtaking.

Peta awoke with a start! She'd been dreaming about the daffodil field again. She glanced at her bedside clock, it was four am. Some habits died hard. Reaching for her walking stick she carefully supported herself as she sat up, swung her legs out of bed, and slowly pushed herself upright. Or as near to upright as she could manage. With difficulty she got herself to the bathroom, always the first port of call these days, and with some urgency. She wound her dressing gown round her spare and angular frame and headed for the kitchen. Every day started with a strong cup of tea, and some gentle stretching exercises while she waited for the kettle to boil.

While the tea brewed she thought again of the field of daffodils, her 'host of golden daffodils', to quote the poet. That monumental achievement by previous generations of her family had gone, ripped up by bulldozers because the new owners of the farm wanted to exploit that gentle slope to make more money. They weren't satisfied with making a decent living from the farm, oh no, they wanted to maximise every square inch to the ultimate extent. And despite having promised to leave the daffodil field untouched, in less than a year it had been ripped out. Peta cried when she heard, but was so thankful that she hadn't been there to see it happen. All she had of the field now was one photograph, and her recurring dreams.

Peta loved her new bungalow with its view of the sea and the Welsh hills. She loved her new garden, with its raised beds, and flowering arch, but especially she loved the corner patch of daffodils. A small triangle of gold in the spring. Smiling to herself she again wondered if she could get the daffodils to spread beyond her fence, and down to the cliff edge. **EE Blythe**

April 28

Excitement In Norwich

Many moons ago, it was just a normal day when a telegram arrived. At that time, John was working in Libya, and we hadn't seen each other for a number of months. The telegram just said (and this was before emails)

Meeting in London. Tuesday.
24 hours home. Flt KLM 45. NORWICH.

You can imagine my excitement and, in that moment, I phoned Norwich Airport to check the time of arrival from Libya, eight-thirty pm. So I made my plans. I couldn't wait to see him and give the girls a surprise too. I collected them from school, gave them tea, put them in the car and set off for Norwich. This was a two-hour drive but I didn't mind, I was going to pick up John as a surprise.

We arrived at the airport at about seven forty-five, early but that didn't matter. By now the girls were in a state of excited anticipation at the thought of seeing their father. Finally, the plane arrived and the passengers started to come through. But no John. We waited, waited some more, then checked with the staff, definitely no John. By now it was after ten so I decided to phone home (just in case we had missed him).

After a couple of rings John answered. When he realised it was me his first words were, "Where the hell are you?" John had arrived in London and headed straight home expecting to see his whole family waiting to greet him. Oops!

On hearing we were in Norwich his response was, "What on earth are you doing there?"

"You said your flight was arriving in Norwich," I said.

There was silence then "No, I had a spare word and NORWICH

was a message for you."

What?

"kNickers Off Ready When I Come Home."

Oops!

My response was, and is, unrepeatable. It took about another two-and-a-half hours to get home very, very late. Try living that down.

Pam Barton

April 29

Sounds like Spring

It's beautiful outside. Spring is just around the corner.
What?
Spring, it feels like spring.
Don't start that.
Don't start what?
To sing.
I didn't mention singing.
Yes, you did. You said you're going to sing.
No I didn't.
You said you feel like singing!
Have you got your hearing aids in?
Of course I have.
Well. Switch them on.
No way.
Why ever not?
Because I sound like a cat being strangled.
What are you talking about?
You just said give us a song. You know I can't sing.
I said no such thing.
Exactly.
Exactly what.
You know I can't sing.
The birds are singing, not you or me.
Leave it to the birds I say.
Those daffs I planted are starting to flower.
Hmm… Right…
And the tulips are up. I love this time of year.
It's far too early.
What do you mean too early?

It's ten in the morning. You turning into an alchy or something?
Why would you say that?
You said you'd love a beer.
I did not!
No good backtracking now. I heard you.
I DIDN'T say I want to sing, OR I want YOU to sing OR that I want a beer. I SAID... I LOVE THE SPRING!
Hmm...Looks like it's going to be a nice day. It's nice to see the sun. Looks like Spring might be here at last.
Oh for goodness sake, I'm going to do the shopping. I'll pick you up some hearing aid batteries while I'm out.
Good idea. Give a man a bit of peace for five minutes.

Rosemary Marks

April 30

Driving North

Who needs Spring when there's a sky like this?

Pure gold, it stretches along the horizon, mile after mile of glory, richer than any Turner skyscape. The great orb of the sun disappeared beyond the fields half an hour ago but left behind such a vast expanse of startling light that it is brighter than day. There are long trailing islands of cloud, underscored with liquid rubies, that make you want to take a boat and sail out to them. And along the fringe of Earth the winter trees enmesh the sky with an exquisite network of branches.

You can keep your fields of nodding daffodils, your clouds of May blossom, your luxurious burst of green foliage, give me bare twigs entwined against this glorious vision of heaven. We were heading north for Christmas, the M6 studded with cars, drivers carefully keeping in line, no reckless overtaking, spellbound by the riches spilled out to the west. And what was odd, the farther north we went, the greater was the expanse of sky, better than any display of northern lights, until, finally, the last golden gleam disappeared beyond the horizon and we were in darkness.

So here we are, back on earth, sitting aimlessly in armchairs while the rest of the family rustle up Christmas dinner. We offer our help, but know as well as they do that it is easier for our hosts to do it themselves rather than explain to us what needs doing. So we try not to feel guilty and relax.

It rained during the night. The air is still, the sky leaden, the lawn soggy. The spring bulbs are still tucked up in the beds, but that golden sunset is still locked at the back of my eyes.

Wendy Goulstone

A Story for Every Day of Spring

May

A Story for Every Day of Spring

May 1

May Queen

Bobby had been determined to be the May Queen, and sit on the plush red and gold throne, on the most important float in the parade. To be wearing the pure white dress, and the green willow garland, and wave to the crowds as the float went past them. Of course, it would be a gloriously sunny day, blue sky and small white fluffy clouds, moving across the sky on a gentle, warm breeze.

Oh, the glory of it; the feeling of being special, if only for the day. Bobby really wanted it. But the chances were slim. So many young maidens had submitted their names, and their photographs. Looking round the village hall, Bobby counted twenty-one girls who had been called for the final stage. Tall, willowy girls, petite girls, a few dumpy girls, and several well-rounded girls. Dark-haired beauties, angels with halos of golden curls, a couple of red-heads, too! The competition was always going to be fierce, Bobby had known that, but today really brought home how difficult the chances of being chosen as May Queen really were.

Each prospective Queen was asked a few questions by the judging panel, usually the same first half-dozen queries, but then came two random ones. Bobby's answers to the random ones had made the judges smile, one even laughed out loud in a sudden burst of lost control, and then looked to the others, apologetically. The ordeal was soon over, and the panel retired to discuss their preferences. The candidates were offered tea, and coffee, and biscuits.

The local doctor, head of the judging panel, appeared, with a single piece of paper in his hand, and the other judges filed in, smiling. The doctor spoke.

"Thank you all for coming today. I wish we could make you all May Queens, but there can be only one. After much deliberation, and an almost unanimous vote, we have chosen…"

+ +

Bobby placed the folds of the long white dress carefully, artfully, across the front legs of the red and gold throne. He couldn't believe he was really there, sitting on the float, getting ready to wave to everyone lining the route to the festival field. Last year's May Queen had just placed the willow garland on his head and gently eased back his heavy dark locks, and as she kissed his cheek she whispered, 'Good Luck.'

Bobby's radiant smile said it all. He had dared. And he had succeeded.

May Queen!

EE Blythe

May 2

Heart of Gold

'We'll have to get her bedroom ready, Martin,' called Hazel as she rushed past me. 'Didn't you hear the phone? They said we can pick her up tomorrow!'

I was surprised, to say the least. 'A bit short notice, isn't it?'

'Well, the sooner the poor little thing comes home to us the better. She's had such a terrible life, and only four years old!'

'Then I'd better phone into work and see if I can get a couple of weeks off. Oh, Hazel, you don't think we're taking on too much, do you?'

Hazel's haughty expression told me everything. This was no time for second thoughts. Ever since our children left home, we've been rescuing waifs and strays. There's always some flea-bitten old cat looking for a new home, or a dog who's fallen on hard times. And injured wild birds! I've lost count of the number of birdcages I've had to make; they're all rigged up in our conservatory, it's like a virtual zoo out there. This time it isn't a baby bird though - it's a little child.

'Don't worry, we're bound to be a bit nervous at first,' said Hazel, giving me a hug. 'Come on, Martin, there's shopping to do!'

+ +

It had all started when my wife picked up a newspaper one night and saw the picture of some orphans and that was it. A heart of gold, she has. After our youngest left to get married, the house was so quiet and empty. I remember saying to her I agreed in principle that people should adopt poor orphaned children, but just not us.

'Why not us?' she had said, just like that. I've never been as quick as her.

'Anyway, we're too old,' I replied.

Well, we weren't apparently. Somehow, I managed to find myself agreeing to a visit. That day, we met so many pairs of soulful eyes it was hard to forget them. But I remember saying to Hazel, 'It's no good, dear, it's going to break our hearts trying to choose one child out of all this lot.' She hadn't answered. She simply squeezed my arm, blinking away her tears.

But then we didn't have to choose, because one poor little girl chose us. With a solemn stare she stole our hearts. So, we found ourselves pouring over application forms, and going through the endless red tape. We loved her already.

+ +

With several bulky carrier bags in the boot of the car, we found ourselves sitting in the coffee shop. It's that one in the arcade that blares out pop music like there's no tomorrow and gives you boiling hot coffee in flimsy paper cups. Perhaps we didn't feel like talking much as we comprehended the possible sleepless nights, chicken pox, and parents' evenings. With our own children grown up and flown the nest I thought we'd seen the last of that so still my doubts hovered.

'Hazel, are you sure we're ready for this?' I asked her as I gazed into her kind blue eyes.

'Yes, I think we've got everything on the list,' she replied happily.

'No, I mean – look, it's not quite like taking on an abandoned puppy, is it?'

She put her hand on mine and said, 'They did say Bobbie can be a bit of a handful. She's been returned to the Home twice already because it didn't work out.' For the first time I noticed a pang of anxiety in her voice.

'Then we'll just have to do our best, won't we, love?' I heard myself saying. Sometimes I sound a lot tougher than I feel. We walked back to the car, carrying bags bulging with pink fluffy toys, new clothes, bedding and pillows. 'Are you sure there's only one little girl coming and not a whole army?' I teased. Hazel's bubbling laughter lifted my spirits and for the first time I began to look forward to seeing our new little daughter.

+ +

Bringing Bobbie home was quite different to how we had expected. She didn't rush into our arms excitedly. She just stood there, a frightened little urchin with big brown eyes. Eventually we persuaded her to get into our car. She sat mute, looking terrified.

'Sit in the back with her, Hazel,' I said.

But when Hazel tried to do up her seat belt she wriggled and squealed. I took charge, buckled her up, wrapped her cosily in a warm blanket and put the teddy-bear we had bought for her on her lap.

'There! How's that Bobbie? Soon be home now!' I added bravely. We actually had a long hour's drive ahead.

+ +

Before coming to us, Bobbie's short life story had been complicated, punctuated with suffering. She was a beautiful child, extremely thin, with a thick mop of curls. And she didn't make a sound. She ate ravenously, but didn't speak. We knew she could talk, but from the moment we brought her home she didn't utter a word. Hazel was so used to talking to all her little charges that she chatted away to Bobbie anyway. Admittedly her new recruits usually only miaowed or whimpered in reply.

One day, after Bobbie had been with us for a few days, Hazel turned to me sadly and said, 'I just wish Bobbie would smile! Just let us know she's happy here.'

'She's eating well,' I replied, watching another plateful of chicken stew and vegetables disappear. 'Would you like some more, pet?' Bobbie didn't nod her head. With her dark eyes watching the saucepan, she simply held out her plate. 'Good girl, there you are then.'

One afternoon I said to Hazel, 'It's a shame when a child has never learnt to play.'

'Here, Bobbie, catch!' I called, tossing a soft fur-fabric ball up in the air. There was no response, but a pensive biting of her lip and dark eyes watching. I tried again, tossing the ball and showing her what to do. 'There! Now you try!' I coaxed. Bobbie stepped forward solemnly but did nothing.

We tried to interest her in the animals. Hazel showed her the birds in their cages in the conservatory. There were four budgies we had rescued from an aviary, two baby finches which she had hand fed and a woodpigeon with a splint on his leg. Bobbie looked worried. She touched the bars of the cage anxiously and looked at Hazel with a frown. Taking Bobbie by the hand, Hazel led her down to the garden shed to where our adopted Collie bitch, Gyp, had recently given birth to a litter of puppies. Now two weeks old, they were just opening their eyes and starting to crawl about.

However, Hazel told me later, 'She didn't even want to stroke them, Martin. I don't understand it. Any little girl loves puppies, don't they?'

'She's had a bad time, darling,' I said. 'She'll come round. A bit of TLC is all she needs.'

Hazel, however, was mystified. 'All abandoned creatures respond to a bit of food and love don't they, Martin?' she persisted.

'Just let her be,' I replied. 'Just carry on being yourself. Keep an eye on her, but don't ask her to join in with you unless she looks as if she wants to.' I felt quite pleased with myself saying this. It's not often I can shed light on these things.

'That sounds sensible, I'll give it a try,' said Hazel. 'Oh, wouldn't it be lovely one day to actually hear her laugh?'

That afternoon, I was busy weeding in the garden when Hazel called me. 'Cup of tea, Martin? It's ready when you are! Can you bring Gyp up from the shed, I'm doing her dinner.'

I went to fetch the dog and she got up wagging her tail, leaving her puppies wriggling and squeaking in protest.

'Come on, old girl. Time for din-dins!' The dog followed me up the garden to the kitchen steps where I started to take off my boots. Bobbie was standing in the kitchen watching Hazel mixing up the dog's meat and biscuits in a bowl.

'Come along then, Gyp, here you are!' said Hazel, putting the bowl down on the floor.

Just as the dog was about to start eating, Bobbie let out a deafening scream and shouted, 'No!' She picked up the dog's bowl and hurled it across the room where its contents spilled all over the floor. Still wailing, she began letting forth a torrent of words neither Hazel nor I could understand.

'It's all right, love, it's all right,' cried Hazel, rushing to calm her down while Bobbie was still crying with anger and frustration. But suddenly the child stopped. She looked up into Hazel's face curiously for a moment and then breaking away from her, she went scrambling up the stairs. We both looked at each other in amazement while Gyp set about clearing up her dinner from the mess scattered on the floor.

I put my arms around Hazel and tried to comfort her. 'Just take some deep breaths, dear, and relax for a moment,' I said. 'She's been starved, remember? I suppose she didn't like you giving all that good food to the dog. Perhaps, to her, it's like throwing it away.'

Within a few minutes Hazel recovered herself, smiled weakly at me and went upstairs where I heard her talking in a soothing tone, possibly reading the child a story.

+ +

When our social worker came on her next visit, we described what had happened. She said it was perfectly understandable considering what she had been through and suggested we started making a scrap book. It could contain pictures of our house, her bedroom, photos of her with her toys and photos of our animals. Then she might begin to identify herself with her new life and feel she belonged. We did as she asked, often with Bobbie helping cut out pictures and paste them in.

The weeks went by. We grew to love Bobbie more and more every day. Most of the time she still had a solemn intense frown. But she began to grow and put on weight. It was time to start thinking about her education. Sometimes we could hear her whispering to herself while she played. Cats purr when they're happy. And birds sing. Little Bobbie only whispered to herself. We were both prepared to wait, hoping she would learn to trust us in her own way.

One day, Hazel was busy in the kitchen making a cake. Bobbie, I thought, was playing with her toys in the lounge. I was upstairs. When I came down, I couldn't see our little daughter anywhere.

'Where's Bobbie?' I asked. Hazel looked at me in alarm. She wasn't in her bedroom or in the dining room. We went through to the conservatory. Through the glass, what we saw astounded us! She was a completely different little girl, smiling broadly and twirling around excitedly.

'Look at her!' cried Hazel. Bobbie was laughing, dancing, and squealing with delight as all the birds were out of their cages and flying around her head.

'What on earth...?' I exclaimed. 'But she's opened all the cages!'

'No wait!' whispered Hazel, putting a restraining hand on my arm. 'Look! Look at her face! She's smiling! Look at her, Martin, she's laughing!'

'But what about the birds?' I asked. 'We'll never get that lot back in.'

'It doesn't matter about the birds, darling, the windows are closed anyway. Just look at her! She's happy, Martin! Bobbie's happy at last!'

We approached the conservatory door, Hazel calling to her as she went. Bobbie suddenly saw us, and rushed towards us, flinging her little arms around us in delight. We've had breakthroughs in our house before: tails that begin to wag; kittens that start to feed; baby birds that learn to fly. But this one was the best result ever: Bobbie had finally let go of her past.

We all three stayed in the conservatory and spent time with the birds. Presently Bobbie was relaxed enough to let them settle on her hand to feed. And that wonderful smile never left her face. Finally, it grew dusk. The birds hopped back onto their perches and tucked their heads under their wings. When Bobbie was ready for bed, she sat up with us, looking at the pictures in the scrapbook book until she grew sleepy, resting her head on Hazel's shoulder.

'Our birds might not be in the right cages,' Hazel said quietly, 'but they know where their home is, just like you do, don't you, Bobbie?'

But already she was fast asleep. **Theresa Le Flem**

May 3

The Bucket List

Elaine helped everyone off the coach, then, pointing to Blackpool Tower clearly visible above the rooftops, she announced, 'Don't forget we're meeting at the Tower at 3:30 sharp.' She smiled as one of the men blew her a kiss and a flash of red caught her eye as Brigid raised a perfectly manicured hand to pat her hair into place.

Freda and Dorothy stood by the coach steps, looking more like sisters in their matching jackets than the close friends they had become. Elaine watched Freda take two silk scarves out of her bag and hand one to Dorothy. As they carefully fixed them over their neatly-styled hair, she marvelled at how much these people had changed in the last twelve months.

'What are you pair up to?' Mabel waddled over, fiddling with the belt on her mac.

'We don't want our hair to get messed up,' Freda explained.

Dorothy nodded in agreement. 'We need to stay smart for this afternoon's tea dance.'

'Who the bleeding hell d'ya think will be looking at you two?' Mabel grumbled, 'You ain't exactly Pan's People.' Stretching stiffly, she announced, 'Me back's sore from that bloody coach. You go on, I'll catch you later.'

Freda and Dorothy obediently set off in the direction of the seafront. Mabel waited a minute then followed slowly at a distance.

'I'll walk with you Mabel,' Elaine said, catching up with her. 'Can I take your bag?'

Mabel quickly transferred the bag to her other hand and despite Elaine's attempts at conversation was uncharacteristically quiet as they made their way to the promenade. Once they reached the front she abruptly announced, 'I'm going off on my own now.'

'Are you sure you want to do this alone?'

'I have to.' Mabel bristled and trundled away.

A Story for Every Day of Spring

'See you at the Tower later...!' Elaine called after her, but there was no reply.

As she watched Mabel cross the tramlines and enter the North Pier, hefting her bag from arm-to-arm, she thought how strong she was, both outwardly and inwardly. She hadn't always felt that way though. Finding a seat overlooking the beach, she allowed her mind to wander back to her early days as warden at Orchard Close.

The community centre had been in a dilapidated state and it had taken her months of nagging before the council finally repaired and re-decorated it. Once it was done, she had found an old bingo machine, arranged for the local library to make regular deliveries of books, and set about trying to persuade the residents to come to coffee mornings and bingo sessions. Gradually they had trickled through the doors, but they had been a quiet bunch then, with one exception. It had taken her a long time to get used to Mabel and her brassy and offensive manner. It's ironic, she thought, that it's because of Mabel we are here now.

+ +

It had been a chilly April morning when Elaine arrived at the Community Centre and found Dorothy already waiting outside.

'I didn't feel like being on my own this morning,' Dorothy explained, placing her handbag carefully on a chair and taking a seat by the window.

'That's alright.' Elaine patted her shoulder. 'I wanted a word with you. I'll make us a cuppa.'

As they drank their tea, Elaine told her about Freda who had just moved into Number Twelve. 'She's recently widowed and finding life difficult. If I bring her across, will you look after her? Mabel did say she wouldn't be here today, didn't she?'

Dorothy smiled knowingly. 'That's right. She's going shopping with her niece.'

+ +

Elaine was showing Freda where to hang her coat when the door banged open. She watched in dismay as Mabel blustered in and, throwing Dorothy's bag unceremoniously on the floor, flopped into the chair and helped herself from the plate of biscuits on the table.

'You all right, Dot?' she asked through a mouth full of lemon puff. 'You look a bit peaky.'

'I'm okay.' Dorothy replied stoically. 'Just feeling my age today.'

'You're as old as you feel, duck.' Mabel grabbed another biscuit and pointed a well-chewed fingernail at the window. 'I wouldn't mind feeling a bit of that, eh!' She guffawed loudly as the gardener whizzed past on his mower. 'Nothing like watching a man at work to cheer you up.' Taking a large bite out of a custard cream, she carelessly swept the crumbs onto the floor.

'I hadn't noticed,' Dorothy replied, closing her eyes, and sniffing the air. 'Although, now you mention it, I do love the smell of freshly-cut grass.'

'Smell of grass, my backside.' Mabel growled, staring enquiringly at Elaine as she approached, trailing a nervous-looking Freda behind her.

'Mabel!' Elaine said, a little too enthusiastically. 'I didn't think you would be here today.'

'Nah. I weren't in the mood for seeing our Debbie. Stuck up madam.'

'That's a shame,' Elaine replied pointedly. 'Freda, this is Dorothy. She's going to look after you this morning.'

Quick as a flash Mabel grabbed Freda by the arm and pulled her into a chair.

'Sit here, gal. Best seats in the house.' She gestured to the window. 'We were just enjoying the view. Been on our own too long, eh!'

'Mabel!' Elaine said sharply. 'Freda has recently lost her husband.'

'Never mind, duck, you'll be all right with us,' Mabel said carelessly. 'I wonder if he'd let me drive that thing?'

'Do you drive, Freda?' Elaine asked through gritted teeth.

'No. My Harry took me everywhere.' She looked tearfully at Dorothy, who patted her arm soothingly.

'Me neither, Freda love,' Dorothy said, 'It's too late for us now.'

'I saw something on the telly the other day,' Mabel announced loudly. 'Some woman had cancer or something and she was making a list of things she wanted to do before she died. I can't remember what they called it, but you could do that, Dot!'

'It's called a bucket list,' Elaine interrupted. 'You can put all sorts of things on them.'

'Mind you,' Mabel continued. 'It'd have to be a bloody short list at your age.'

Elaine had stared at this loud, coarse woman who had become the bane of her life yet had unwittingly come up with an idea which might benefit them all.

'We could make a bucket list for Orchard Close.' Elaine said thoughtfully. 'It might be fun; give people something to look forward to.'

'A bit like *Surprise, Surprise*,' Freda offered shyly.

'Trust me, gal, there won't be many surprises with this lot.' Mabel lifted herself out of the chair and went off in search of more biscuits.

+ +

The community centre was full for the first Bucket List meeting and the ideas flowed thick and fast. Elaine was aware throughout, though, of Mabel waiting for an opportunity to floor each speaker with a cutting comment. The final straw came when quiet little Brigid confessed that she had always envied the film stars their manicured nails and would like hers done the same.

'You wait,' Mabel declared in a stage whisper. 'The minute she gets them nails done, she'll be off to confession like a shot. With her gloves on of course.'

'Right, Mabel,' Elaine had announced sternly. 'We've listened to everyone else. What shall we put on the list for you?'

'I ain't discussing my business in public.' Mabel crossed her arms defensively. 'I'll have a word with you in private later.'

'If that's what you want.' Elaine shrugged her shoulders. She wasn't surprised. The Mabels of this world could dish it out but couldn't take it. 'It looks like the Orchard Close Bucket List is underway. Well done everyone' She turned and headed for the office. 'Mabel, come with me. I can't wait to hear what you have to say.'

+ +

The residents threw themselves into their new pursuits with gusto, and she knew that several of them were looking forward to showing off their recently acquired ballroom dancing skills later. Smiling, she remembered how busy the mobile beautician had been this week, making sure the ladies looked their best for today's trip. Glancing along the seafront she waved at a couple of residents who were getting off a horse-drawn carriage; and spotted another three petting the donkeys on the beach. Yes, she thought, it's been an all-round success.

No one could have prepared her for that talk with Mabel though. She had been sworn to secrecy when Mabel had announced firmly that she wanted to go to Blackpool, and by the time she had told her story they had both been in tears. Glancing towards the pier, Elaine wondered how Mabel was getting on.

+ +

Mabel marched along the boardwalk, barging through anyone unfortunate enough to be in her way. Spotting a stray chair, she dragged it to the end of the pier and sat down, hoisting her bag onto her lap. A large seagull landed on the rail in front of her, surveying her with beady eyes.

'Bugger off, you!' Mabel waved her arm and the gull hopped onto the floor and walked nonchalantly away.

Pulling her bag closer, she closed her eyes and whispered, 'It's taken a while, Bill, but we're here at last. It hasn't changed a bit.' As the sounds and smells of the resort buzzed around her, she felt a gentle, fleeting touch on her cheek, and she knew he was with her. This had been their special place when they were courting, and Bill had proposed on this very spot and promised to take care of her forever.

She opened her eyes, staring blindly as the seagulls soared and swooped and cried over the water, an unsuspecting backing group to her sad love song.

They had been young and full of plans. She used to laugh when Bill said that, when his time came, he wanted his ashes to be scattered off this pier, but fate had intervened, and his time had come much sooner than they expected. Mabel had straightened her back and hardened her heart and got on with life as best she could, but she couldn't let him go.

'Are you proud of me, Bill?' she asked him. 'I never thought I could do it, but I did.' Opening the bag, she peered inside. 'You've been with me every step of the way, lad, but now it's time. Like I said to Elaine, if I don't carry out your wishes now, heaven knows what will happen to you when I'm gone.'

Standing up determinedly, she retrieved the urn, removed the lid, and briskly emptied the contents over the side. The wind caught the ashes, whirling them swiftly upwards, then casting them down. As they danced on the waves, Mabel turned and walked purposefully away.

+ +

When Elaine spotted her returning along the pier, she ran ahead to join the rest of the group.

As Mabel approached them, a concerned Dorothy declared, 'Your eyes are all watery, have you been crying?'

'Don't be so daft, what have I got to cry about?' Mabel wiped her face with her sleeve. 'It's the bloody wind, blown salt spray into my eyes. I got a bit lost, that's all.' She pinched the arm of Dorothy's jacket. 'You buggers went off without me.'

Dorothy and Freda looked guilty, but Elaine intervened. 'Now Mabel, you can't get lost in Blackpool.' She took her by the arm, giving it a quick squeeze. 'It's time we went up to the ballroom. The tea dance will be starting soon.'

Mabel shrugged her off and pushed herself to the front of the group, yelling, 'Get a move on, I want a good seat so I can spot the talent.'

Elaine caught her up and, leading everyone through the entrance, she whispered in Mabel's ear affectionately, 'Mabel, you are incorrigible.'

'Better than being bloody boring.' Mabel winked at her then hollered over her shoulder. 'Come on, you lot! Chop, chop! I reckon Anton might be here today!'

Rosemary Marks

May 4

The Enemy

The mysterious light was there again. Red and malevolent, it danced in the air as if it were taunting her. Delilah crouched in the shadows, watching carefully to track the light to its source so she could deal with the threat and save her family. It was a self-appointed task – she knew where her duty lay – so they could continue their lives without a care. Thankfully she was there, ready to save them, whether they appreciated her or not. And she felt very unappreciated!

The light vanished and would not return until the next evening – it never did. She had failed to find the enemy's base. She stretched and went in search of food, then an early night to be ready for the next day.

The following evening, she concealed herself in the shadows. This time she would succeed and eliminate the enemy. She was a patient hunter, remaining motionless in a dark corner, her prey unaware of her presence.

The light appeared, swirling in the air in graceful curves and loops, up and down, side to side. Her eyes tracked its path, waiting for her family to notice the threat – and her hunting skills. They did not. The light was hypnotic and she began to sway. What did the enemy want? Why didn't her family understand the threat?

Delilah jerked awake as the light vanished, leaving no trace of its presence. She glared at the people sitting and chatting, ignoring her and her efforts to protect them. Serves them right if the light swallows them up, she thought, as she stalked off to the kitchen. Laughter followed her but she held her head up and ignored them in return.

"We really should stop doing this," Jane said.

"But it's funny," Bob said. "Did you see her going cross-eyed trying to follow the light?" He put the laser pointer down.

Jane shook the box of treats and Delilah rushed back in, all thoughts of strange evil lights gone. Jane picked her up and stroked her. Delilah purred.

Fran Neatherway

May 5

Roses And Poppies

I stood marvelling at the painting in front of me. Blown away. Gobsmacked.

As a mere beginner, a retirement hobby painter, I could never equal the skill of it, or so I thought then. Now I know I can.

It was about the size of a double *Daily Mail* spread, a watercolour of roses, each perfect specimen unerringly drawn, the colouring exquisite, a realistic capturing of beautiful flowers, and a composition of commanding grace. Amongst this exhibition of local amateur painters, it just looked, well, professional. The painter knew what she was doing. After years of looking at art, I was acquiring something of what's called 'a good eye', but there's nothing like trying it for yourself for developing real insight.

A weekend course had got me started on a huge still-life of a shell, a representation in oils of a whelk, a large hole at one end, spiralling along to a point. Next, I enrolled on a course of instruction, starting, curiously enough, with another whelk and the requirement to enlarge it. Another larger than still life. Soon I could do shells.

I joined a group and moved on to flowers, in watercolour. It was roses, roses all the way. I learned how to get the paint to flow, from the surprisingly deep colour at a petal's base out to the paler frills of the edge – before it dried. Important. Otherwise, it became tiny clumps of cauliflower-like colours. A tricky business - as was doing the leaves, trying to reproduce that hazy shine or the different colour of the veins. Then came poppies, which were harder! That crumpled silk effect of the petals and the exact shade of scarlet were impossible to reproduce. It was quite beyond me. I was never one of the stars of the group, but it was an absorbing hobby and I made progress that kept me happy. I learned to look at things.

The course ended. I had a break booked to meet friends, on a regular spring opera package, in Llandudno. It was a browsers' paradise and there I discovered the ideal book for beginners of watercolour flowers. Technically I was more Improver now than Beginner but not only did it show how to reproduce fuchsias, it also did roses – as well as poppies! It even had tracing paper and outlines at the back - I wouldn't need them. That was one step away from *Painting by Numbers,* but it showed you exactly how to mix the required paints, the names of the colours and the required quantities. It was worth it just for that. Back home it sat among my books, giving me confidence. I'd get that scarlet yet. When poppies came back in fashion, I would know what to do.

A more skilled local group than mine was holding its annual exhibition. So there I was in front of that perfection of a painting. Some of this group were so good – that large watercolour of poppies, the colour so convincing, and the composition spot on. By the same painter as the roses. I stood, knowing by now how accomplished it was. Torn between wanting to possess it or to emulate its skill, I eventually moved on.

Lots of elephants this time. Last year it was cows: gentle, bovine eyes gazing from every fourth frame. A few careful portraits of children, marked not for sale. Grandparent portrait painters. One or two of royalty, a poor portrait of a politician, identifiable mainly by its blond hair. And that quirky painter of farm landscapes had submitted some of his again - and there, yes, there, was the Painter of the Roses herself. I had come across her a few times before. I think I had once attended a talk by her, and felt emboldened.

'Your paintings are brilliant. These poppies are perfect. So realistic. Your colouring is so exact – just wonderful. And those roses are exquisite.'

Was the enthusiasm of my admiration embarrassing her?

I explained, 'I've been trying to paint poppies for ages in watercolour, but I could never do anything as good as these. You're so talented. That colour, spot on.'

She smiled modestly and volunteered, 'I, er, I use watercolour inks.'

'I've never heard of them. But, well, you've got them exactly right.'

'Thank you.' She shyly gazed down at the floor. I felt she deserved further encouragement.

'No, but the best thing is the wonderful composition. That elegant curve of the main stem, and the way the placing of the other stems enhances it. And your roses are just as perfect. That same sense of rhythm in the arrangement of them. Brilliant composition! I can't paint like you, but I can recognise what makes a good painting - and you've got it in spades.'

'Thank you.' She didn't say much, not even wondering if I was interested in buying, but her humility was encouraging, so I continued.

'How long've you been painting? You must grow roses yourself, and fuchsias, too. And poppies! You've got a real understanding of flowers.' Etc, etc, until I eventually let her go.

For some time I regretted not purchasing those roses myself. The exhibition was on for a few days. I could go back, but no, I'd have a go at painting the flowers myself. I was a painter not a collector. Wouldn't be half as good, but at least I'd try – a poor thing but mine own.

Some months later, maybe the start of the poppy season, the connection was made. Those poppies, I'd seen them before. In that book. And there they were: at the back, along with their tracing paper. Those exquisite forms of roses and poppies flaunted their elegant curves, ready to be copied.

Chris Rowe

May 6

Drama In The Hen House

It had been a lovely week's holiday camping in North Wales, with the entire family together. We arrived home at our house tired but happy. As the family all went inside to make a cup of tea, unpack, and put on things to wash and dry, my first priority was to check on the hens. I wanted to ensure they were all right, talk to them, and give them fresh water and feed.

Upon opening the hen house door, I noticed four eggs at the back on the floor, just out of reach. My husband had built the house off the ground, so I decided to climb in and retrieve them. As I began to walk across, I suddenly heard a crunch, and before I knew it, I found myself going straight through the boards. One leg was stuck through one board, and the other through another. I could feel blood trickling down my legs. I shouted for help, but no one in the house heard me.

Eventually, Kerry, my neighbour from the farm at the bottom of our garden, heard me shouting and came to investigate. I explained what had happened, and she sent her son to inform Monty that I was stuck. Monty came down and helped me climb out of the predicament.

Later, when my husband came to mend the hole, he discovered woodworm in the boards. It turned out that it wasn't my weight that caused the boards to give way. Needless to say, I have never stepped into the hen house again. It was definitely an "oops" moment.

Ruth Hughes

May 7

Grey

She was glum. No other word for it. She was sitting in an old easy-chair, on the far side of the small room, facing the large window that looked out onto her tiny front garden, the mostly empty road, and the big house opposite. The curtains were closed over there, which she thought strange, but couldn't be bothered to wonder for long why they would be.

The radio burbled on, but she wasn't really listening. The odd word intruded now and again, but they passed without sparking any interest. Radio Four, *Woman's Hour*, not her sort of thing, but she couldn't find the energy to get out of her chair and re-tune the radio to another station. It was a grey day, and she was in a grey mood.

And she feared it might turn darker. Lower. She'd known a few people who'd had bleak and black times, and had sunk into depression. And how they'd changed, and become strangers. She wondered why people always said 'sunk into depression', or that they were 'down'. Why was the term depression used for this condition anyway? Surely suppression was a better fit. Then again, who was to say what was the right mental state to be in, that everyone was supposed to live in, anyway?

"But we're all different," she said out loud.

She'd noticed she had been talking to herself, talking out loud, a lot more just lately, and at first she'd been worried someone would think she was going senile. But then, who would know? She hardly ever had visitors, hardly ever left the house, and always felt so stressed in the company of others that she rarely spoke to anyone, and scurried back to her home as quickly as she could. There she could talk to the washing machine, the radio or the television as she pleased. But, she had to admit that her days were empty, her life had shrunk, and nothing engaged her interest. Apart from the books she read. When she could be bothered.

That just about summed her up, and her life. Her life had no excitements, no highs, no lows, no disasters, mainly because she just couldn't find the energy to change things. Apathy had set in. She was afraid to mention this state of being to anyone in case the authorities waded in and forced her to take medication. She didn't want that. In the past she had seen the effect that drugs for depression and anxiety had had on people she cared for. They'd had complete personality changes, or gone noisy crazy, or committed suicide. No. She'd just stay here, and look after herself, and never bother anyone, or give any cause for anyone to interfere in her life thinking they knew best for her.

But now and again, on empty days like today, with a grey sky, a blustery wind keeping the little birds tucked away, and nothing to watch going on in the road, she wished she could be bothered to change things.

EE Blythe

May 8

VE Day

Edna ran out of the house in her red, white and blue dress that had been made by her mother especially for the occasion. It was 8th May 1945 and the party in the street to celebrate VE Day was in full swing.

As she joined her brothers (at that point she was the only girl of five), the overriding emotion she felt wasn't happiness. It wasn't joy or excitement either. It was hope.

The day the war started flashed through her mind. It would be a moment she'd never forget. The terrible news was announced on the radio and then, at only three years old, she was told to pop to the shop to get some groceries. Life had changed but everything seemed normal still.

It wouldn't be normal for long, but maybe now, six years on, it could get back to being normal again.

There would be no more running to the air raid shelter. Or on the odd occasion when it was flooded out with water, they all had to hide under the table. Edna even had to sleep under the table at times. She'd never have to do that again.

What would happen to her Mickey Mouse gas mask? Could she throw it away now and safely know it would never need to be used?

What would the view be like through her bedroom window, as for years she'd only seen the barrage balloon that was masking the factories below?

As she mingled with her neighbours, she noticed how all the faces were smiling, but she knew not everyone's smiles were the same as hers. She'd been lucky. She'd lost no one. Only her oldest brother had been old enough to enlist, but he'd stayed at home as his job was too important. He'd then joined the Home Guard to help out around his work, whenever he could.

Edna also felt hopeful that he may stop grumbling now as he

wouldn't have to go out at night anymore.

Edna hadn't been afraid over the past six years. Even when her mother had read out from the paper every day the names of all the soldiers who had died, Edna still hadn't felt scared. Perhaps because she knew no different; perhaps because no one she loved was over there.

In fact, there were days when Edna was very happy, too young to appreciate the full picture of what she was experiencing. Like that time when the bomb had dropped over the road from her school. It wasn't terror that struck Edna but delight. She could now cut through the damaged building and she had a much shorter journey each morning.

She might not have felt fear, but she'd struggled with the difficulties like everyone else. Edna would sleep with her arm over her ear to block out the traumatic noises, and she hated that she could never play in the garden in case she ruined the precious vegetables, food that was so desperately needed. Little did she know that these small things would stay with her forever. She'd always sleep with her arm over her ear, and she'd never get over her hatred of cabbage because it ruined all her fun!

What would life hold for her now, Edna considered as she sat in the street with the other children. Birmingham was damaged; rubble everywhere. Much of it had gone unreported, as if the true extent of the war had been hidden from view in an attempt to keep the spirits of the people up. Even though they could all see it with their own eyes.

But all of that was behind them now. Life was starting anew, and this nine-year-old girl had so much ahead of her. She was full of hope, and it was the best feeling she'd ever experienced.

Lindsay Woodward

May 9

Vera Lynn

On VE day in 1945, the Prime Minister, Winston Churchill, broadcast to the nation on the radio that the war in Europe was at an end after Germany had surrendered. Some people decided that London was the place to be and crowds gathered in front of Buckingham Palace and in Trafalgar Square. The crowds at Buckingham Palace called for the Royal Family to appear on the balcony - several times. King George VI broadcast to the nation.

Winston Churchill addressed the crowd at Whitehall. Ernest Bevin declined to come forward and share the applause, saying, "No, Winston. This is your day," but conducted a sing-song of *For He's a Jolly Good Fellow*. Princess Elizabeth joined the crowds in her ATS uniform.

Around the country more than a million people celebrated in the streets. People organised parties with drinking and dancing. At my mother's school they built a big bonfire in the playground. In Rugby someone put a pair of fluorescent tubes in a shop window to make a big V symbol. Later, the torch in the Statue of Liberty in New York was re-lit.

But where was Vera Lynn?

Vera Lynn had come to the fore as a singer shortly before the Second World War broke out, but she's best remembered for the songs *We'll Meet Again* and *The White Cliffs of Dover* which were popular during the war. Perhaps more than this, she was greatly respected in the armed forces for visiting Egypt, India and Burma to entertain the troops. To do this she had to travel almost to the front line, and in Burma this meant long journeys in an army truck on what must have been little more than a track hacked out of the unforgiving Burmese jungle. Much later when she was awarded the Burma Star, I think many veterans thought it only fitting.

But on VE Day Vera Lynn was celebrating at home in East Ham, in the garden.

Jim Hicks

May 10

Italian Job Allowance

"Hang on a minute, lads. I've got a great idea." Charlie Croker sounded much more confident.

"Put the window out, jump through and let the tyres down. That will stop some of the wobble. Then I'll let the fuel out through this access hatch. Mind you we might be a little while."

"Hold on. How long, Charlie?" said Coco.

"About four hours, so you won't be visiting any of the Italian birds."

The rest of the plan meant getting stones to balance the gang members one at a time. The hours went by and the well-disciplined gang were over the worst and looking forward to getting their share of the gold bars. However, four hours is a long time to carry out a plan in the Italian Alps when pursued by the Mafia.

No sooner had they and the gold left the incapacitated vehicle than they were surrounded by twenty swarthy mafiosi, indignant at a crime carried out on their home turf.

"Senor Croker, you were warned about this. Now you will all face the fate of the hanged man."

"At least it'll be quick, Charlie."

"You don't understand. We hang you by the leg over the cliff edge. We brought plenty of ropes. Then we leave you for the crows."

Twenty minutes later, Charlie and the boys looked like the worst abseiling accident there had ever been in the whole of the 1960s, with their gold left at the edge of the cliff, quite on purpose, tantalising them.

"Hang on a minute, lads. I've got a great idea," said Charlie.

Chris Wright

May 11

Food

'You are what you eat,' they say! Whoever 'they' are. It is imperative I never eat gluten ever again. I am a Coeliac with a gluten free diet. I've confessed. Now to make this gf (gluten) piece interesting. It is a challenge that I am prepared to undertake.

Gluten is a protein found in wheat, barley and rye. Oats can be eaten if produced in an uncontaminated field where the three previously mentioned cereals have been grown. Sounds far-fetched, however it is true.

It is a strict diet that I've been on for nearly fifteen years since losing weight and so ill that I thought I had cancer and would die. It was a relief to learn that my weight loss was due to Coeliac disease, which I hasten to add is not infectious! Previous to my diagnosis I had been eating too often and not absorbing any nutrients.

Après diagnosis, I put on ten pounds in weight in two months. This had to stop and I had to control what I ate.

However horrendous I had to stop eating gluten in all my favourite foods - fresh bread, cake, biscuits, crisps, anything with gluten. Label reading was the order of the day. A friend told me in which aisles in Sainsbury's I could not eat any foods.

I decided never to knowingly eat gluten again nor to feel so ill.

Thinking positively, foods I can eat are whole foods including fruit, vegetables, meat, milk, eggs, cream and gluten free processed foods such as gluten free bread and pasta. On the whole a gluten free diet can be healthy if I avoid products with too much sugar and/or high fats.

Keeping healthy is paramount. Keep walking and keep fit. I don't drive and probably walk more to buses rather than jumping in the car. Travelling by car is great on a freezing cold day or when it is pelting down with rain. I usually have to walk.

A recent walk was a day with a white freezing layer on the ground.

It was a thrilling day as I stood quietly by a pond. Then I saw the most beautiful deep turquoise and orange underfeathers of a kingfisher. It was unmistakable, only a few yards in front of me as it flashed across the water and gone. Five minutes later I saw a muntjac, a small deer cross my path and disappear into the hedge.

Nature is an amazing distraction from my sometimes boring food diet.

Keep positive and on a healthy diet.

Kate A Harris

May 12

Midsomer Move

Dear Auntie Jean,

Thank you for your letter. I'm very excited about your move to the West Country but was concerned to hear that you are moving to Midsomer Hemlock. In this village alone, there have been ten murders since 2003, including:

- an old lady, special operations trained, who murdered a young nephew,
- a bizarre game show style killing involving drowning with a fish tank,
- landing of a fake UFO on the gamekeeper's head, and
- a lethal argument about the quality of local wine leaving 26 people in the hospital with poisoning. Fortunately, no fatalities that time.

The culture of the area seems to be at fault. When, for example, in a murder weekend, the host was brutally impaled in an "accident on purpose", the attending guests applauded the show. Considering the Midsomer reputation, the guests could just as easily read the local papers as attend. The Causton CID seems to consist of a harassed sergeant and a chief inspector only. Their 100% clear-up rate is also suspicious.

If in the area and a theremin or bass clarinet is heard, the advice is to walk to somewhere well-lit very quickly.

Can I suggest a move to a less crime-ridden zone of the country such as central Liverpool, the East End of London, or Birmingham in the middle of a Peaky Blinders style gang war?

Sincerely yours,

Chris, former police statistician, collar number 9195

Chris Wright

May 13

Horror In The Car Park

The other day I parked the car in front of Wickes. Dolores, my wife, noticed a charity recycling bin in the corner, just opposite the beef burger van.

"Ooh, stop please," she said. "I've got some old clothes in the boot."

I dutifully stopped and she rushed round to the boot to retrieve a bag, then walked briskly over to the charity bin. It was one of those with a sort of compartment at the front in which you placed your donation and it then rolled away from you and dropped into the depths of the bin.

I decided to turn the car around whilst Dolores was dealing with the donation. When I had finished reversing, I glanced over to the bin and could see that my wife was having some difficulties. The bag of clothes just wouldn't roll away from her and seemed to be caught on something. She continued to struggle with the machine, pushing and shoving the package so that it might disappear. Deeper and deeper she reached in, her legs eventually levitating from the ground, so determined was she to ensure the charity received my old trousers.

At this point, I decided she might need assistance, but first decided to change the CD in the car. When I looked in the mirror again, there was no sign of our charity bag, and, more worryingly, no sign of Dolores either.

This was serious. I got out of the car and walked over to the bin. It was as if nothing had happened. Total silence. Or was it? I pulled down the cylinder carefully and sneaked a peek inside. There was only darkness. Where had Dolores gone?

Ah well, I thought, it's getting late. Maybe she had decided to nip into PetZone to get some Tasty Chunks for King, our pet Rottweiler.

I set off walking across the car park. Only then did I hear what sounded like two separate noises. One was definitely a scream which appeared to come from the depths of the earth beneath the charity bin. The other sounded more like laughter followed by the gnashing of teeth.

This had turned into a very strange day.

John Howes

May 14

Pyrenean Spring

Yves Durand had lived in the mountains for only six months, but already felt more content than at any other time since he left the family home on the island of Corsica at age nineteen. Perhaps it was because mountain and island people are similar. They get by on less and can handle a degree of isolation without worry or complaint. Back then, he'd joined the Armée de l'Air as an officer cadet, with the hope of becoming a helicopter pilot: a dream he realised six years later. Fifteen years of military flying was followed by five years as an aerial firefighter, one of the legendary Pompiers du Ciel, based in Nimes in Southeast France. The role came with a price: frequent secondments all over Europe for months at a time, establishing new firefighting operations and training the pilots to be water bombers. It was anything but a settled existence.

At age 41 he was headhunted by the European Civil Protection and Humanitarian Aid Operation, the so-called rescEU, to manage the Europe-wide aerial firefighting effort, based in Brussels. At first, he relished the idea of routine, but that quickly turned into a bad case of 'be careful what you wish for'. He didn't take to life in an office one little bit. The desk-bound days, exchanging emails with 'his' helicopter operators around Europe, interspersed with the interminable policy and budget meetings, weren't his bag. After so many years living on his wits, where a split second's indecision could mean the difference between life and death, the banality of office life repulsed him.

During the nomad years as a pilot and while he'd been in Brussels, he'd never owned a property he'd lived in. Five years ago, he'd wisely bought a small house with a two-car garage in the village of Cazeaux-de-Larboust in the French Pyrenees, between the ski areas of Les Peyragudes and Bagneres-de-Luchon. It was a sturdy two-storey house, set four-square to the winds. It had an entrance door in the middle of the façade and tall, narrow, shuttered windows on either side. Its outer stone walls were two feet thick, and it was built to withstand the punishing Pyrenean winters. Yves's brother, Francois, had mused that its brutalist exterior suited his persona perfectly, fashioned as it was to be impervious to outside influences, however harsh.

The other thing that had thus far passed him by was a relationship that lasted more than a few months. Sure, there had been a few girls that had come and gone over the years. All but two relationships hadn't survived his long secondments, and he'd ended those himself due to a distinct lack of long-term interest on his own part.

There was someone he did like, however. Adriana was a colleague at rescEU. She ran the external communications team. Her job was to tell the world all about the fabulous work that their department did and, indirectly, ensuring that the funding tap from the EU stayed firmly 'on'. She did her job with enthusiasm and flair. Yves admired her no-nonsense approach to the many high-ranking EU officials who regularly visited the rescEU offices on Rue Joseph II. They always left with a crystal clear impression of how important rescEU's work was and how deserving of increased funding they all were.

She was originally from Bucharest, was thirty-five years old, one point seven five metres tall and had long, black hair and brown eyes. She kept herself in shape by swimming a hundred lengths of the twenty-five-metre pool near her flat in the Ixelles neighbourhood of the city twice a week, walked to the rescEU offices every day and cycled everywhere else in the city, preferring that to taking the Metro. Her athletic figure belied her age and except for the laugh lines around her eyes, most strangers thought she was at least ten years younger than her true age.

Their relationship had never progressed beyond friendship, even though it was clear to them and to others that they liked each other. When Yves announced that he was leaving rescEU, she had become more open with him about her hopes and dreams for the future over their daily coffee at Café Pera, across the street from their office. The café's motto 'more expresso, less depresso' had made them both smile on their first visit, and they soon struck up a rapport with the serving team, to the extent that their caffeine fix was ready and waiting for them each day at eleven am sharp.

On their last visit to the café together as colleagues, the five-strong Pera team gave him a send-off with a cake they'd baked themselves and a standing rendition of *He's a Jolly Good Fellow*. He was touched and slightly embarrassed. He didn't like a fuss. Adriana and the other customers were all highly amused, however, which made him feel better. He smiled at her and, for an instant, he thought he detected a small tear in the corner of her eye, but she blinked, and it was gone. It was then that he suggested that she visit him in Cazeaux for a few days when he got settled. She gave him her usual non-committal 'why not', which infuriated and excited him in equal measure, and he agreed to let her know when the place would be ready for visitors.

Saturday 6th March 2023 was the day. She was due to arrive at Toulouse Blagnac airport at noon. The airport is an easy two-hour drive from Cazeaux, so Yves had plenty of time for his morning routine and to drive to collect her. He got up at seven am, put on his running gear and headed out onto the D76 for his regular five-kilometre run to the neighbouring village of St. Aventin and back. Spring was slowly seeping into the valley, with streams gushing where before there was just a trickle, and icicles hanging from eves becoming visibly smaller every day. Returning from his run sweating, breathless and exhilarated, he walked over to the large water butt at the side of the house, which at this time of year was full to the brim with ice-cold meltwater, and plunged his head and upper torso into it. Seconds later, he pulled out violently, with a gasp for air and an enormous grin on his face.

He returned indoors, showered, shaved, and dressed in black jeans, a lightweight steel grey merino wool polar neck jumper over a plain, white tee-shirt and a pair of black leather ankle boots. This was his favourite outfit for winter driving: it was warm enough for the conditions but still gave him plenty of freedom of movement. Feeling clean, refreshed and pin sharp, he moved downstairs to the kitchen. Here he made himself a two-egg mushroom omelette with a splash of Tabasco Sauce, a glass of grapefruit juice and an exquisitely bitter little espresso, prepared on his Treviso coffee machine: one of his favourite gadgets.

By now, it was nine am. Yves washed up after breakfast, collected his work-worn leather flying jacket from a peg next to the front door, and locked the house. He pulled the jacket on as he walked over to the garage, lifted the single door with a flick of his wrist, and allowed himself a satisfied smile as the early spring sunshine glinted off the bonnets of the two cars that lay within. On the left was his pride and joy: a 1972 Porsche 914-6 in its striking original paint colour of Zambezi Green. On the right was a car he had only slightly less admiration for: a white 1989 Peugeot 205 diesel. He didn't like modern cars, with their automatic systems for this and that: 'bloody washing machines'. He'd given both cars a full overhaul when he bought them from their first owners, and they were better than new. He also maintained them like his aircraft, not just in line with the motor manufacturer's scant and infrequent schedules, which were barely sufficient to keep a lawnmower running.

It was slightly too early in the year to risk the 914 on the salted roads, so he decided to take the Peugeot, which had left the factory better rust-proofed than the Porsche anyway, something he'd augmented further when he took ownership. He joked with himself that it could be used as a taxi in a salt mine and wouldn't rust. He opened the driver's door and settled himself into the seat, slipping the ignition key from above the sun visor as he did so. He turned the key to the first position and waited until the glow plug light went out, which took about fifteen seconds at this time of year. He then twisted the key all the way and the engine sprang to life with barely a turn of the starter motor.

'If engines could talk,' he whispered to himself, 'this one would say, why the hell did you turn me off last time – I just want to GO!'

He drove out of the garage, stopped to close the door, then headed out onto the D618, D125 and then the D825, in the direction of the A64, which would take him straight to the Toulouse ring road. Once on the autoroute, he settled into a steady one-hundred-and-twenty-five km/h cruise, which the Peugeot easily held on the route north-east, tracking the Garonne River towards the city.

He pulled into the short-stay car park at Blagnac Airport at eleven thirty, took a ticket from the machine at the barrier, and found a parking space in the covered section, away from other cars but close to the walkway to the terminal building. He locked the door and made his way on foot to Arrivals. He hadn't been waiting long when a stream of travellers started to amble through the sliding doors from the baggage reclaim area. After about three minutes, he spotted her walking in step with the others. She hadn't seen him yet, so he took the time before she did to re-familiarise himself with her face, which looked even more beautiful that he remembered on that last day in the café. She was wearing black leggings, black leather knee-high boots, a white cable knit polar neck jumper and a royal blue hooded puffer jacket by JOTT: one of her favourite brands. She was pulling a small, carry-on suitcase and had a slim, tan leather handbag slung over her left shoulder. He subconsciously logged another point in her favour, for travelling light.

As soon as he'd finished his scrutiny of her and as if on cue, she waved to him across the crowded hall. They rushed towards each other and when they met, they hugged each other, with all the formalities of former colleagues forgotten. She pulled out of the hug, kissed him lightly on the cheek, looked straight at him with her warm, smiling eyes and said, 'Hello Yves, take me home.'

Simon Parker

May 15

To My Dear Departed Son

How I wish I'd been with you more before you left us so tragically at the age of twelve in the blink of an eye on that dreadful day. You were our first-born son and even though I had to spend most of my days away from home, I was so immensely proud of you.

I'm so sad you didn't know me when you were a child but I had to work to pay the mortgage and put food on the table. It was only when I returned home early one day and you shouted, 'mum there's a man in the kitchen', I realised you didn't know me and what my job was doing to our relationship and our family.

I left my vocation driving and lost the freedom of the roads to work in the confines and constraints of a warehouse so I could be with you and then your brother John, who was born exactly two years after you on your birthday. All was well in my world and we became not only son and father, but friends sharing many laughs and adventures as a family.

Ten years later another brother Joe arrived and our family was complete. What could possibly spoil our happiness? Why, I often ponder, did I give you my bike? Why didn't I say no when you wanted to go fishing with your friends? Why didn't I get up that morning to say goodbye? And so many other whys, ifs and buts that I've lost count.

I never saw you alive again after that dreadful day but I play it over and over in my mind. Even though it's now forty years since the accident, it still breaks my heart. Every now and then tears roll down my cheek quite unbidden if I'm taken off guard by some insignificant thing that triggers your memory. You would just have celebrated your fifty-second birthday. Would you have found yourself a sweetheart, married and given us grandchildren? Would you have become a famous writer as you loved writing stories, or followed any manner of other paths your life could have taken? I shall never know.

My life changed beyond description after that tragic day. I write this letter on your birthday and will leave it on your grave under the flower pot.

From your dear old dad. Only a heartbeat away.

Regards

Patrick

Patrick Garrett

May 16

The Lobby Of The Ritz Carlton Hotel

Elvira was up early. It was spring, the sun was shining, and the birds were making a racket. Elvira hadn't slept well, probably due to all the excitement. She had spent the night in a budget motel in Laplace on the outskirts of town, and today she was going on her first date in, she couldn't remember, but it had to be at least five, possibly even ten, years.

She was to meet Tom, an old school friend whom she had not seen since the day they left school thirty-five years ago. They had re-connected over the internet, had struck up quite the rapport, and when it became apparent that they both had single status, they decided to make a date.

Elvira turned on the TV and busied herself around the motel. She decided to take a shower even though she had one the previous evening just before she got into bed. She put on fresh underwear and put another pair of clean panties in her shoulder bag. Just in case, you never know, she thought.

Just about all she could remember about Tom from school was his name. She remembered talking to him, she couldn't remember ever going on a date with him, but that was neither here nor there. They were both over fifty now. They were adults. They were mature grown-ups. She couldn't even envisage what he looked like, but that didn't really matter either - a fifty-five-year-old man wasn't going to look anything like an eighteen-year-old guy. Will he still have hair? she thought. We'll soon find out. She wondered whether Tom would remember her. At school, she had shoulder-length mousy hair, now it was short, tight, smart, and bottle blonde.

+ +

She waited outside the motel in the warm spring sunshine. Presently the cab turned up and came to a halt right outside the door. She opened the rear door and climbed in.

'Good morning, lady,' said the cabbie, 'where are we heading?'

'The Ritz Carlton Hotel, please,' said Elvira.

'Oh nice, very posh,' said the cabbie. 'You on a date, lady?'

Elvira paused before saying, 'Well actually, as a matter of fact I am. Is it that obvious?'

'Well, you do look neatly turned out. Did you meet on the internet?' asked the cabbie.

'Yeah, but not like that. He's an old school friend from back in the day, we're just having a catch-up get together.'

'Well, that sounds swell,' said the cabbie. 'There's some nut jobs out there on the internet, and they just mess it up for all the good folk. But if he's an old school friend, then you've got nothing to worry about.'

'I wasn't worried, I'm just nervous,' said Elvira, adding, 'Should I be worried?'

'Aah no. You look from out of town so you probably didn't hear.'

'Hear what?'

'There's been a couple of murders in the last month. Well, hey, this is New Orleans, I won't lie, there's a couple of murders every hour.'

'No, I didn't hear anything, tell me,' said Elvira.

'Well, the thing is the cops don't even know if they are murders. Two women went missing from downtown hotels, apparently unconnected, two weeks apart, never seen again. All their stuff still left in their room, one was on vacation with her husband. Can you believe that? No trace.'

Elvira was quiet. They drove along in silence. Louis Armstrong International Airport glided by on the passenger side of the cab. 'Well, thanks for telling me that. I shall certainly be on my guard,' said Elvira.

The cab made a left on Tulane and headed towards Canal Street.

Traffic was heavy. 'What time is your date?' asked the cabbie.

'Eleven,' said Elvira.

'Oh well, you've got a whole bunch of time to kill,' said the cabbie. 'If I drop you off on Canal Street, would that be okay?'

'Is it far to the Ritz Carlton?' asked Elvira.

'From where I drop you, it's a two-minute walk, straight along Canal. They have the street dug up outside the hotel so I can't park. Lord knows what they're doing, it's been dug up about three weeks.'

'Well, it's been really nice to meet you, sir,' she said. 'My name's Elvira, by the way.'

'Well, it's been really nice to meet you too, Elvira. My name's Jerry. You take care now.'

'Thank you, Jerry.' She reached her arm into the front of the cab, and they shook hands. When they let go, Jerry pointed his finger at her and said, 'Now you promise me you'll take care, young lady.'

'Hey, go steady with the "young" there, Jerry.'

'I mean it.'

'I know you do. Thanks. I'll be fine.'

+ +

Elvira stood on Canal Street and lifted her jacket sleeve so she could see her watch. Although she was still a good half hour early, she decided to go straight to the hotel, not least to get out of the heat. Elvira walked over to the maître d's desk and asked if she could wait in the lobby as she was expecting a friend. 'Of course, madam, by all means. Would you like a drink while you are waiting?'

Elvira wondered how much a drink would cost in the Ritz Carlton Hotel, but the words 'yes please' came out of her mouth regardless.

'Excellent, madam. Take a seat anywhere, and I'll have someone come over to take your order.'

'Thank you,' said Elvira, and she walked over and took a seat in front of a low glass coffee table adjacent to a piano. There were about twenty-five to thirty people seated in the lobby, a few couples and a smattering of folk on their own. A waiter came over and handed Elvira a drinks menu. She ordered a small glass of Australian

Cabernet Penfolds at twenty-three dollars a glass. When it arrived, she took a couple of sips and then started to observe the other folk in the lobby. When she'd exhausted this endeavour, she took out her phone to make it look like she actually had something to do. First, she Googled the wine that she'd just ordered and wasn't surprised to learn that she could buy a bottle for considerably less than what she'd just paid for a glass. There was still no sign of Tom, so she continued to waste more of her life by looking at her phone.

After a while, completely bored and somewhat frustrated that she'd wasted minutes looking at absolute drivel, she turned her phone off and shoved it into her shoulder bag. She checked her watch again. It was now approaching half-past eleven, and she was half-resigned to the fact that Tom wasn't going to show. She'd considered this eventuality in the last few days and thought, quite reasonably, that it wouldn't be the end of the world if he didn't show. She would still be a tad disappointed though, and consider Tom quite rude to stand her up in this way.

She looked around the lobby again; it appeared to be the same people who were there when she first came in. She turned right round in her chair and glanced behind her. There she saw a man seated two tables away, though he had his back to her and was facing the entrance to the hotel. He seemed to be engrossed in his phone. Wasn't everybody these days? Elvira wondered how long he'd been there and why she hadn't noticed him before. Well at least he has hair, she thought. She drained the last of her overpriced Cabernet and decided to make her move.

She walked over and gently touched him on the elbow. 'Hello,' she said. The man looked up, slightly surprised. 'Hello,' he said in a friendly voice.

'Tom?' she enquired. The man considered this for a moment and then said, 'Why, yes.'

'Elvira,' she said, extending her hand. They shook hands. 'Have you been here long?' she asked 'I thought you weren't going to show.'

'Well,' said Tom 'I apologise, I've been here about ten minutes but had some work stuff I had to sort out on my phone, but it's all sorted now, I do tend to get a bit distracted.'

'It's awfully good to see you,' said Elvira. 'I must say you're looking very well.' The years did appear to have been very kind to Tom. 'Would you like to get out of here?' she asked, 'the drinks are so expensive, and it's such a lovely spring day out there, we could just go for a walk.'

'Sure,' said Tom. 'Tell you what, I know a great little bistro on Jackson Square, and they have tables outside. We can cut through the French Quarter.'

'Sounds lovely,' said Elvira, 'I just have to settle my tab.'

'Hey, I'll take care of that,' said Tom. 'Hand it to me, I have to settle mine too. Give it to me, I'll be back in a minute.'

Elvira went over and waited by the entrance to the hotel. Her spirits had certainly lifted. She wasn't sure how Tom would've turned out after thirty-five years absence, but he seemed perfectly fine. Better than fine. *Much better*. She was starting to feel that the whole trip from Baton Rouge, the motel, the cab fare, was all worthwhile.

Presently Tom came back. 'All set?' he asked with a beaming smile. Elvira nodded, she was smiling too. Two people smiling and walking down what some folk claim is the widest street in the world. They walked along Canal, then took a left into Royal Street walking to the heart of the French Quarter.

And this is the last we see and hear of Elvira and Tom, but not quite the end of the story. For that we have to re-trace our steps back along Canal Street and into the lobby of the Ritz Carlton Hotel.

The lobby was filling up now with the luncheon crowd. The Maître d' had collected the glasses from Elvira and Tom's tables and wiped them down. About midday a tall thin gentleman entered the hotel and made his way to the Maître d's station. He was clean-cut and casually dressed. What was left of his hair was cut short and neat. The Maître d welcomed him as he welcomed everyone, with a broad smile. 'Good afternoon, sir, can I help you?'

'I hope so,' said the gentleman. 'I was supposed to meet someone here about eleven o'clock but I got terribly waylaid.'

'I'm sorry to hear that, sir. Nothing serious I hope.'

'Well, actually I was mugged. Some good for nothing snatched my phone, in broad daylight. Can you beat that?'

'Oh no, that's awful, sir, but welcome to New Orleans,' said the maître d'.'

'It's okay,' said the gentleman. 'It's sorted now, I've reported it. I just don't have a phone. So anyway I was wondering if anyone left a message with you, or maybe made any inquiries?'

'I don't think so, sir, I've been on since ten, but I'll just check the ledger.' He produced a large leather-bound book from under the desk and opened it to reveal a blank page. 'Sorry nothing today, sir.'

'Okay,' said the gentleman. 'Thanks anyway. Do you mind if I wait for a while?'

'Not at all, sir. Feel free. Would sir like a drink while he's waiting?'

'Yeah, sure,' said the gentleman. 'What do ya have?'

'If you'd like to take a seat, sir, anywhere in the lobby, I'll send someone over.'

Martin Curley

May 17

Unexpected love

Kit looked around whilst waiting for his suitcase. He liked to people watch. He glanced over at the second luggage carousel and spied a young-looking guy in a black leather jacket and jeans. He had a handsome face too. Kit looked back at his conveyor belt. Still no sign of his suitcase.

Kit looked back over at the handsome guy and caught him turning away.

Had he been looking at me?

No.

Can't have been.

Kit realised he was staring but before he could look away, Handsome Guy turned his head and their eyes met. The guy smiled and looked back at the second luggage carousel. The guy had checked him out. Kit looked over and saw the guy looking back at him with that same smile on his face. Kit couldn't help but smile back.

This exchange of looks happened a few times more until Sanj elbowed Kit.

'Is that yours?'

Kit spotted his luggage and it almost passed by him. He quickly grabbed it off the conveyor. He looked back over to Handsome Guy. His heart sank. He had gone.

Ten days passed and although Kit enjoyed his holiday, not once did he catch sight of Handsome Guy. Finally it had come time to fly back home.

It wasn't until he was at the luggage carousel that he looked over at the second one on the chance that Handsome Guy was there. He was. He was looking back with that smile on his beautiful face. Again they exchanged a few glances and, again, he was gone when Kit looked after retrieving his luggage.

Feeling a little despondent, they headed for passport control. That was when he spotted him again. Handsome Guy was ahead of him and Kit just raced to catch up with him. He didn't think. He just went for it.

'Hi. Hello,' Kit said as he approached handsome guy. 'I saw you smiling at me again and thought I'd say hello this time. I'm Kit.'

'Gregory,' Handsome Guy replied

'Nice to meet you.' Now butterflies started to dance in Kit's stomach; now it was do or don't. 'I think you are very handsome. Would you like to go on a date?'

Kit realised his hands were clammy and it seemed like forever before Gregory responded. In reality it was a few seconds.

'Okay.'

Christopher Trezise

May 18

Blue Dye

It was a sponsored walk — twenty-five miles, thereabouts — around the Outer Circle bus route in Birmingham. I'd expected my parents to say no, but because the information had come via my school, they said yes! I arrived at the Fox And Goose, the nearest starting point, and was directed to a group of four girls who were waiting to start. We set off for the next checkpoint, but I soon got frustrated as the others walked so slowly.

At the checkpoint, having been rained on, the girls wanted to get dry and were not going to go on. Luckily, I came across some boys from my year. They were just leaving and were OK with me joining them. They were more fun.

The heavens opened, and the rain pelted us every step of the next five-mile section. Soaked and dripping, we arrived at the checkpoint, and the boys were already talking of stopping. I knew I'd have to carry on, as I had no idea where I was or how to get back home from this point. Tom said he wanted to keep going, so we set off together as a twosome. So many walkers had given up that the rule of five was not being enforced.

Tom was wearing a Donovan cap, now soaking wet, and as we went along, the blue dye from it was running down his neck and face. In my head, I sang a little ditty about it. It made a great 'walking song', especially with the musical accompaniment coming from my soaked shoes! The last eight miles or so passed in a sort of blur of laughter, talk about new music, and the squish-squish of my shoes to the music in my head.

Then suddenly, there was the Fox And Goose again. We'd done it. Walked over twenty-six miles for a few pounds for charity. I can't even remember how I did get home. But the strongest memory of the day is Tom's Donovan cap and the blue dye. **EE Blythe**

May 19

Wizards

The bargee was happy to take my cash and welcome me on board as a passenger.

For this mission, I thought travelling by river would be the simplest and quickest way. I went below to my berth. In my line of business it doesn't pay to attract attention.

But staying out of sight can attract attention too, so after the first night I came out on deck. The steersman looked as though he didn't want to be disturbed so I contented myself with looking at the box containing... whatever was moving the boat. Being unlearned in these matters, I assumed it was some kind of magic contraption. How wrong I was.

Suddenly a figure in a pointy hat emerged from behind a tree and pointed his wand at us. To his credit, the boat's look-out raised the alarm immediately and the defence wizard went into action.

In my experience, in situations like this whichever wizard gets the drop on the other usually wins. Our wizard had been quick, but not quick enough. The enemy wizard's spell hit us first.

To judge by the visual effects, I recognised it as Cancel Magic. Clever: disable the boat's motive power and then we'd be sitting ducks.

But nothing happened. The boat continued along the river as before. Then our wizard's spell hit, and the enemy found himself restrained by a tangle of very stiff ivy.

"He won't be giving us any more trouble," said our wizard with an air of satisfaction. In this world, leaving a trail of dead bodies tends to attract unwelcome attention.

"Excuse me." The Third Mate had appeared. "The captain sends his regards, and invites you to his cabin for brandy and cigars."

Of course I agreed, but I was on my guard.

I thought I'd better make polite conversation.

"Is the boat powered by magic?" I asked. I knew it wasn't.

"No."

"Is it powered by some kind of elemental being, then?" I asked, taking a sip of the brandy.

"No - it's powered by a very big spring."

Jim Hicks

May 20

Goodbye, Humphrey

An extract from my diary

I'm up fairly early to take Humphrey to the garage. He is my cheerful little red Kia Picanto. I have owned him since new and he has served me faithfully for the past seventeen years, including a run to Scarborough as an emergency stand-in when our main car failed us.

I have not been kind to him, neglecting him out on the drive in all weathers, allowing nature to colonise him - as my friend, Jim, once commented: "Is that moss growing on the number plate?"

As I drive to the garage, I am especially careful not to crash into any other vehicles. About an hour later, the garage staff ring. They are always upbeat and friendly, but I realise at once that this is going to be a bad one. ¶

"It's not good news, I'm afraid," I am told. Humphrey has failed his MoT big time and needs a considerable amount of expensive welding to have a chance of passing the test again. The garage can't do this and suggest another company in the town centre who might be able to help. I look at the test report - brake problems, axle problems, seat belt problems, windscreen problems. This isn't going to end well. In fact, the repairs are going to be much more than the car is worth.

I drive Humphrey home, turn his engine off, and softly pat the bonnet, whispering the word 'Thank you' to him for years of sterling service. He has never let me down. His body work might be faltering but he has never - not a single time - failed to start for me. He has a perky little engine, full of cheer and spirit, and was so easy to manoeuvre around town and into parking spaces. Once he went a little too fast and I had to pay a fine, but I forgave him. He was a willing and loyal friend whom I should have treated better. Goodbye, Humphrey. It's been a blast.

John Howes

May 21

A Village Evening

An extract from my diary, May 1960

I need my mum to order me two Young Farmers' booklets for me. There is so much I need to learn about farming. I will offer to send a postal order to pay for them. I want *No 7, Implements and Farm Machinery*. Also, I will remind her I need more socks, else I might be working in bare feet.

This diary is about a month behind due to milking and haymaking plus rehearsals for the play now that I have joined Young Farmers and volunteered for the play. I am in the chorus, but I do have a solo.

I am going to write about the last performance. I am writing this on Sunday morning. I dragged myself out of bed at ten am, had some breakfast. My head is so full with the play and everything. We were at Holsworthy Village Hall; it holds three hundred. It was packed, with people standing at the back too. I started to feel miserable and sad, but it was so exciting that I soon forgot. I had been given the morning off; no milking today. I just got ready and picked up my bike and cycled the five miles to Bradworthy, parked my bike by the garage, and got picked up to be driven the eight miles to Holsworthy. I will keep my program and newspaper cutting in my journal too.

At the end of the performance, Ivor, the director, made a speech and then drew the raffle, a box of chocs and fifty cigarettes. Then we did one last chorus and scooted off to get changed. The man who had won the chocolates sent them backstage for me, for singing so beautifully, he said. I was thrilled.

Then a man brought in a tray filled with glasses of champagne and sherries. We had a drink, and Ivor played his organ, and the company entertained us. Ivor got out his community songbook. After some more champagne, we got stuck into singing. I did *Ilkley Moor* for them. I was the only one who could do the accent. I think I sing better with alcohol. Then we had some sherry. At twelve o'clock, we sang some hymns and spirituals. At twelve thirty, we hurriedly packed up, and everyone went around kissing everyone. I'm glad the lights were low to hide my blushes. Then we all piled into Ivor's old crock, and I was dropped off at Bradworthy where I claimed my bike and cycled back to our farm.

Oh, it was a wonderful experience. I shall never forget it. I seem able to cope with the alcohol. I cycled home safely at one o'clock and went to bed quietly by candlelight.

Ruth Hughes

May 22

Friday The Thirteenth

Lawsie always had the window seat because I got off the bus before him. He probably saw first my parents waiting and signalling at the even earlier stop outside Grandad George's bungalow one afternoon in our second year at grammar school. I did not realise anything was amiss until I had alighted to join them. Mum as usual came straight to the point.

'David, I'm sorry but your grandad's dead.'

I hope my relief was not too obvious to Dad when Mum quickly clarified that it was Grandad Bailey who had suffered the fulminating heart attack or stroke, coming to the end of a day on the potato field of his allotment. I pictured him lying on his back against a slope of spuds.

Mum and Dad had waited only to break the news to me before heading to Sutton Bridge, leaving me in the care of my other grandparents. I was shocked at the thought of death rather than deeply upset. Grandad Bailey had always been a remote and somewhat forbidding figure, right back to when I had spent a lot of time at his house. In later years, while I suppose we must have visited them at least over the Christmas season and there was one memorable evening when we all went to King's Lynn to see professional wrestling (Steve Logan topped the bill), there was little other contact.

Dad would have been well suited to take the family lead in a situation like this, while Mum would have been keen to ensure he was allowed to do so as the oldest son (and oldest child too). There was no question of any will existing, nor any doubt that everything would go straight to the widow. Ironically it was Elsie rather than Cecil who had been taking regular medication for a heart condition – angina.

I would only have been in the way at the preparations for the funeral, which I noted as a day of ill-omen since it fell on Friday the thirteenth. It was the first time I had seen my grandmother since the death. There was nothing unusual to me in her wearing black. I had no conception of offering my sympathies, but she did find time in the kitchen as everyone prepared to leave for a few words with me, squeezing my hand.

I was pleased to see my cousin Susan again, even in such circumstances. Naturally more affected than I, she remembers us walking into the church together. My memories of the funeral, at Sutton Bridge, do not go much beyond Nana collapsing as the coffin was carried into the church.

It was only back in Railway Lane that I learned Elsie had joined her husband in death. The organist happened to be the village doctor and had told Mum at the church there was nothing to be done for her, but the service went ahead. Dad was not told until it was over. His father's coffin was placed in the grave three days after his death, without the widow living to see it.

I am told I saw Nana propped in a chair in the living-room. I remember wanting to be outside, standing at the bottom of their garden. I somehow found my way to Princes Street, nearly a mile away, to Uncle Norman and Aunt Maude's. Norman came quickly to Railway Lane to reassure my parents I was OK, and could stay as long as I wanted rather than return to what was no longer my grandparents' house.

The flight to Aunt Maude's was a buried or forgotten detail Mum gave me years later. It was a very foggy day, but Grandad George made it over from Outwell to fetch me back. I would have stayed at his that night, though Mum and Dad eventually returned to Outwell to sleep. She also said I missed school the next day, amending that at my insistence on the funeral's day of the week to say I missed football. But I didn't think I was being picked for the school team at that time... My only solid memories are of the cawing sound Nana made, on and on, as she fell at the front of the church. I was keen to establish that as a 'death rattle', which I had read of as always signalling a person's last moments. I was in bed that Friday night when, thinking back how she had squeezed my hand, I realised it was outside the covers. I quickly pulled it back in, fancying a sudden chill had struck it. Those are my two solid memories.

In Sutton Bridge, I was told later, the remaining members of the family had one of their best nights ever together, full of laughter as they reminisced. Much of the laughter was probably close to hysteria, naturally enough after the day's initial stress then shocking close. The events at the funeral made it onto the local television news.

There were four new orphans. Margaret was always spoken of as highly strung. Her husband Jack died as quietly as he had lived, whether before or after the fatal funeral I am not sure. We learned of his death in her annual Christmas card. I can imagine Aunt Jean's natural vivacity could turn quickly to tears of either merriment or regret.

Uncle Brian I picture as the most silent, not necessarily because he was the most deeply affected (though he was certainly that, in terms of impact on his daily life), but because he was usually so in any group. Twenty years younger than my dad Allen, he perhaps heard stories that night of a father and mother he could barely recognise.

I never saw Dad cast down by the double loss, nor heard him mention his parents subsequently any more than he had before. Mum, as if anxious to ensure I knew the filial pieties were being observed, assured me he had been crying in bed every morning.

There was no thought of me attending the second funeral. But really, what worse could have happened?

David G Bailey

May 23

The Ghost of Grandma

My dad worked on the farms, and we moved quite often if he could get a penny an hour more elsewhere. I was about five or six when we moved into a farmhouse that was part of the farm buildings. The entire affair was encompassed in a large square with two main entrances, two storeys high, through very large doors/gates on each side. Our house was part of the entire structure tucked into a corner.

As there was no mains electricity, next to us in a shed that was part of the square was a generator that produced electricity during the day for us. The mansion called East End was a short way away in the woods. Early every morning my father's responsibility was to start it up. It only had one cylinder and a huge flywheel that sounded like some monster's muffled heartbeat in the distance.

In the middle of the square was the farmyard. On the other side from our house was a deep, sunken midden surrounded by a four-foot wall where all the manure and slurry were thrown. It formed a deceptively thick crust on the surface that could, with great care, be walked on. As the detritus of the farm built up, the midden became a living thing, digesting and transforming the waste into useful manure.

Being in a family of eight, my older brother and I slept in a small room over a large echoing garage. At night we could hear rats scurrying around the vast attic spaces that extended all the way round the farm buildings and, depending on the wind direction, eerie, unidentifiable sounds sighing and groaning like some tormented creature.

The first few nights were fine, and I felt I had my older brother to look after me. On the third night, quite unbidden, a misty apparition of an old lady and young girl drifted through a solid wall. We were petrified and hid under the blankets till we could scarcely breathe.

Next day we told our parents, but they didn't believe us, which was odd because my dad told the most amazing, scary ghost stories. The apparitions turned out to be a regular occurrence once or twice a week, and we became accustomed to the visits and lay watching as our visitors wandered about the room, looking at furniture that was no longer there, showing not the slightest interest in us.

As the weeks passed, we told an old farmhand we had befriended about the apparitions as he was more receptive to our experience than our parents.

The story he told was of a grandmother and possibly a young servant girl who were extremely close. Grandma used to live in the mansion that owned the farm, but as she suffered from dementia, the owners, her now grown-up grandchildren, regarded her affliction as if she was mad. Back then it held a great deal of stigma, so she was sent to the farm out of visitors' sight. She lived a relatively free existence and would wander during the night with the young servant carer responsible for her well-being. One night grandma slipped out into the yard and entered the midden followed by the child. They were not seen again even after extensive searches in the fields and woods that surrounded the farm, only to be found in the autumn when the midden was emptied to fertilise the fields, bleached white and partly consumed by biodegradation and rats. They had been swallowed and drowned in the deep midden slurry as the child was leading her back to their bedroom. The slurry crust had reformed over them giving no hint they were there.

I'm still a sceptic about such things as ghosts, believing there is always a logical explanation, but Shakespeare's Hamlet says it all: 'There are more things in heaven and Earth, Horatio, Than are dreamt of in your philosophy.'

Patrick Garrett

May 24

Dear Cousin Blanche

Dear Cousin Blanche,

Thank you for the letter and the photos you sent us from your new home. You're so lucky to have found such a quiet place, right in the middle of that deliciously dark forest! Your room looks simply divine with that darling quilted wallpaper – you must tell us where they get it? The jacket they've given you to wear is so in vogue too. They feed you after all – lucky again – so why do you need your arms free anyway? We're all jealous of the electric shock treatment you get free twice a week. You have no idea how much we have to pay for it, but we simply can't live without it!

The children are well, and they send their best regards. Wednesday is doing awfully well at school, especially in biology. Only last week, while all the other students were dissecting rats and frogs, she was busy collecting the pieces and sewing them together. She brought them home and got busy with an old car battery and - hey presto – she's made some of the friendliest pets you can imagine!

Pugsley's favourite subject is woodwork. This semester he's made a rack, which we all love to have a stretch on every Friday evening. Lurch especially loves it. Wouldn't you think he's tall enough already?

Fester is up to all his old tricks, electrifying anything he touches. He can make cousin Itt's hair stand on end just by staring at him. That's quite a furball when it happens, let me tell you!

Gomez has bought another swamp, which is keeping him even happier than usual. He says he's preparing it for us both to go moon-bathing together, so I cannot wait.

That's about all our news. Keep your spirits up and we'll see you in a few weeks at our annual winter picnic!

Hauntingly yours, Morticia Addams.

Simon Parker

May 25

Sorry You Are Not Well

Dear Christine,

I am sorry you are in hospital and not well. I am not a very good hospital visitor due to having a phobia, so I will send you letters instead to amuse if I can.

I will start with the saga of the lettuce snatcher in our village. One of the allotment owners noticed one of his beautiful Webb's lettuces was going missing each week in the night. He decided to don dark clothing and hid in his gooseberries to catch the culprit red-handed, or perhaps green-handed, and he did. By the time next everyone in the village knew about him and who he was. He was nicknamed the lettuce thief until he left our village.

My own husband was the source of one such legend. He had to drive an old JCB from the farm up to someone from Clifton to borrow. It was very hot, dry weather, and the JCB had a broken exhaust pipe on the top. It was behind Monty while he drove happily along, and unbeknownst to him, sparks came out and set the hedge on fire. He had no idea. A fire engine came along and put the hedge out. For the next twenty years, he was called The Fire Starter.

Just one more story for you. This one was described by friends as just like *The Last Of The Summer Wine* series. New people have moved into our village, good people who want to help improve things. They were doing good work on Great Central Way. They wanted to dig some post holes on the bank, so they hired a small JCB digger.

But of course, none of them had ever operated one; they all drove cars and thought it wouldn't be any harder. What could go wrong? They managed to overturn the digger on the leg of one and the arm of another. They were injured for quite a few weeks. If they had asked around, they would have discovered that my husband had used many of these types of diggers.

Heyho Christine, love Ruth. **Ruth Hughes**

May 26

Write What You Know

Jeanette Wivenhoe wanted to be a best-selling author of cosy crime fiction. However, she'd never written a word. She researched every *How to Write* book she could find and distilled all the various methods down to the following:

1). Never open with the weather.
2). Write what you know.

The first was easy enough, but write what you know was causing her problems. She'd never done anything interesting or been anywhere exciting. And she'd certainly never murdered anyone.

Jeanette lived in a bleak, ugly village in Staffordshire, not in a pretty village like the ones in *Midsomer Murders*. The houses were all bland, most of them dating to the nineteen-sixties, not a thatched roof among them. The pub belonged to a chain. Even the church was ugly. No-one would ever print postcards of it.

However, the village soon became notorious when, for two months, it was plagued by a series of unnatural deaths. The tabloids named it "the village of doom" and "the death village".

The vicar was battered to death with the guitar he played badly at morning service. A farmer was trampled to death by his cows. Another farmer was run over by a baler, which was exceedingly unpleasant for the person who found him. The postmistress was stamped, addressed to the North Pole, wrapped up in brown paper and string, then left by the pillar box. And the pub landlord was stuffed into a barrel of best bitter.

The police were, of course, baffled. Although, unlike TV, the crimes weren't investigated by only one inspector and one sergeant. The village was full of police officers. They interviewed and re-interviewed the inhabitants, to no avail.

Brown Owl drowned in the duck pond. The president of the WI was crocheted to death. The owner of the corner shop suffocated under a large pile of baked beans tins. The really annoying young man, who played his car stereo very loudly at two in the morning, was run over by his own car. Two pensioners totally disappeared.

After eight weeks, the deaths stopped and everyone was relieved. The police put out a statement that the deaths were a series of tragic accidents. The fuss died down.

+ +

Several months later, Jeanette self-published her first novel. Hardly anyone read it, except for a reporter on the local paper. She got in touch with the police.

Police officers and forensic specialists in white coveralls raided Jeanette's house. They found photos of every death, with a detailed description of how she'd done it. The two missing pensioners lay in a pool of dried up blood in the cellar. They'd been hacked to pieces with an axe.

Jeanette had to be dragged out in handcuffs by two policemen. She was screaming, 'Write what you know! Write what you know! Write what you know!'

But her book didn't open with the weather.

Fran Neatherway

May 27

Two Days In May

Monday May 1st, 2023

I am sitting in a coffee shop in Tissington, Derbyshire, a rather quaint Peak village not far from Dovedale. I wonder if my grandfather, known as 'Pap', visited here on his cycling journeys. He was an avid cycling club member and used to cover vast distances. It is a pity he gave it up and exchanged the bicycle for a Ford Cortina, though that was also a classic, with its bag of extra strong mints sitting permanently between the front seats. He had his own way of turning the steering wheel which I've never seen anyone else do. In the afternoons, he would go out for a drive with my gran just for the pleasure of driving around some country roads. Does anyone do this anymore?

There is an interminable wait in this cafe which isn't particularly busy. Why can't anyone work out how to run a coffee shop properly? A rally of Minis has just passed by, about a dozen of them on some sort of fun drive. Very noisy. I wonder what the locals made of it.

The coffee eventually arrives and is pleasant enough. We then head off to the trail, walking first down a gorgeous country lane, out into the fields and then about a mile along the trail back to the car park where two horses are getting refreshment. We have lunch at our cottage then head off for another walk across the fields; none of these is too far, not approaching two miles, but each one gives me a little bit more confidence. Then a lazy cup of tea with some YouTube videos to watch. Now a daily routine.

After supper, we walk to the lane again. Someone has left both gates open to the public footpaths which run across the farm. On this occasion, I am not to blame.

We watch the *Star Trek* movie tonight. Noisy but fun. Lizzy lights the fire late on when it starts to get chilly then she goes outside to watch the stars and look at the solar lights in our little garden.

Tuesday May 2nd, 2023
On the way to Cromford, we stop off at the village shop in Parwich for a newspaper, except the shop is shut. A basset hound is wandering around the garden and car park. A woman eventually emerges and says I would have to order in advance if I would like a newspaper. We get to Cromford and go in search of a newsagent. The woman in the post office informs us there is no such thing in the village and we could try Wirksworth, which is a couple of miles away. We end up calling there on the way home and find a good Co-op, get *The Times* and fill up on petrol.

The mill complex is interesting, though we don't do the guided tour. We would have preferred to go round ourselves but this is not on. The story of Richard Arkwright is fascinating though and so transformational for the English way of life. We visit a couple of smelly secondhand bookshops and Lizzy buys some coloured thread, which is sweet. We have coffee by the canal and spot two grey wagtails, which are actually yellow, visiting a nest by the water. Glorious. We take our packed lunch to the bank of the River Derwent which is running at quite a pace. It is a lovely sunny spot. We walk round the church graveyard and find some of the Arkwright graves, then along the river bank for a while. Opposite is the castle which Arkwright moved to once he had made his fortune. Now it is some sort of conference centre with archery targets set up in the grounds. Our drive back is a different route, getting up close to three majestic wind turbines slowly turning on the top of the hill.

In the evening, Lizzy chooses *Bank Of Dave* as our movie, a joyous and charming feel-good movie, if not totally true.

John Howes

May 28

Cheese Rolling

Spring Bank Holiday Monday, and today is the day for the great event at Cooper's Hill, Gloucestershire.

The crowds arrive, and so do the runners. They have trained for weeks every day after work, after office and school and field and factory floor. They've built up their strength, their speed, and determination to win the race and be village hero for twelve months. They've studied the turf for humps and bumps, dips and holes, and clumps of grass. They know every inch of the hill and the best position for the start of the race.

Their nerves are twitching as they fiddle with laces and flex their muscles at the top of the slope. Now it is time to take up their positions, jostling shoulder to shoulder to claim the best spot. This year there's a great number of competitors they've never seen before, from rival villages, towns, and cities, and overseas.

The crowd at the bottom of the hill lick their ice creams and fizz open cans of beer and chat with their neighbours, or lay last-minute bets in aid of the village hall, so it's for a good cause.

A local chap with the loudest voice organises it all every year and won't give up now after forty-five years and several broken bones as a competitor. He moves to his place and takes a deep breath.

'One to be ready. Two to be steady. Three to prepare. And four to be...' The cheese is sent on its way, rolling down the hill...'OFF!'

And the cheese is bouncing its way from tuft to tuft, and they're off down the hill, tripping and stumbling, leaping and rolling head over heels, with a great shout from the crowd, screaming for husbands, lovers, fathers, and brothers, and before you know it someone has gone a cropper, and they are all in a tumble of rolling and kicking of legs and arms flailing and heads banging until they all arrive in a heap at the bottom, laughing or groaning, depending on injuries.

The wives, mothers, sisters, lovers all rush to inspect the damage.

The ambulance folk are at the ready, trying to get to the injured before they get trampled to death by the press, and off the injured go on stretchers or on the arms of a green-coated paramedic and someone is clutching the cheese but no-one knows who for there is much confusion, and the police shake their heads and make their annual plea to everyone to go home and be thankful they haven't been put on a charge for disorderly behaviour, and for participating in banned games. But they are ignored as usual and no-one has any intention of going home until hunger and crying children drive them in.

Wendy Goulstone

May 29

Mr Jeff At The Park

A beautiful day for a dog walk in Bravesham, but Mr. Jeff was surprised that the park was empty. Usually, lunchtime was dotted with children, couples, and other dog walkers.

Mr. Jeff hated his name. He hated his flat. He hated the low-rent neighbourhood, but he didn't hate his dog; he loved his dog. But most of all, he hated his city and the feeling of powerlessness. Crime was a problem. When the superheroes retired, it settled a little.

If they're giving up, why shouldn't we give up? thought Mr Jeff. The family name had been Gurdjieff, like the mystic, but his grandfather changed it. Partly because of the pronunciation and partly because of those associations evoked. He walked his little Jack Russell down the steps past the oak trees dedicated posthumously to Captain Peregrine.

Wishy the dog, or Wishy-Washy, trotted jauntily. The dog's home named him WishBone Ash II after the famous rock group of long ago.

Mr Jeff was deep in thought. In this city, it was always advisable to have eyes in the back of your head, in case some pumped-up criminal or super do-gooder blasted by. Since Dr Doomer and Speed-Girl retired, things seemed quieter. Until that new gang, self-identified as the 'Psycho Crew', started robbing banks and terrorising citizens. However, looking at their green overalls and evil attitudes, the paper splattered the name 'Rubbish Men' on the kiosks; three despicable types who used their gifts to get the general public to do their dirty work.

Wishy was getting impatient and stared at Mr Jeff, trying not to whine. Mr Jeff picked up a stick, which he didn't really need but made him feel a lot safer against the super-powered menaces in Bravesham.

The park was suddenly ablaze with streaks of a familiar yellow blur. Mr Jeff felt something else, a hideous feeling of dread, reportedly exuded by Misery, the leader of the Rubbish Men.

What a time for Wishy to do his business!

Mr Jeff had forgotten his poop bags again, and with the background noise of fighting, he panicked.

"I'm out of here!" he announced to the evacuated benches. "To hell with the dog doo!"

In fact, no one had seen the expulsion except for a middle-aged man on the short side with yellow eyes that seemed to stare right through Mr Jeff.

"That's it. Just leave it there, Mr Jeff. Nobody cares, so why bother? Everybody else is doing it." How did he talk without moving his lips? Stick dropped in fear.

This was Shrink, a telepathic psychologist, which automatically made him one of the most hated men in the city. Before Mr Jeff could refocus, a black energy ball enveloped the villain, and it delivered him instantaneously into Dr Doomer's energy cage.

"Still, I have no poo bags," said Mr Jeff. Suddenly Shannon from upstairs was in front of him.

"Here's a green one, Mr J. Keep our city tidy." She walked off. Where had his neighbour come from? A puzzle. He turned to thank her, and she wasn't there, again.

He and Wishy walked back to the flats and, twenty-five minutes' strolling later, he saw Dean and Shannon leaving the block.

"You youngsters," he laughed. "So much money and time."

"Early retirement." Dean seemed almost to be complaining.

"Very early. We're off to the movies. *Schindler's List*. Wanna come?"

"Three's a crowd, dear, and Liam Neeson films leave me cold, but have a good time."

Up four flights of stairs. Mr Jeff had no appreciation of his good health in contrast to his neighbour Mrs Collins who was compelled to use the lift, unknown to Mr Jeff.

He trudged, still laughing, to the second floor where he heard the radio playing Ed Sheeran, but he knew Mrs. Collins hated pop music so he knocked on the door.

"Dawn! Are you OK? Mrs Collins? Can you hear me, Dawn?" No answer. Without thinking, he kicked the lock which fortunately was only waist height.

They both walked in to see Mrs Collins collapsed on the floor and unable to use her emergency button to call for help.

A familiar voice behind him...

"Let me help you both." Shannon again! Her fingers were a blur while dialling the emergency services. They were on the scene in minutes. Dawn was on her way to the hospital already.

Shannon grinned at him.

"Now you're a hero. I should call you by your first name, Jerome."

"Can I call you Speed-Girl?" Finally, it was Jerome's turn to smile.

Chris Wright

May 30

One May Morning

We were going to the Welsh Bat Conference and decided to stop off at our favourite beach for a swim before signing in at the venue.

Accordingly, we set off early on a beautiful May morning, armed with several cassettes (I'm not a good traveller, and we found that music helped) for the four to five-hour journey to North Wales, including a stop in Welshpool. The journey was not uneventful.

I remember Sparks' latest single was on Radio Two just as we approached Shrewsbury, and that was probably the last time the journey went smoothly. We got stuck behind someone going even more slowly than us on the long hill just after turning onto the A470, heading for Dolgellau, and the vibrations generated by the severely uneven deck of the Toll Bridge at Penmaenpool caused the cassette player to cut out, right in the middle of *Don't Pay The Ferryman* by Chris de Burgh!

With great anticipation, we drove our aged Škoda into the car park at the end of Beach Road, walked through the golf course and the dunes, and out onto Harlech beach, only to find it covered in jellyfish of all colours and sizes. Some of the smaller ones had already evaporated away, leaving just a shadow of their presence, in the shape of a slightly indented circle in the sand. Much as I love to swim in the sea, it was decided to give it a miss. I didn't want to swim alone.

So, shortly after leaving the beach, we chugged up yet another steep road and arrived at Plas Tan-y-Bwlch, stopping in the courtyard, not by choice, as the engine ground to a halt. Steam poured out from under the bonnet even as water drained from underneath. The journey home was going to be fun! Not.

+ +

It certainly wasn't. We travelled home with umpteen bottles of water stashed in between all our luggage, all thoughts of possibly having a few days break cancelled. We needed to stop every few miles, stand around waiting for everything to cool down a bit, then pour in more water. We took every chance we could to refill the bottles, and oh, were we so relieved when the glowing red mast lights of Rugby Radio Station came into view, and we knew we were almost home.

She (the Skӧda) always managed to come up with something to prevent us having a straightforward holiday or journey, but she always managed to get us home each time, in the end. And when it came time to let go of her, I felt we were betraying her in some way. Her much-needed replacement was bigger, much newer, more reliable, and easier for me to get into, but we only had 'Saffy' on the road for three months. A stroke took away her driver. I never learned to drive.

Saffy moved on, to my son and his new family.

EE Blythe

May 31

Plat du Jour

The photos were spread over Jean's table. Pauline must've printed every single one, Jean thought, as she tried not to show what she was feeling: envy. The terracotta warriors gazed back blankly at her. The Great Wall wound its way through twenty-four pictures. Resentment seethed. Jean wanted to travel. She yearned for wide-open spaces, for crowded streets full of mysterious people selling strange and marvellous things, for exotic food, for adventure and excitement. Travel was wasted on Pauline; she was only interested in the shops.

Pauline chattered on, telling her where every photograph had been taken, what it was a picture of, and where she, Pauline, had been standing. Jean knew how many inoculations Pauline had needed, what the side effects were, how long the flight had been, what each hotel was like, and, more importantly, exactly how much it had cost. Her special subject: Pauline's holiday. She tuned Pauline's voice out; she'd had plenty of practice at that when they were children, and stared out of the window at the dull skies and the rain, longing for sunshine and warmth, anywhere that wasn't here.

Pauline started talking about the food, so different from Chinese restaurants. She described it in lavish detail. Jean didn't wish to eat duck's feet, but at least food was more interesting than Pauline's Hong Kong shopping expedition. Then she felt guilty; Pauline had bought Jean a beautiful silk robe. Completely impractical, of course, but it was lovely.

Finally, Pauline left. Jean felt relieved to be alone again. A little of Pauline went a long way. Thank God they were both grown-up now and didn't have to live under the same roof anymore. The visit had unsettled her. She felt so envious of the trip to China. Her own holidays seemed confined to a weekend away or a week spent painting her flat. But why shouldn't she spend her money on something frivolous? What was she saving it for? A rainy day? She looked out of the window again. That rainy day was here, now.

+ +

Two weeks later Jean stepped off a bus at a crossroads in the middle of nowhere. Perhaps she was too old to backpack round Europe, as Pauline had so charmingly reminded her, but what the hell, it was an adventure and it was time she had one. She had been travelling for five days, zigzagging across the countryside on the local buses, staying overnight wherever she ended up. This region of the country was renowned for its food, but so far she had been disappointed. The meals she had eaten were, at best, indifferent and she hoped the food in the next town would be better.

She dropped her rucksack and looked around, hoping that she had understood the bus driver correctly. The signpost pointed towards a narrow lane winding through olive groves. A fellow traveller she had met at her last stop had told her this was the place to come for great cooking.

"Marvellous pork," he'd raved. "Succulent, cooked to perfection."

Jean couldn't wait to try it. Two kilometres wouldn't take her long to walk. Her stomach rumbled as she picked up her bag. The sun beat down on the dusty road and the air smelt like lemons. She walked slowly, inhaling the scent with pleasure, taking her time to enjoy the scenery. Woods covered the slopes of distant hills and goats grazed on close-cropped grass among the gnarled olive trees. Jean had never felt so alive as she entered the town.

Whitewashed buildings leaned across cobbled streets. Narrow alleys wound in and out, disappeared into dark passages leading into a warren of medieval houses. Silence followed her. She didn't see a soul until she reached a flight of steps leading down into the marketplace. It was full of people: plump grandmothers in black, greying hair pulled back into tight buns; old men with gappy smiles propped open by thin hand-rolled cigarettes; young wives in headscarves shopping for the evening meal; swarthy young men with gleaming white teeth who looked as if they'd be carrying knives; and children running in and out of the stalls, dodging the adults.

Jean was delighted. She had found the true Mediterranean at last. Food was everywhere: huge legs of ham hanging above curled up salami and sausages; plump figs and ripe olives; sunshine-yellow melons, tart lemons, juicy oranges, and succulent grapes; bunches of herbs, basil, rosemary, thyme, sage, and others that Jean didn't recognize; sun-dried tomatoes; freshly baked bread; and cheeses, soft or hard, runny and smelly, blue-veined and crumbly. The smells mingled in a wonderful mélange. Her mouth watered.

She wandered around, looking at everything. Among all the food Jean found other things that seemed somewhat out of place. A man was selling second-hand mobile phones and rucksacks, all fairly new, and an elderly woman presided over a pile of clothing, jeans, T-shirts, and trainers, mostly designer labels. Her stomach growled, reminding her that it was well past lunchtime. She bought a baguette, goat's cheese, and a large slice of melon.

Another flight of steps led up to a large square. A church dominated one side, opposite a closed café. A fountain stood in the middle. Jean sat down on its edge, enjoying the cool spray of water cascading down, and ate her lunch. It tasted as good as it looked. She rinsed her fingers in the water. There was no shade from the hot sun overhead. One of the church's great oak doors was slightly open, beckoning her. Jean wandered over and went in.

It was cool and dim inside. A statue stood in a niche opposite the door, a man pierced by arrows and writhing in agony. I suppose that's Saint Sebastian, Jean thought. She sat down in a pew to rest her tired feet and looked at the stained glass window. She couldn't make out what it depicted, but there was a lot of red, casting a crimson glow over the altar. It occurred to her that it was the first time in her life that she had dashed off on a whim, no plans made, nothing organised. Even Pauline didn't know exactly where she was. No one did.

A solemn procession entered, led by the priest in all his robes and vestments. The coffin was placed in front of the altar and covered with flowers. Jean wanted to leave, but she didn't want to disturb the mourners. There weren't many: an old woman in the obligatory black; a young man barely out of his teens; an older man with a big bristling moustache, rather like a bandit; and three small children, two boys and a girl in their Sunday best. Jean was worried her presence would offend them, a morbid tourist gate-crashing their loved one's funeral, but she noticed that none of them seemed very upset, their blank faces showing no emotion. Even the children didn't seem disturbed by their proximity to death.

The service didn't last long; it was solemn and incomprehensible, full of ritual and incense. The coffin was carried out of the church, Jean shrinking back into the shadows as the mourners passed. She waited another five minutes before following them out.

The square was empty. It was still very hot, but it would soon be evening and Jean needed to find somewhere to stay. The café was open now and there was an immediate hush as she entered. All the customers were men and she felt a little awkward. With the aid of a phrasebook, she tried to ask for a room and a meal. Once the proprietor and his cronies had understood her, they made her feel welcome. A glass of wine was handed to her and Madame escorted her upstairs to her room. It was small, containing only a bed and a chair, but it was clean. Jean put her rucksack down and opened the window. The room faced the church, overlooking the square and its fountain. Madame showed Jean the primitive bathroom and she washed away the day's grime.

The proprietor seated her at a table by the window. There was no menu. He brought her a plate of stew, fresh bread, and a salad. It was wonderful. The meat was cooked in cider with wild mushrooms and onions. Jean tried to identify the herbs. Thyme, she thought and bay leaves, hard to disguise, and others. The meat melted in her mouth. She was surprised how different the pork tasted. No factory-farming here. Pigs that roamed free and ate only natural food would taste better. This pig certainly did. She'd never tasted anything like it.

Her long day had caught up with her. As she headed for the stairs, she noticed the family of mourners, tucked away in a corner. She hadn't seen them come in. Her bed was surprisingly comfortable, the cotton sheets cool against her skin. She slept well, lulled by the fountain's splashing.

In the morning, she dawdled over croissants and freshly brewed coffee, watching the people going to work and housewives going to the market, baskets in hand. The water in the fountain sparkled in the morning sun, and the sky was as cloudless as the day before. Jean thought she might stay for another day, explore a bit, and see if tonight's meal was as good. The proprietor was agreeable. As she left, she saw another funeral procession crossing the square to the church. Two funerals in two days. The coffin was followed by an old woman, two men, and three small children. Jean shivered in spite of the heat. The people looked the same as yesterday, but that was silly. She rubbed her eyes, but the procession had disappeared inside the church.

Jean followed the road out of town, soon forgetting the funeral and its familiar mourners. She spent the morning walking up a steep hill to the old crusader castle that stood on the cliffs overlooking the sea. Her guidebook told of a long siege. More than half of the town's people had died and the rest were starving. Jean stood on the battlements, wondering how they'd managed to survive and what they'd found to eat. She pictured knights in armour and archers shooting arrows down on the invaders, huge engines of war hurling boulders through the air and defenders pouring boiling pitch on soldiers trying to scale the walls.

There was a path down to the beach and Jean spent the afternoon swimming and sunbathing. It was strange there weren't more tourists; the scenery was lovely, the natives friendly, and the food was so good. She hadn't seen another soul all day.

By the time she'd walked back to the town, Jean was ready for her meal. She was surprised to see the mourners were eating in the café again, greedily clearing their plates, but she soon stopped thinking about them when she tasted her food. It surpassed the previous night's. The meat was even more tender, more tasty. She wondered if Madame would part with the recipe, or at least tell her which herbs she'd used. Perhaps the secret lay in the way the butcher prepared the meat. Jean didn't know, but she would be buying organic meat and vegetables when she got home. Unfortunately, the wine was a little sour, but Jean didn't let it spoil her enjoyment of a wonderful meal. She decided she would leave in the morning, but she was beginning to feel rather sleepy.

+ +

It was another lovely morning in the small town. The sky was blue and free of clouds. The sun was bringing warmth to the cobbled streets. The room above the café was empty and the bed had not been slept in. The bus drove straight past the crossroads without stopping. Another coffin was carried into the church, accompanied by one old woman, two men, and three small children.

In the little café that evening, the roast pork was exceptional. The old woman, the two men, and the three children enjoyed it.

Fran Neatherway

Collect all four of our seasonal anthologies.
Visit us at www.rugbycafewriters.com

Also from The Cafe Writers of Rugby

Our first anthology of short stories, poems and essays
211 pages

A thought-provoking collection of poems
251 pages

WHAT OUR READERS HAD TO SAY

'Books to dip into and read an item in just a few minutes, or sit down with for a longer session.'

'It's hard to pick a favourite because they are so different. I'm looking forward to reading more from this group.'

'An easy read. Great as a gift.'

---

www.rugbycafewriters.com

About the authors

David G Bailey from East Anglia has also lived in Europe, the Caribbean, North and South America, with a base in Rugby for over forty years. He has published three novels since 2021: *Them Feltwell Boys*, parallel narratives of a schoolboy's first love affair and his career and marriage unravelling twenty-five years later; *Them Roper Girls*, tracing the turbulent lives of four sisters (including the marriage of one to a Feltwell boy) from their 1950s childhood; and *Seventeen*, an adventure fantasy story aimed at and beyond young adults. His contributions to this volume are edited extracts from a first volume of memoir *The Sunny Side of the House: When Life Gives You Strawberries - Memories of a Fenland Boy*. To read more of and about David's work, including a quarterly newsletter and new content daily comprising extracts from diaries and other writings, visit his website www.davidgbailey.com.

Pam Barton began writing again recently after many years. In the past, she has had a radio programme for children, been a D.J. and put through the landing on the moon for the Australian Radio in the Indian Ocean. On returning to England, she was a busy parent with John, and became a skin care consultant up to District Manager. After moving again, she went to Luton University for a marketing course. She retired to Rugby with John. Now she is enjoying writing again, painting is also a great pleasure although, as with the writing, hard work is needed.

EE Blythe is compelled to write. And that's all that needs to be said.

Martin Curley has recently retired from a lengthy career as a long-distance lorry driver. This career allowed him to read many books and listen to numerous radio plays. It also allowed him plenty of time to literally talk to himself, often out loud. This talking out loud usually took the form of two-way conversations of which Martin, obviously had to adopt both parts. He believes that talking to yourself is the first sign of creativity. These conversations then formed the basis for many of his short stories. He lives in Rugby with his wife and three dachshunds. He stopped watching television about forty-five years ago, citing that ten minutes spent watching TV is ten minutes spent not listening to music.

Patrick Garrett was born in a farm cottage in Perthshire, Scotland before the NHS came to be and spent the first nine years of his life on farms in Perthshire, Peeblesshire, Wigtownshire and Lanarkshire before moving to England, then two more farms in Princethorpe and Dunchurch. His father then moved to Rugby.

As Patrick is blessed with mild dyslexia, his academic career was not stellar but once he learned to read, the world became his oyster. His careers ranged from apprentice, shop assistant, removals, HGV one driver and positions in the warehouse industry. He learned to fly gliders then qualified as a CAA Microlight aircraft pilot having his flying stories published in a flying magazine. After he retired, he decided to take up local history research and write about Rugby's history. He then found Rugby Cafe Writers and says the future is yet to be written.

Wendy Goulstone has been writing for as long as she can remember. She won the Stafford Children's Library playwriting competition when she was 10 years old and hasn't stopped since. This year she was joint winner of Stafford Library's Staffordshire Countryside poetry competition. Her poems have been published in *Orbis* and *The Cannon's Mouth*, and one was long-listed in the Words out Loud competition about the Covid outbreak, with a poem in the ensuing anthology, *Beyond the Storm*. She has been short-listed several times by Poetry on Loan. She is a member of several writing groups in Rugby and online, including Rugby Theatre Playwriting Group and Rugby Cafe Writers. Her furniture lies under a layer of dust and her culinary skills are basic.

Christine Hancock, originally from Essex, lived in Rugby for over forty years. A passion for Family History led to an interest in local history, especially that of the town of Rugby. In 2013 she joined a class at the Percival Guildhouse with the aim of writing up her family history research. The class was Writing Fiction and soon she found herself deep in Anglo-Saxon England. Based on the early life of Byrhtnoth, Ealdorman of Essex, who died in 991AD at the Battle of Maldon, the novel grew into a series. She self-published four volumes followed by the first volume of a new series, *The Wulfstan Mysteries*.

Sadly Christine passed away in March 2021. We remember her with great fondness.

Kate A Harris and her three siblings lived on their farm near Market Harborough. She left home at 16 to pursue her career with children. After training in the Morley Manor, Dr. Barnardo's Home, in Derbyshire from 1966 to 1968, she qualified as a Nursery Nurse. Kate met and married her Royal Naval husband in Southsea when working in a children's home. As a naval wife, she was in Malta for two years with her two sons when they were shutting the naval base. They have two sons and two grandchildren. She worked on the local newspaper and discovered a love of writing at 50! Now she is writing her story mainly featuring Barnardo's. It's a major challenge with intense and fascinating research. She's had an incredible response from diverse and fascinating resources. Kate is interested in hearing from people who worked in Barnardo's, mainly in the 1960s.

Jim Hicks was born and raised in Rugby. After leaving school, he studied computing at Imperial College, London and the University of Cambridge. He worked in the Computing Services department of the University of Warwick for nearly twenty-six years before being made redundant in 2011. His mother is a little surprised that he joined a writers' group. He thought someone might want some help with the technical side of using a computer to prepare documents, and has remained ever since.

John Howes was born and raised in Rugby. He was a journalist on local newspapers for 25 years before retraining as a teacher. He has self-published two books – *We Believe*, a collection of his writings on spirituality, and a guide on how to teach poetry. He plays the piano and writes music for schools and choirs. John is working on a memoir and dabbles in poetry. He runs a book group and a lively theology group. He presents a Youtube Channel dedicated to the music of Elton John.

Ruth Hughes was born in Sutton Coldfield but has lived in Rugby for 50 years. She says, "I think I have a book in me but so far I just enjoy writing poems and recollections of my life." Ruth belongs to Murder 57, which enacts murder mysteries around the country, and to Rugby Operatic Society.

Chloe Huntington started writing at the age of five or six and since then she hasn't stopped. She has written short stories for school projects and essays for homework, but she has never published any of her works. She hopes that she can one day publish one (or more) of her stories and introduce the world to her world of fantasy, fiction and romance. Chloe lives with her Mum and her five chickens and wants to hopefully write a story from the point of view of a dog that she loves. What will Chloe write next?

Theresa Le Flem, a novelist, artist and poet, always wanted to be a writer. With four novels now published, and also an anthology of her poetry and drawings, her dream was first fulfilled when her first novel was accepted and published by Robert Hale Ltd. She never looked back. Born in London into an artistic family, daughter of the late artist Cyril Hamersma, she has three children and five grandchildren all who live abroad in America and New Zealand. Her creative life began by writing poetry, painting and later in running her own studio pottery in Cornwall. But she has had a succession of jobs too – from factory-work, antiques, retail sales, veterinary receptionist and sewing machinist to hairdressing.

Over five years ago, Theresa formed a group of local writers, Rugby Café Writers, who meet fortnightly to talk about their work over a coffee. Writing remains her true passion. Married to a Guernsey man, Theresa shares a love of the sea with her husband and they have bought an almost derelict cottage in Guernsey. Gradually they are working to bring it back to life. Situated only a short walk to the sea, it might one day become the perfect writer's retreat where a new novel might emerge out of the dust and cobwebs. Theresa is a member of the Romantic Novelists' Association, the Society of Authors and The Poetry Society.

Rosemary Marks has lived in Rugby all her life and has three children and three grandchildren. She has always been an avid reader and was lucky enough to work at Rugby Library for 23 years, a Bibliophile's dream. She is now retired and enjoys travelling with her husband, writing, painting, researching her family history and spending time with friends and family.

Madalyn Morgan was brought up in Lutterworth, where she has returned after living in London for thirty-six years. She had a hairdressing salon in Rugby before going to Drama College. Madalyn was an actress for thirty years, performing on television, in the West End and in Repertory Theatre. She has been a radio journalist and is now presenting classic rock on radio. She has written articles for music magazines, women's magazines and newspapers. She now writes poems, short stories and novels. She has written ten novels – a wartime saga and a post war series. She is currently writing her memoir and a novel for Christmas 2023.

Fran Neatherway grew up in a small village in the middle of

Sussex. She studied History at the University of York and put her degree to good use by working in IT. Reading is an obsession – she reads six or seven books a week. Her favourites are crime, fantasy and science fiction. Fran has been writing for thirty-odd years, short stories at first. She has attended several writing classes and has a certificate in Creative Writing from Warwick University. She has completed three children's novels, as yet unpublished, and is working on the first draft of an adult novel. Fran has red hair and lives in Rugby with her husband and no cats.

Simon Parker grew up and lived on The Wirral until 1985. He arrived in Rugby in 2003 via Coventry, Bristol and Seattle. He's an aerospace engineer by training, with a love of the open road whether by bicycle, motorcycle or car. His travels galvanise his writing and he writes fiction for pleasure. He lives with his wife, two teenage children and a small collection of interesting vehicles: 'on the button' and ready for their next adventure.

Steve Redshaw was born and raised in Sussex. Over the past forty years he has taught in primary schools in the South of England and East Anglia. Now retired, he is living aboard his narrowboat, Miss Amelia, on the Oxford Canal near Rugby. Passionate about music, he sings and plays guitar in pubs, folk clubs and sessions around the area. He also is a dance caller for Barn Dances and Ceilidhs. His creative output is perhaps best described as emergent and sporadic, but when inspiration strikes, he finds himself writing songs, poems and short stories.

Chris Rowe. Just before covid, Chris tried to write poetry: lockdown gave the time to attempt different poetic forms, some of which appeared in Press Pause. From childhood, Chris has been interested in reading prose: such as Richmal Crompton (Just William), Alison Utley (Sam Pig), Henry Fielding, Mark Twain, Jane Austen, and Terry Pratchett. Shakespeare has always been a favourite and long ago the ambition was achieved of seeing a performance of every play: Antony and Cleopatra being the hardest to track down (all those scene changes deter production.). Favourite performers of the Bard are Oddsocks.

Christopher Trezise was born and raised in Rugby and pursued a professional acting career on theatre stages culminating in work for Disneyland Paris. Christopher has held many jobs from kitchen assistant through to risk management consultant but he has always had a passion for writing. He runs several table-top roleplaying groups which he writes scenarios for and has self-published a fantasy book based upon one of those games.

Lindsay Woodward has had a lifelong passion for writing, starting off as a child when she used to write stories about the Fraggles of *Fraggle Rock*. Knowing there was nothing else she'd rather study, she did her degree in writing and has now turned her favourite hobby into a career. She writes from her home in Rugby, where she lives with her husband and cat. When she's not writing, Lindsay runs a Marketing Agency, where she spends most of her time copywriting, so words really are her life. Her debut novel, *Bird*, was published in April 2016, and Lindsay is now working on her 10th book. She writes love stories with a twist.

Chris Wright is a local author who has just published a collection of light poetry and prose on Amazon under the title of *Tomfoolery*. The collection features poems, prose and comedy from a 20-year span on topics like: medicine, secret agents, work - the funny side, animals and the environment. Usually, he tries to add a comical twist. Chris is a long-time member of Rugby Cafe Writers and has found their support invaluable. He lives in Cawston and is married with three children and a rescue greyhound.

Printed in Great Britain
by Amazon